When the Chat Paused

A Platinum Chocolate Bond

By LongTemple

When the Chat Paused – A Platinum Chocolate Bond

Published by Platinum Chocolate Publishing

An Independent Imprint of LongTemple

ISBN: 978-1-972217-23-8 (paperback)

Cover Design: LongTemple

Interior Layout: LongTemple

First Edition

Printed in the United States of America

10 9 8 7 6 5 4 3 2 1

Dedication

To the women who believe in sisterhood—

in laughter that heals,

in conversations that hold us together,

and in the quiet strength found in simply being understood.

To the women who show up,

who stay,

who grow—together.

This is for you.

With warm regards,

- LongTemple

Table of Contents

Prologue: When the Chat Paused

The sound didn't disappear.

It changed.

At first, nobody noticed it—not in a way that demanded attention. Life had a way of shifting tones without asking permission. What used to hum could quiet down. What used to buzz could soften. What used to be constant could… hesitate.

But it was still there.

Somewhere between a notification chime and the echo of laughter that used to follow it.

Marlie heard it first.

Not with her ears—with her rhythm.

Her mornings had always begun the same way. Phone in hand before her feet touched the floor. A soft stretch beneath satin sheets. A glance at the clock. And then—

Tap.

Unlock.

The glow of connection.

Facebook notifications stacked like layered conversation. Instagram hearts resting beneath last night's photos. A TikTok draft she'd recorded and almost posted—her in soft lighting, head tilted just enough, talking about *grown love and second chances like she was teaching a masterclass without ever calling it one.*

And then—

The group chat.

The Ebony M. Elites.

It lived at the top of everything.

Pinned.

Protected.

Priority.

There was a time when opening it felt like stepping into a room already filled with voices.

Marsha would have said something bold before sunrise. Mary would follow with something measured and grounding. Mia would add something warm—faith, humor, or a quiet truth that landed deeper than expected.

And Marlie?

Marlie would read it all first.

Always.

Because even as the most expressive one in the room, she liked to *feel the temperature before she added to it.*

That morning—

She opened the chat.

And the room…

Wasn't empty.

But it wasn't full either.

A single message sat there. Hours old.

No replies.

No rhythm.

No laughter trailing behind it.

Just… stillness.

Marlie stared at the screen longer than necessary.

Her thumb hovered.

Then she locked the phone and placed it face down on the nightstand.

she said out loud, her voice soft against the quiet of her room.

But the silence didn't agree.

By the time she reached the kitchen, she had already shaken it off.

Coffee brewing.

Jazz playing low from the speaker near the window.

Something smooth—horns drifting, bass steady, a rhythm that didn't rush her into the day.

Marlie moved through her space with intention.

She always had.

Fifty-five had taught her that style wasn't about what you wore.

It was about how you moved through your life.

She set her phone upright against the counter this time.

Not face down.

Not ignored.

Observed.

It lit up.

A notification.

Not the group chat.

Discover.

She smiled.

Now *that*… she enjoyed.

Marlie picked up her phone and tapped into the app, glancing at the sleek interface like it had personally congratulated her for being exactly who she was.

Organized.

In control.

In the know.

She reached for her bag on the chair, slid her fingers across the smooth band resting inside.

Her **Discover Dot Band.**

She still remembered the first time she used it.

Tap.

Just like that.

Information exchanged. No fumbling. No explaining. No "hold on, let me find it."

Clean.

Modern.

Effortless.

She had tapped it against a man's phone at an event once—watched his eyebrows lift just slightly, watched respect settle in before conversation even began.

"Oh... you're one of those."

Yes.

Yes, she was.

Marlie slid the band onto her wrist and admired it for a second longer than necessary.

"Stay ready," she murmured.

Because she did.

She always did.

The phone lit again.

This time—

The chat.

Her body reacted before her mind did.

She picked it up quickly.

Opened it.

And waited.

A message from Marsha.

Short.

Uncharacteristically short.

"Good morning, ladies."

Marlie blinked.

No follow-up.

No second message.

No joke.

No spark.

She stared at it.

Then typed.

Paused.

Deleted.

Typed again.

"Morning."

Sent.

She watched the screen like it might breathe.

Nothing.

Across town, Mary noticed too.

But Mary didn't react.

Mary observed.

She sat at her dining table with her tea—no sugar, no distraction—and scrolled through the chat with the kind of focus that came from a life of paying attention.

Patterns mattered.

Energy mattered.

And this?

This was a shift.

Not dramatic.

Not loud.

But present.

She placed her phone down gently.

Not concerned.

Not yet.

But aware.

Mia had already been awake for hours.

But her phone sat untouched.

Face down.

Silent.

By mid-afternoon, Marsha broke the quiet the only way she knew how.

Direct.

"Okay… y'all good?"

It landed in the chat like a knock on a closed door.

Marlie saw it immediately.

So did Mary.

Three women present.

One missing.

Again.

Marlie leaned back against her counter, arms crossed loosely, her eyes narrowing just slightly—not in worry, not yet, but in recognition.

Something had shifted.

And whatever it was…

Hadn't announced itself.

That night, Marlie stood in front of her mirror longer than usual.

Not adjusting.

Not correcting.

Just… looking.

Her reflection met her without apology.

She saw the woman she had fought to become.

The woman who had survived silence.

Who had relearned desire.

Who had stepped back into rooms not to be chosen—

But to choose.

She smiled slowly.

"Whatever this is," she said quietly, *"we'll handle it."*

Because they always did.

The Ebony M. Elites didn't fall apart.

They adjusted.

They realigned.

They showed up.

Together.

But this time…

The pause wasn't just a moment.

It was a message.

And none of them knew yet—

That everything they had built…

Was about to be tested in a way no conversation could prepare them for.

Chapter One: Silk, Swagger, and a Little Trouble

The group chat didn't wake up—it activated. By 10:47 a.m., Marlie's phone was already lit, messages stacking in rhythm, the cadence so familiar she could hear each voice without needing to press play.

She leaned against her kitchen counter, coffee warm in her hand, thumb moving slowly as the thread built itself into something alive.

Marsha: *Dresses picked up. If this zipper breaks, I'm blaming sequins and Jesus.*

A quiet smile pulled at Marlie's mouth before the next message slid in.

Mia: *Not Jesus catching strays this early.*

Mary: *Zippers don't fail without reason. Respect the garment.*

Marlie took a slow sip of her coffee, letting the warmth settle before she typed, her tone already wrapped in control.

Marlie: *The garments will be respected. The bodies inside them? That's between us and prayer.*

That did it.

The thread picked up speed—not chaotic, not scattered, but layered, like instruments finding their place in a song.

Mia: *Tonight is silk. I'm telling you now—I'm not leaving without at least one man questioning his life choices.*

Marsha: *Please don't ruin nobody's household.*

Mary: *Admire. Don't audition.*

Marlie paused over that one, reading it twice, because Mary always knew where the line lived—and how to draw it without raising her voice. Her reply came steady.

Marlie: *We are not auditioning for anything. We are the main event.*

The chat stilled, just for a second. Then —

Marsha: *Say that again slower.*

Marlie didn't respond. She didn't need to. The statement had already landed.

—

By early evening, her living room had transformed into what it always became before a night out—not just preparation, but intention made visible. A staging ground. Garment bags hung neatly along the wall, each one holding shape and promise.

Shoes lined up beneath them like they had been briefed. Jewelry rested nearby in quiet coordination — silver, gold, nothing loud, everything deliberate.

Marlie moved through the space with quiet authority, adjusting a hem here, smoothing a sleeve there, stepping back to take it all in as if she were studying a finished piece instead of preparing one.

Because to her — this was art.

A knock broke the rhythm.

Marsha.

Always first.

Marsha's voice came through the door before she did, energy already present as she called out, *"Let me in before I change my mind and wear sneakers with this dress."*

Marlie opened the door without rushing, stepping aside as Marsha entered and immediately paused, her body turning slowly as she took everything in.

Marsha let out a slow breath, her tone caught between admiration and disbelief as she said, *"Okay... wait."*

Marlie lifted a brow slightly, her voice calm, measured. *"What?"*

Marsha pointed toward the lineup, her expression settling into appreciation as she added, *"This? This right here? You've outdone yourself."*

Marlie didn't smile wide—she never did—but something settled in her posture, something satisfied, something certain as she replied, *"I told you... tonight is intentional."*

—

By the time all four of them stood together, the room didn't get louder or brighter—it got fuller. Four women. Four bodies. Four expressions of the same understanding.

We know who we are.

Mia adjusted her neckline, her movements smooth but aware. Mary checked the clasp of her bracelet, precise and measured. Marsha turned sideways in the mirror—once, then again, then once more, because she wasn't finished admiring the work.

Marlie reached into her bag, her voice cutting gently through the room as she said, *"Before we leave—new rule."*

Three heads turned toward her at once.

She held up something small, sleek, almost unnoticeable—black, controlled.

"A clicker."

Marsha blinked, her tone immediate. *"A what?"*

Marlie stepped closer, holding it between her fingers, letting the simplicity of it speak before she did, her voice steady as she explained, *"Bluetooth remote. Sync it to your phone camera—set it up—and we don't ask anybody to take our pictures ever again."*

The room paused.

Then shifted.

Mia leaned forward first, curiosity leading as she said, *"Wait."*

Mary followed, already engaged, *"Show me."*

Marlie set her phone against a stand, tapped the screen with quiet efficiency, then stepped back into position. She lifted the clicker slightly.

Click.

The flash captured them mid-curiosity—real, unposed, unguarded.

Perfect.

Mia's mouth dropped open, laughter rising right behind it as she said, *"Oh, this is dangerous."*

Marsha shook her head, already amused, her tone full as she added, *"You mean to tell me we've been trusting strangers all this time for no reason?"*

Marlie tilted her head slightly, her answer simple, final. *"Not anymore."*

Mary nodded once, slow and thoughtful, her voice grounded. *"Efficient."*

Marlie placed the clicker into her hand like it belonged there, her voice lowering slightly as she added, *"Stay ready."*

—

The venue didn't overwhelm—it received. Low lighting softened the edges of the room while gold accents caught just enough shine to feel intentional. Jazz drifted through the space, curling around conversations, settling into corners, never competing, only guiding.

The Great Gatsby theme wasn't announced.

It was understood.

Tailored suits. Structured dresses. Movement that respected space.

When the Ebony M. Elites entered, the room didn't react in fragments.

It responded as a whole.

Marlie felt it immediately—the subtle recalibration of attention, the quiet shift in posture, the way presence announced itself without introduction. Men didn't stare.

They assessed.

And tonight — they approved.

Marsha leaned slightly toward them, her voice low but amused as she murmured, *"Okay... this is already better than the Sneaker Ball."*

Mary lifted her glass, her gaze moving across the room with quiet analysis, her voice calm. *"Let's see how the conversations behave."*

Mia smiled, slow and certain, her energy steady. *"I'm ready."*

—

The first man approached with intention—not rushed, not unsure.

He greeted them evenly, his tone balanced as he said, *"Good evening."*

Points.

Marlie clocked it without reacting.

He continued, his attention distributed with care, *"May I ask—are you all together?"*

Mia answered first, her tone smooth, controlled as she replied, *"We are."*

He nodded slightly, adjusting easily. *"That explains the energy."*

Better.

They spoke—about music, about fabric, about the quiet difficulty of finding a proper tailor who understood structure and movement at the same time. The conversation stayed where it belonged—light, aware, respectful.

Then came the question.

His voice shifted just slightly as he asked, *"So… what do you ladies do?"*

The air didn't tense.

It sharpened.

Mary answered without hesitation, her voice even, grounded. *"We live."*

Marsha followed, a smile threading through her tone. *"Very well."*

Marlie watched him—not suspicious, not defensive—just measuring.

He adjusted.

Didn't press.

Didn't retreat.

He smiled instead, accepting the boundary as he said, *"Fair enough."*

Respect restored.

—

Later, near the bar, Marlie placed her phone carefully against a glass partition, angling it just enough to capture without asking. Her voice carried just enough to gather them.

"Come here."

They moved toward her naturally—arms linking, shoulders aligning, laughter already forming before the moment even settled.

Marlie lifted the clicker slightly, her tone light but certain. *"Ready?"*

The answer came together, layered, familiar.

"Always."

Click.

This time, it caught them exactly as they were—not posed, not performing.

Present.

Alive.

Behind them, a woman leaned toward her friend, her voice soft but sincere as she whispered, *"I love that."*

Marlie heard it.

She didn't turn.

She didn't need to.

—

By the time the night settled into itself, it had already given them what they came for. They had danced, deflected, admired, released, chosen—and somewhere between silk, swagger, and a little trouble, the Ebony M. Elites reminded the room of something it had quietly forgotten.

Desire didn't belong to youth.

It belonged to confidence.

And confidence — they wore that better than anything else.

Chapter Two: The Morning After the Music Slowed

Morning didn't rush them. It never did after a good night. It lingered—soft light stretching itself across Marlie's bedroom walls, catching the edge of her mirror and the curve of the chair where last night's dress rested, draped like it still had something to say. The room held onto the evening just enough to feel it, like the music had lowered but never fully stopped.

Marlie's feet met the floor slowly, carefully, her body reminding her that heels always came with consequences.

"Mm..." she murmured, rolling her shoulders once before reaching for her phone.

Tap.

Unlock.

The glow met her the way it always did—ready, waiting, layered with everything she had missed while she was busy being present.

Instagram first.

Always.

Notifications stacked neatly, not overwhelming but active, a steady climb of likes gathering beneath the photo she had posted just before midnight—the one where the four of them stood shoulder to shoulder, gold and silver catching light like they owned it.

And they had.

She tapped it open, her eyes moving slowly this time, not rushing the moment, letting the comments settle instead of passing through.

"This is how grown women step out."

"Y'all are everything."

"I need friends like this."

Marlie's smile didn't stretch wide.

It settled.

Satisfied.

She moved next without thinking, opening her Discover app for a quick glance, a quiet check-in—because staying on top of things wasn't work to her. It was rhythm. Information. Movement. Control.

Then — The group chat.

Pinned.

Always.

She opened it, already knowing what she would find.

Alive again.

Marsha: *Tell me why I woke up sore in places I did not dance with.*

Marlie laughed immediately, soft but real, the sound filling the quiet room as she leaned back into her pillows.

Mia: *Because you danced like your bills were due at midnight.*

Mary: *Good morning. Hydrate before you exaggerate.*

Marlie let the conversation settle into her chest before her fingers moved, her tone sliding easily back into rhythm.

Marlie: *Good morning. Please confirm we looked as good as I remember.*

The responses came without delay.

Marsha: *Better.*

Mia: *Illegal, actually.*

Mary: *Memorable.*

Marlie exhaled slowly, her head resting against the headboard as she stared at the screen just a moment longer.

There it was.

That feeling.

That ease.

That… them.

—

Across town, Marsha was already in her kitchen, robe tied tight, hair wrapped, moving with purpose that didn't depend on how she felt. Her phone rested between her shoulder and ear out of habit, even though no one was on the line yet, her free hand already reaching into the fridge as she shifted her weight from one foot to the other.

She pulled the phone down, tapping into the chat as she muttered, *"Let me see these pictures..."*

She paused.

Zoomed in.

Tilted her head.

"Okay... wait."

Her fingers moved quickly, capturing the moment she saw something she liked, and she dropped the screenshot into the chat without hesitation.

Marsha: *LOOK AT THIS.*

The responses stacked quickly.

Mia: *Oh wow.*

Mary: *That is a strong frame.*

Marlie: *Clicker doesn't miss.*

Marsha laughed out loud, the sound bouncing off her kitchen walls as she reached for her coffee.

Marsha: *That little button just changed our lives.*

Mia: *We really out here self-sufficient and fine.*

Marsha shook her head, pleased in a way that didn't need to be explained, lifting her cup as she repeated softly to herself, *"Self-sufficient and fine."*

—

Mary sat near her window, tea cradled in both hands, her posture upright but relaxed, the morning light settling gently across her shoulders.

Her phone rested lightly in her palm as she scrolled through the photos—not quickly, not for reaction, but for understanding.

Angles.

Expressions.

Presence.

She paused on one image longer than the rest, her gaze moving with intention—Marlie slightly turned, controlled even in stillness; Mia mid-laugh, unguarded but composed; Marsha caught in motion, energy visible; and herself—still, centered, grounded.

She nodded once.

Mary: *These will age well.*

Marlie's response came almost immediately.

Marlie: *So will we.*

Marsha followed without missing the moment.

Marsha: *Speak for yourself—I'm already there.*

Mia added easily.

Mia: *You've BEEN there.*

Mary smiled into her tea.

—

Mia sat on the edge of her bed, still wrapped in last night's bonnet, her phone held in both hands as her thumbs moved slower than usual—but steady. She opened the photo again, zooming in, then out, then back in, not searching for flaws but for something else entirely.

Recognition.

She let out a soft breath, her voice quiet, thoughtful. *"Mm..."*

Not critique.

Appreciation.

Her thumbs moved carefully as she typed.

Mia: *I will say this… being seen without being bothered? I like that.*

Marlie read it once, then again, before responding.

Marlie: *That's because we're not presenting confusion.*

Mary followed, grounding the thought.

Mary: *Clarity is attractive.*

Marsha layered her truth on top.

Marsha: *And expensive.*

Mia smiled as she typed.

Mia: *And worth it.*

—

Marlie finally rose, tying her robe as she moved toward the kitchen, her steps unhurried but intentional. Coffee came first—always—and as it brewed, the faint echo of last night's jazz still lingered in the room, like the space hadn't fully released the mood.

She set her phone upright on the counter—not tucked away, not silenced—included.

It buzzed.

Instagram.

A direct message.

She opened it, her expression neutral as she read.

"Good evening—well, good morning now. I saw you last night. You and your friends… that was something special."

Marlie tilted her head slightly—not impressed, not dismissive—just aware.

She didn't respond.

Not yet.

Instead, she returned to the group chat, her fingers moving with intention.

Marlie: *So… hypothetical.*

Marsha responded immediately.

Marsha: *Already sounds like trouble.*

Mia followed.

Mia: *Proceed.*

Mary grounded it.

Mary: *We're listening.*

Marlie leaned her hip against the counter, coffee now in hand as she typed.

Marlie: *If a man says he noticed the group energy before anything else… is that a point or a warning?*

The responses came layered.

Marsha: *Point.*

Mia: *Strong point.*

Mary: *Depends on what he does next.*

Marlie nodded to herself, the answer settling without needing debate.

There it was.

—

The conversation flowed easily after that, revisiting the night in pieces, flipping through moments they already knew they would keep.

Marsha: *The one in the velvet jacket? Immediate no.*

Mia: *Too close. Too fast.*

Mary: *No awareness of space.*

Marlie: *Released.*

A pause.

Then—

Marsha: *Gently.*

Mia: *Respectfully.*

Mary: *Efficiently.*

Marlie laughed again, pouring her coffee into a fresh cup, the word settling comfortably as she echoed softly, *"Efficiently..."*

—

By late morning, the energy softened on its own—not fading, just settling into something quieter, more grounded. Plans surfaced naturally, without pressure, each woman already moving into her own rhythm for the day.

Marsha: *I'm cooking today. Real food. Not vibes.*

Mia: *Choir rehearsal. Pray for me.*

Mary: *Service, then a walk.*

Marlie: *Fabric store. I have an idea.*

Marsha didn't miss the opportunity.

Marsha: *Of course you do.*

Mia: *She never stops.*

Mary: *That's why we look the way we do.*

Marlie didn't respond.

She didn't need to.

She just smiled.

—

Before the thread slowed, Marsha sent one last message, the kind that didn't try too hard but landed anyway.

Marsha: *Last night was fun... but I love us the morning after.*

There it was.

The truth of it.

Not the dresses.

Not the attention.

Not even the music.

Them.

Marlie's fingers moved slower this time, more deliberate.

Marlie: *Same.*

Mia: *Always.*

Mary: *That's the part that lasts.*

The thread quieted after that—not ended, not paused—just resting.

—

Marlie stood at her counter a moment longer, coffee warm in her hands, her phone glowing softly beside her. She glanced at the photo again—the four of them, captured without interruption, without interference.

No strangers.

No distortion.

Just them.

Click.

She reached for her Discover Dot Band, sliding it onto her wrist with a small, satisfied motion, the gesture already becoming habit.

"Stay ready…" she murmured softly.

Because something in her—quiet, steady, undeniable—felt it.

More moments were coming.

Moments worth capturing.

Moments worth holding.

Moments that would matter later—

in ways none of them could see yet.

Chapter Three: Posted, Seen, and Slightly Shifted

By noon, the night before had already begun living again—just not in memory.

It moved through light, through screens, through quiet observation, finding its second life online as Marlie stood in her living room with her phone in hand, sunlight stretching across the floor and catching the soft highlight of her cheek.

She studied the photo without rushing, letting her eyes move across it slowly, not searching for flaws but for confirmation, for alignment, for that exact moment where everything had come together without effort.

Not the first shot. Not the safe one. The one. The one where Mia was caught mid-laugh—unguarded but still precise, where Marsha's body held motion like it belonged to her, unapologetic and alive, where Mary stood composed, grounded in a way that didn't ask to be noticed but always was, and where Marlie herself stood centered and still, not posed, not performing, just knowing exactly when the moment had arrived. The clicker had done its job—clean, intentional, no interference—and she adjusted the brightness slightly, tilting the phone just enough to watch how the light held on their skin before opening Instagram, her thumb hovering only briefly before moving with quiet certainty.

The caption had already formed in her mind before she even touched the screen. She typed it exactly as she heard it, letting it sit there for a second before committing to it.

"We don't chase moments. We create them."

She read it once, not to correct it but to feel it settle into place, then tapped *post*, lowering the phone slightly as if the moment itself had just been released into something larger than them.

Across town, Marsha's phone buzzed before she even made it fully back to the table, her hands still half-busy in the kitchen as she wiped them quickly on a towel and reached for the screen.

"Oh… here she go," she muttered under her breath, leaning into the counter as the comments began stacking faster than she expected, her eyes moving quickly but her expression slowing into appreciation. *"Who are these queens?"* one read, followed by *"This energy is different,"* and then *"I need to know where y'all were at."*

Marsha let out a soft laugh, shaking her head as she typed back into the group chat without hesitation.

Marsha: *You done started something.*

response came almost immediately, Marlie's tone steady and grounded even through the screen.

Marlie: *We didn't start it. We showed up.*

Mia slipped into the rhythm easily.

Mia: *Same difference.*

And Mary, as always, anchored the moment.

Mary: *Visibility always invites curiosity.*

Marsha smirked, her fingers already moving again.

Marsha: *And commentary.*

Marlie's reply came softer but firmer, not dismissive, not defensive, just resolved.

Marlie: *Let them talk.*

Mia sat near her window with her legs tucked beneath her, her phone resting lightly in both hands as she scrolled more slowly than she usually would. Not distracted—present. She wasn't just looking at the photo. She was feeling it.

There was something different about being seen like that, something that didn't press or demand or distort. It didn't feel like exposure. It didn't feel like judgment. It felt like recognition, like something had been understood without explanation.

She paused on the image again, her thumb resting against the screen as her gaze softened just slightly before she typed.

Mia: *I will say this… we looked like we knew something.*

Mary's response came almost instantly, as if she had been waiting for that exact sentence.

Mary: *We do.*

Marsha jumped in, unwilling to let that sit without challenge.

Marsha: *We do?? What we know?*

Marlie read the exchange, her lips curving just enough before she responded, her words landing with a quiet certainty that didn't need emphasis.

Marlie: *That we don't have to rush anything.*

The message settled into the space naturally, not as a declaration but as a truth they already shared.

The engagement continued to build without them needing to tend to it—likes stacking, shares moving quietly beneath the surface—and then Marlie's phone lit with a tag that made her pause just long enough to shift her attention. She tapped it open and found a short video—unpolished, distant, clearly not staged.

TikTok.

Someone had captured them walking into the venue, the four of them moving in that same unspoken rhythm, their steps unhurried, their presence contained but undeniable.

At first there was no sound, just the visual of it—the entrance, the spacing, the stillness within motion—then music slid in, smooth and intentional, wrapping itself around the clip like it belonged there.

The caption read, *"When grown women enter the room and don't need permission."* Marlie watched it once, then again, then a third time, not out of vanity but out of curiosity, wanting to understand what they looked like from the outside, what their presence translated into when they weren't controlling the frame.

"Hmm..." she murmured softly, her expression unreadable but settled.

Not bad.

Not bad at all.

She dropped the link into the group chat.

Marlie: *We've been documented.*

The responses came quickly, overlapping in tone and timing.

Marsha: *WAIT.*

Mia: *Oh no...*

Mary: *Let me see.*

A few seconds passed before Marsha came back louder than the others.

Marsha: *Oh I LIKE THIS.*

Mia followed, her tone softer but sincere.

Mia: *This is actually beautiful.*

Mary completed it, as she often did, with clarity.

Mary: *This is what presence looks like when it's not forced.*

Marlie didn't respond. She watched the video one more time, then locked her phone, letting the image sit with her instead of reacting to it.

Outside, the day continued exactly as it always did—cars moving without pause, people rushing through conversations they weren't fully present for, voices overlapping and dissolving into the background—but inside their separate spaces, something had shifted.

Not loudly. Not dramatically. Just enough to be felt. It wasn't excitement. It wasn't ego.

It was awareness.

Later that afternoon, Marlie stepped out, not dressed for attention, not performing for anything, just herself—clean lines, soft structure, elegance that didn't announce itself but didn't hide either.

The café greeted her with quiet familiarity, the low hum of conversation blending with the hiss of espresso, the kind of space that held people without demanding anything from them.

The line moved easily, and when it was her turn, she stepped forward, placed her order, and waited with the same calm she carried everywhere.

When the total came, she didn't reach for her bag. Her wrist lifted instead.

Tap.

The Discover Dot Band met the reader with a soft, confident contact, and just like that, it was done. No digging. No pause. No break in rhythm.

The man behind her noticed immediately, leaning just enough to catch her attention as he asked, *"Wait... what was that?"* Marlie turned her head slightly, acknowledging him without fully turning.

"Convenience."

He smiled, intrigued. *"That looked... smooth."*

She met his eyes briefly, her tone even.
"It is."

She picked up her coffee, gave a small nod, and moved on without lingering, leaving the moment exactly where it belonged—simple, complete, unextended.

Back in the group chat, the rhythm had changed. It wasn't broken. It wasn't cold. It just… spaced itself out. Messages no longer stacked on top of each other.

They arrived, then rested. Mary noticed it first, not because she was looking for it, but because she always noticed the shifts that didn't announce themselves.

The pauses stretched just a little longer between messages—nothing alarming, nothing to name—but enough to register.

She didn't comment on it.

She simply observed.

Mia had gone quiet again. Not absent. Still present in the thread, still reading, still there—but not moving with the same rhythm. Her phone sat beside her, screen dimmed, her thoughts traveling somewhere the chat didn't follow.

Marsha filled the space the way she always did, naturally, without forcing anything back into place.

Marsha: *Okay important question—what are we doing next? Because I refuse to look this good and stay in the house.*

Marlie saw it and responded steadily.

Marlie: *The Sneaker Ball is coming back next month.*

Marsha didn't hesitate.

Marsha: *Say less.*

Mia didn't respond.

Mary did.

Mary: *That could be interesting.*

Marsha grinned, already leaning into it.

Marsha: *Interesting?? I'm wearing sneakers and attitude.*

Marlie added, her mind already ahead of them.

Marlie: *I already have ideas.*

Marsha shook her head.

Marsha: *Of course you do.*

Evening settled without announcement, the light shifting, the air softening, and the chat slowing again—not abruptly, not noticeably, just gradually, like music lowering instead of ending.

Marlie sat near her window with her phone resting loosely in her hand, though her attention had already drifted beyond it.

The TikTok video replayed in her mind—the way they moved, the way they entered, the way they didn't ask. Something about it stayed with her, not the attention, not the commentary, but the image of who they were together.

Aligned.

Unbothered.

Whole.

She opened the group chat again and scrolled slowly through the day, letting each message settle before moving to the next. Then she paused, her thumb hovering as she typed something, stopped, deleted it, then typed again.

Marlie: *We looked... settled.*

Mary responded first.

Mary: *We are.*

Marsha followed, her tone light but grounded in truth.

Marsha: *Speak for yourself, I'm still a little dangerous.*

Marlie smiled, but her eyes softened slightly as something quieter moved beneath the surface.

Because in the spaces between the messages, in the pauses that stretched just a little longer, in Mia's absence from the rhythm—something didn't feel wrong.

But it didn't feel the same either.

That night, the group chat didn't close. It didn't end. It simply… didn't continue. No goodnight. No last laugh. No final thought to carry into sleep. Just a thread resting where it was—open, waiting.

And somewhere beneath the ease, the laughter, the visibility, and the quiet pride of being seen, something subtle had shifted. Not loud enough to name. Not sharp enough to fear.

But present enough to matter.

Chapter Four: Sneakers, Silk, and Signals

The next morning didn't arrive with urgency—it unfolded, slow and deliberate, like the day itself understood there was no need to rush what had already found its rhythm.

Soft light stretched across quiet rooms, brushing along walls and tabletops, catching the edge of mirrors and the faint sheen of fabric left draped where it had been removed the night before.

Curtains breathed gently with passing air, and phones rested exactly where they had been left—some face down in quiet resistance, others face up as if still listening for something more.

Marlie reached for hers without thinking, her hand moving before her mind caught up.

Tap.

Unlock.

The screen lit her face softly as the group chat appeared exactly where it always did—pinned, present, waiting. Still. She watched it for a moment longer than necessary, her thumb hovering without movement, not impatient, not concerned, just aware of the quiet before she opened it anyway.

Nothing new.

Not yet.

She set the phone down and moved toward the kitchen, bare feet steady against the floor as the coffee maker came to life in low, familiar sound—water heating, breath building, the beginning of something simple and necessary.

The scent followed, warm and grounding, filling the space before she returned to the counter, drawn back not by urgency, but by habit.

Her phone lit again just as she reached for it.

Marsha: *Good morning, beautiful women. Don't forget—today we move with intention.*

Marlie's lips curved slightly, not into a full smile, but into recognition, into rhythm.

Marlie: *Morning. Already in motion.*

Mary followed, her presence as steady as ever, her words carrying that same grounded clarity.

Mary: *Good morning. Hydrate. Stretch. Proceed wisely.*

A small pause settled between them, not empty, just… open.

Then—

Mia: *Morning.*

Short.

Simple.

But there.

Marlie exhaled just slightly, her chest softening in a way she didn't name—not relief, not quite—but acknowledgment. She lifted her coffee and leaned into the counter, letting that single word settle into the space around her, letting it exist without asking anything more from it.

By mid-morning, her living room had already begun to shift under her hands. Space cleared. Fabric laid out in quiet order across surfaces that now held intention instead of rest.

Her sketchbook lay open, pencil placed exactly where she needed it, though her mind had already moved ahead of what the page could hold.

She moved through color like it spoke back to her, like each shade carried a voice she understood without translation. Textures responded beneath her fingertips. Structure mattered—not as restriction, but as language.

Because it did.

Her phone buzzed again, pulling her just slightly from that space, not enough to disrupt, just enough to connect.

Marsha: *So we doing this Sneaker Ball or we just talking about it?*

Marlie didn't answer immediately. Her pencil finished its line first—clean, intentional—before she set it down and reached for her phone.

Marlie: *We're doing it.*

Marsha: *Say less.*

Mary entered where clarity lived.

Mary: *Theme?*

Marlie didn't hesitate.

Marlie: *Structured casual. Elevated street. Clean lines. No confusion.*

The words landed with precision, shaping something that already existed in her mind.

A beat passed.

Then—

Marsha: *You lost me at structured.*

Mia's response came in smooth, effortless translation.

Mia: *She means we still look expensive.*

Marsha's understanding followed quickly.

Marsha: *Oh. I understand expensive.*

Marlie's smile stayed faint, her eyes already dropping back to the page, her hand moving again as if the conversation had simply fed the work instead of interrupting it.

Across town, Mia sat with her phone resting in her lap, her body still but her thoughts moving in quieter, less visible directions.

She read every message. Didn't skip. Didn't rush. Her thumb hovered longer before responding, her presence felt more in the space she occupied than in the words she offered.

But she stayed.

And that mattered.

Mary, seated near her window with tea warming her hands, watched the thread unfold with the same steady awareness she carried into everything. The messages didn't stack the way they once had.

The rhythm wasn't as layered, not as immediate—but it was still there. Still connected. Still intact. She added her voice where it mattered, not filling space, but shaping it.

Mary: *Shoes matter this time.*

Marsha answered without hesitation.

Marsha: *Shoes ALWAYS matter.*

Marlie refined it.

Marlie: *Sneakers must be intentional. No randomness.*

Marsha laughed softly to herself.

Marsha: *No randomness is crazy.*

Mia's response came quieter—but precise, anchored in something deeper than the moment.

Mia: *We are not random.*

The message didn't rise.

It settled.

Firmly.

Marlie paused before answering, her eyes lingering on the words just long enough to feel what sat beneath them.

Marlie: *Exactly.*

By early afternoon, the conversation shifted into visuals, moving from words into form. Marlie sent the first sketch, the lines clean and deliberate, balanced in a way that didn't ask for validation but received it anyway.

Marsha: *Oh… okay.*

Mia: *Yes.*

Mary: *That works.*

Marlie added, already adjusting in her mind, already seeing beyond what they were looking at.

Marlie: *I'll adjust for body and movement.*

Marsha leaned into it immediately.

Marsha: *Adjust for snacks too.*

Mia followed without hesitation.

Mia: *Always adjust for snacks.*

Marlie shook her head, a soft laugh slipping out as she leaned back from the table, letting the room hold both her work and their voices at once, the balance of it settling naturally around her.

Later, she stepped outside—not for attention, not for presentation, but for movement, for air, for the simple act of existing within the city without absorbing its urgency. Cars passed without pause. Conversations overlapped and dissolved.

People moved as if already late for something they hadn't fully decided mattered.

Marlie walked through it all without taking it on, her pace her own, her presence contained.

The boutique greeted her the way it always did—quiet, intentional, unbothered by trends or noise.

She moved through the space with ease, fingertips brushing fabric, her eyes scanning without rushing, her body recognizing what it needed before her mind named it.

A woman approached her, not interrupting, just observing long enough to speak.

"You always look like you know what you're doing."

Marlie glanced up just enough, her response immediate, grounded, without edge or performance.

"I do."

At the counter, her selections rested neatly before her, her movements clean and unhurried as the total appeared. She didn't reach into her bag.

Her wrist lifted instead.

Tap.

The Discover Dot Band met the reader with quiet certainty, the transaction complete without disruption.

The woman blinked, watching the simplicity of it.

"That's... efficient."

Marlie nodded once, gathering her things.

"It should be."

And just like that, she was gone, the moment left exactly as it needed to be—complete, unextended.

Back in the group chat, Marsha had already picked the rhythm back up, filling the space the way she always did—naturally, without forcing energy where it didn't want to sit.

Marsha: *Okay but real question—who's actually dancing this time and who's pretending?*

Marlie responded first, her tone even.

Marlie: *We don't pretend.*

Mary followed, refining without softening.

Mary: *We participate appropriately.*

Marsha laughed.

Marsha: *That sounds like pretending.*

Mia answered simply.

Mia: *I'm dancing.*

Marlie read it once.

Then again.

Then typed.

Marlie: *Good.*

One word.

But it carried.

By evening, the tone softened again, not fading, not disconnecting, just settling into something lighter. Messages spaced themselves out.

The rhythm loosened. Mary noticed, of course she did, but she didn't interrupt it. She adjusted to it, the way she always did when something shifted without asking permission.

Marlie stood in front of her mirror that night, not dressed, not preparing, just present.

Her reflection met her calmly, without correction, without question. Her phone rested nearby, the screen dimmed but waiting.

She picked it up, opened the chat, and read through the day slowly, letting each message land differently than it had the first time.

Then she typed.

Paused.

Then sent.

Marlie: *The Sneaker Ball is going to be ours.*

Marsha responded without hesitation.

Marsha: *It better be.*

Mary followed, steady as always.

Mary: *It will be what we make it.*

A pause settled between them, not empty, just… held.

Then—

Mia: *I'll be there.*

Marlie read it once.

Then again.

Her expression softened, something quieter moving beneath the surface, something she didn't name but didn't ignore.

Marlie: *Of course you will.*

The thread didn't continue after that.

It didn't need to.

The plan had formed.

The intention was clear.

And the connection — still held.

But beneath the planning, the laughter, the fabric, and the quiet confidence of knowing they could shape any space they entered, the rhythm remained slightly off—not broken, not lost, just shifted, like music playing from another room, familiar enough to recognize, but not as close as it used to be.

Chapter Five: The Moment Between Messages

Evenings told the truth—not the loud version people performed in daylight, not the polished one dressed up for rooms and reactions, but the quiet truth that waited patiently until everything settled and there was nothing left to distract from it.

Marlie stood by her bedroom window, the city stretching out before her in soft pulses of light, buildings blinking in the distance like a conversation she didn't have to answer.

The glass held a faint reflection of her face, steady and unreadable, while her phone rested in her hand, the screen dimming, lighting, dimming again, as if it too was breathing in rhythm with the room.

The group chat had carried them all day—pictures layered over laughter, voice notes spilling personality into seconds, outfit ideas building into something bigger, memes that made no sense outside of them but landed perfectly where they lived.

It had been full. Alive. Moving. But now it had quieted, not abruptly, not uncomfortably, just… paused, like music lowering without ending. And for the first time since all of this had begun, Marlie felt it—not absence, not distance, but that space that exists between connection and something else, something harder to name.

Her phone buzzed.

She didn't look right away.

She exhaled first, her breath slow and controlled, before her thumb moved and the screen came to life.

Ebony M. Elite

Marsha: *So nobody's going to talk about how we shut that brunch DOWN?*

Mia: *We didn't shut it down. We elevated it.*

Mary: *There's a difference.*

Marlie's smile came soft, almost automatic, her fingers hovering over the screen as she leaned her shoulder lightly into the wall, letting the moment settle before she responded.

Marlie: *We were present.*

The typing bubbles appeared immediately—three dots rising, disappearing, returning like breath being held and released.

Marsha: *Here she go…*

Mia: *Let her cook.*

Mary: *No… let her finish.*

Marlie tilted her head slightly, her gaze drifting toward the window again, not searching, not performing, just allowing the words to find their place before she gave them shape.

Marlie: *We didn't need the room to react to us. We were enough in it.*

The silence that followed wasn't empty.

It held.

Then—

Mia: *That's the part that scared me.*

The air shifted.

Not dramatically.

But undeniably.

Marlie straightened just slightly, her body responding before her mind fully caught up, while the city outside continued blinking like nothing had changed.

Mary: *Why?*

Mia's response came slower this time, the pause between her words carrying weight.

Mia: *Because I didn't realize how long I'd been... waiting to feel like that again.*

No one rushed to fill that space.

No jokes followed.

No quick deflection.

Because that wasn't light.

That was truth.

Across town, Mia sat on the edge of her bed, still dressed from earlier, her shoes kicked off but everything else left exactly where it had been, like she hadn't fully transitioned out of the day.

The mirror across the room held her reflection without judgment, without critique—just honest, just present. Her phone lit again, pulling her attention down just as the private message appeared.

Marlie: *Talk to me.*

Mia shook her head slightly, a small smile touching her lips, something warm and knowing in the gesture.

Of course.

Her fingers moved slower this time.

Mia: *I'm not sad.*

The response came back immediately, steady, grounded.

Marlie: *I didn't say you were.*

Mia paused, her thumb resting against the screen as she let the truth settle before she shaped it into words.

Mia: *I just forgot what it felt like to be seen without explaining myself.*

Across the city, Marlie closed her eyes briefly, her head tipping back against the wall as the words landed deeper than she allowed herself to show. Because she understood that. Not in theory. Not in passing. But in a way that sat quietly in her own chest, unspoken but always present.

Marlie: *You don't have to explain anything here.*

A pause.

Then—

Mia: *I know.*

And that — That was the shift.

Not the brunch.

Not the laughter.

Not the pictures that had traveled farther than they expected.

This.

Right here.

Marsha's house carried its own rhythm, the low hum of television blending with the sound of dishes clinking in the background, life moving the way it always did around her. But her attention stayed on her phone, her thumb hovering longer than usual as she read Mia's words again, then once more, her expression softening in a way she wouldn't announce.

Then she typed.

Marsha: *Well… don't get used to me being emotional because I still have a reputation.*

There it was.

The release.

The breath the room needed.

Mary: *Too late.*

Mia: *We've seen you cry over a commercial.*

Marsha sat up slightly, already defending herself with energy returning to her tone.

Marsha: *That dog FOUND HIS WAY HOME. Respect the moment.*

The laughter returned, not loud, not forced, but real, easing the weight without erasing it. And underneath it—something steadier had taken root.

Understanding.

Mary sat at her desk, her pen finally moving across her notebook, not writing in full sentences, not organizing thoughts into structure, just letting words land where they needed to.

Presence.

Alignment.

Witness.

She paused, underlined the last one twice, then reached for her phone, her message measured and intentional.

Mary: *We're not just spending time anymore.*

We're witnessing each other.

The chat stilled again.

Because that word — Carried weight.

Marlie read it slowly, her eyes moving across the sentence once, then again, letting it settle into her. A quiet exhale left her lips.

Marlie: *That's it.*

Time passed—not long, but enough for the moment to breathe, enough for what had been said to settle into something that didn't need to be repeated. Marlie pushed off the wall then, her body moving with quiet intention as she walked back into her living room. She set her phone down on the table, letting it rest there for the first time that evening before her attention shifted to something else.

A slim black band.

Sleek.

Minimal.

Elegant.

She turned it slowly in her fingers, the same way she had the clicker before—testing it, understanding it, claiming it. Then she slid it onto her wrist, adjusted it once, and lifted her phone again.

Click.

The image captured exactly what it needed to—clean lines, quiet luxury, the band resting against her skin like it belonged there.

She dropped it into the chat.

No caption.

Just the image.

The typing bubbles appeared instantly.

Marsha: *Okay... what is THAT?*

Mia: *Don't tell me you bought something else.*

Mary: *No... she didn't just buy it. She's about to introduce it.*

Marlie leaned back into her couch, her smile slow, deliberate, confident.

Marlie: *Dot band.*

A pause.

Then—

Marlie: *Tap to pay. No wallet. No phone. Just this.*

The chat lit up again, energy returning in waves.

Marsha: *Oh now we futuristic?*

Mia: *Wait... you serious?*

Mary: *Show us.*

Marlie's response came without rush, already knowing she had them.

Marlie: *Tomorrow.*

Marsha: *Where?*

Marlie: *Out.*

Mia: *That's not a location.*

Marlie: *It's a vibe.*

Mary smiled to herself, already aligned.

Mary: *I'm in.*

Marsha followed, practical as ever.

Marsha: *If we're outside, I need notice on what we're wearing.*

Mia added, her tone lighter now.

Mia: *Of course you do.*

Marlie leaned deeper into the couch, her laughter soft in her chest, not loud, not performed—just full, just real.

The chat slowed again, not because it was fading, but because it was settling, becoming something steadier, something less dependent on constant motion.

Marlie looked at her phone one more time, her gaze lingering just long enough to feel the connection still there, then she placed it face down beside her.

For the first time that day — she didn't need it in her hand.

Because what they had wasn't fragile.

It didn't disappear when the messages paused.

It lived in the spaces between them.

Across four different homes, four women sat in four different kinds of quiet, the noise of their individual lives moving around them, but none of them feeling alone.

Not tonight.

Not anymore.

And somewhere between the last message and the next moment waiting to unfold, something else began to take shape—not announced, not explained, just felt.

A rhythm.

A bond.

A becoming.

Because sometimes it isn't the conversation that changes everything — it's the moment that comes right after it pauses.

Chapter Six: Tap, Pay, Repeat

The city felt different when you stepped into it on purpose.

Not rushing.

Not reacting.

Arriving.

Late afternoon light slid across the sidewalk in warm bands as Marlie adjusted her sunglasses and stepped into the day with the kind of ease that made everything around her seem slightly overdone.

Her outfit was effortless in the way only carefully chosen things ever are—neutral tones layered with precision, soft gold catching light at her wrist and throat, crisp sneakers grounding the whole look like punctuation at the end of a sentence.

She felt her phone buzz once inside her bag and didn't reach for it.

Not yet.

Because today she wasn't leading with the phone.

She was leading with presence.

The café met her with its usual low hum—espresso machines hissing, cups touching saucers, conversations folding into one another in soft waves. It was the kind of place where people brought laptops to look busy but mostly watched each other exist.

Mia was already there, of course, seated near the window with her tablet open in front of her, posture relaxed but alert, one elbow resting lightly against the table as she moved between Instagram and Facebook with the focused drift of someone who was scrolling, yes—but also feeling something.

Her finger paused over the brunch photo.

The one Marlie had taken.

All four of them.

Natural.

Unposed.

Beautiful.

The likes had climbed. The comments had multiplied.

"Y'all look amazing."

"This is grown woman energy."

"Where was this at?"

Mia exhaled softly as she read through them, not overwhelmed, not flattered in any childish way—just… noticed.

Marlie slid into the seat across from her so seamlessly it felt less like arrival and more like continuation, her voice low and certain as she said, *"You saw it."*

Mia looked up, the corner of her mouth lifting.

"You knew I would."

Marlie leaned back slightly, her gaze dropping briefly to the screen before returning to Mia.

"It's the picture."

Mia shook her head once, slow and certain.

"No… it's the feeling in it."

That sat between them for a beat before Marsha's voice entered the café a full second before her body did.

"Okay—FIRST of all—y'all not about to start without me."

Mia laughed immediately. Marlie didn't even turn right away.

"You're loud before you arrive."

Marsha dropped into her seat with purpose, setting her bag down like it had been part of the entrance.

"And still right on time."

Mary arrived last, as always—not late, just perfectly placed. She greeted them with that soft, knowing smile of hers, her eyes taking in the table, the room, the light, the energy before she even sat down.

"This place has good light."

Marlie tilted her head, already amused.

"For pictures?"

Mary settled into her chair, glancing once toward the window before answering.

"For truth."

Mia leaned back with a small sigh of affection.

"Here we go..."

Menus came. Orders were placed. Glasses sweated quietly against the tabletop.

But none of that was the moment.

The moment was coming.

Marlie reached for her wrist with deliberate calm, turning her arm just enough for the slim black band to catch the light. Marsha noticed first—of course she did—and narrowed her eyes in immediate suspicion.

"Okay—what is that AGAIN?"

Marlie smiled, not fully, just enough to suggest she had been waiting for this.

"Dot band."

Mia leaned forward.

"You serious about this?"

Mary didn't say anything yet.

She watched.

She always watched first.

Marlie sat a little straighter, her tone even, her confidence completely unforced.

"Watch."

The server approached just then, placing drinks down with a polite nod and the practiced softness of someone who knew how not to interrupt a table with its own rhythm.

"Whenever you're ready."

Marlie nodded once.

No wallet.

No phone.

No digging through leather compartments, no shifting bags around, no fumbling for cards with names and numbers and unnecessary steps.

She simply lifted her wrist.

Tap.

A soft confirmation tone sounded from the register.

Done.

The server blinked.

"Oh—wow."

Marsha's mouth dropped open.

"No. No no no. You did NOT just pay like that."

Mia leaned in close, eyes narrowed with real curiosity now.

"Let me see that."

Marlie extended her wrist slightly, turning it just enough for all of them to see the band resting there with quiet authority.

"Tap. Pay. Move."

Mary smiled then, slow and thoughtful, because she had already seen past the object itself.

"It's not just about the band."

Marlie glanced at her.

"No."

Mary folded one hand over the other on the table and gave the truth its proper shape.

"It's about the ease."

Marlie nodded once.

"Exactly."

Marsha sat back, shaking her head as if she had just witnessed something suspiciously elegant.

"I'm not ready. I still like to feel my card."

Mia laughed.

"You like to struggle."

Marsha pointed at her with immediate offense.

"I like control."

Marlie leaned back into her chair, gaze steady.

"This is control."

A pause passed, and then Mia's hand was already moving toward her phone.

"Wait—hold on."

She opened Instagram and lifted the camera.

"Say that again."

Marlie raised one brow.

"You're recording?"

Mia didn't even blink.

"For content."

Marsha turned toward Mary.

"Oh now we content creators?"

Mary, unbothered, reached for her glass and took a small sip.

"We've been documenting. Now we're curating."

Mia grinned, her hand steady, camera trained exactly where she wanted it.

"Say it again."

Marlie looked straight into the lens.

Not performing.

Not pitching.

Just being exactly who she was.

"This is control."

Click.

Saved.

Minutes later, the video was up—Instagram first, then Facebook, then clipped down for TikTok. Not overproduced. Not staged. Not trying too hard. Just real enough to feel expensive. The caption sat beneath it with the same confidence Marlie carried at the table.

"Grown women. Smart choices. Soft life."

The engagement came fast.

Too fast.

Comments rolled in. Shares stacked. DMs began arriving before Mia finished refreshing the page.

"Where you get that band?"

"Is that Apple Pay?"

"I need that."

She stared at the screen, blinking as the numbers shifted upward almost in real time.

"Oh... this is moving."

Marsha leaned over so far her shoulder nearly touched Mia's.

"Wait—refresh that."

Mary watched all of it first, then lifted her eyes to Marlie.

"You knew this would happen."

Marlie gave the smallest shrug, her fingers circling the base of her glass.

"I felt it."

Outside, the world kept moving with its usual indifference—traffic dragging itself through intersections, people crossing streets with coffees in hand, somebody laughing too loudly into a headset half a block away. But inside, at that table, the atmosphere had shifted again.

This was no longer just four women meeting up.

No longer just friends catching up over drinks and digital proof that they looked as good as they felt.

Something else was forming.

Something with momentum.

Mia's phone buzzed again.

This time it wasn't Instagram.

Not Facebook.

WhatsApp.

Her eyes dropped. Her fingers opened the message before she had fully decided to. A name she hadn't seen in a long time sat at the top of the screen, and although her face didn't change immediately, something in her posture did. It was small. Easy to miss if you didn't know her.

But they knew her.

Marlie saw it first.

Of course she did.

"You good?"

Mia locked the phone too quickly and looked up.

"Yeah."

Marsha raised one eyebrow.

"That didn't look like 'yeah.'"

Mary said nothing at all. She simply watched Mia the way she watched weather—carefully, patiently, noticing what changed before anyone else named it.

Mia exhaled slowly, then reached for her glass.

"It's nothing."

But her voice didn't fully agree.

The moment didn't explode. It didn't tip into drama or demand immediate unpacking. It simply sat there—quiet, unresolved, real. Marlie didn't push. She didn't ask again, because she understood something most people missed in the name of care: not every moment needs to be opened the second it appears.

Some things need room first. Some truths arrive better when they've had air.

Mia took a slow sip, then forced a small smile that almost reached her eyes.

"So... we not going to talk about how I just went semi-viral?"

Marsha clapped once, loudly enough to turn heads.

"NOW we talking."

Mary smiled softly, and the energy lifted—but not completely, because something had entered the room, and even though no one named it, they all felt it.

Marlie glanced down at her wrist again. The band sat there—simple, sleek, powerful. She tapped it lightly with one finger, not to use it, just to feel it.

A quiet reminder.

Of control.

Of movement.

Of stepping forward without asking permission.

And as laughter returned to the table, as phones lit up again with fresh notifications, as the café continued humming around them and the city outside kept spinning on schedule, the rhythm held.

Stronger.

Deeper.

More connected than before.

Because now it wasn't just about showing up.

It was about what followed them once they did.

Chapter Seven: What Followed Them

The night did not end when they left. It followed them—not loudly, not in a way that demanded attention, but in quiet echoes that settled into the corners of their individual spaces, lingering in fabric, in memory, in the soft glow of screens that refused to let the moment close.

Marlie felt it first when she stepped into her apartment, the door closing behind her with a soft, controlled click as her heels were placed neatly by the entrance, not discarded but set down with the same intention she carried through everything.

Her bag followed, resting along the table's edge, her body moving through the space with practiced awareness, but beneath that control, something quieter had shifted—something that did not disrupt her rhythm, but deepened it.

She crossed into the kitchen, reaching for water instead of wine, the glass cool against her palm as she leaned lightly against the counter, her phone still in her hand, still active, still pulling.

The notifications had not stopped.

Not overwhelming. Not chaotic. Just steady.

She opened one, then another, her eyes moving without urgency, absorbing rather than reacting as messages layered themselves into something consistent.

"Y'all walked in like the room belonged to you."

"This is how grown women carry themselves."

"I need to understand this energy."

Marlie tilted her head slightly, her expression composed, unchanged, but her awareness sharpened—not because the attention surprised her, but because it confirmed something she had already understood before anyone else had named it.

"We didn't perform," she murmured softly, her voice barely rising above the quiet of her own space as she lifted the glass to her lips. *"We arrived."*

Across town, Marsha's entrance carried none of that restraint, her shoes kicked off the moment she crossed her threshold, one landing near the couch, the other disappearing somewhere behind it as her bag dropped onto the nearest chair like it had traveled with her through something that required release.

"Jesus..." she exhaled, rolling her shoulders as her hand reached immediately for her phone, her body settling but her energy still moving.

The chat was open.

Alive.

But she bypassed it.

TikTok.

She tapped.

Paused.

Her body stilled—not dramatically, not frozen, but caught in recognition as her posture shifted and she leaned forward just slightly.

"Oh."

It wasn't just Mia's video.

Another angle.

Another perspective.

The same moment—but reframed.

Marsha watched it once, then again, her eyes narrowing slightly as she moved into the comments, her thumb scrolling slower now, her attention sharpening as the numbers climbed.

Hundreds.

Still moving.

"Wait a minute..." she said quietly, her tone changing, not louder but more focused, as she pushed herself upright and dropped the link into the chat without hesitation.

Ebony M. Elite

Marsha: *Y'all... we outside OUTSIDE.*

Mia saw it almost immediately.

She was seated on the edge of her bed, her dress half-zipped, one earring already removed while the other still caught the light as she turned her head toward the mirror, her phone resting loosely in her hand, her thumb slower now, her body not fully settled between where she had been and where she was returning to.

She opened the link.

Watched.

Once.

Then again.

Her expression did not shift right away, but something behind it moved—something subtle, something internal, something that recognized the moment not as performance, but as reflection.

"That's us..." she said quietly, her voice steady, not surprised, not questioning, just acknowledging what was already true.

Mary, seated near her window with a cup of tea resting between her hands and her notebook still open from earlier, read the message with the same composed attention she gave everything. She opened the video, her gaze steady as she watched it through once, then placed her phone down, only to lift it again moments later and watch it again, her lips pressing together slightly—not in disapproval, but in thought.

"This is visibility," she said softly into the quiet of her room, her tone neither celebratory nor cautious, but grounded in recognition.

Back in her kitchen, Marlie opened the video without hesitation, her eyes scanning not for reaction, but for alignment—the way they moved, the way they held space without asking for it, the way the room adjusted without invitation. She watched it again, then locked her phone, setting it down without ceremony.

"That's accurate," she said simply.

The chat shifted.

Not abruptly.

But noticeably.

Marsha: *No—this is DIFFERENT.*

Mia: *It is.*

Mary: *It will bring attention.*

There was a pause—not long, not empty, but deliberate.

Marlie's fingers moved with intention.

Marlie: *Then we decide what to do with it.*

The message settled between them, not closing the moment, but stabilizing it, giving it shape without limiting its direction.

Time moved differently after that.

Not faster.

Not slower.

Just… more aware.

Mia rose from the edge of her bed carefully, her body adjusting as she moved toward the bathroom, her hand brushing lightly along the wall for balance, not out of weakness, but out of presence, her reflection catching her before she had fully prepared for it.

She paused.

Looked.

Not critically.

Not harshly.

Just honestly.

Her head tilted slightly as she studied herself—not searching for what had changed, but recognizing what had remained.

"You look..." she began, her voice quiet, her brow softening as the word formed not from expectation, but from truth.

"...like yourself."

And for the first time, that felt complete.

Across town, Marsha had moved into her kitchen, her phone propped against the paper towel holder as the video replayed again, her body shifting with a kind of restless energy that had less to do with nerves and more to do with direction.

"Okay but now we gotta move right," she said aloud, her tone firm, her thoughts already organizing themselves into action as her fingers moved quickly across her screen.

Marsha: *I'm just saying—if people are watching, we not about to be out here looking regular.*

Mia responded without hesitation.

Mia: *We don't look regular.*

Mary followed, her tone as steady as ever.

Mary: *We don't behave regular either.*

Marlie read both, her expression softening just slightly—not with amusement, but with recognition—as her response came measured, aligned.

Marlie: *Exactly.*

Mary closed her notebook then, the word she had written still visible beneath her pen.

Presence.

She underlined it again, slower this time, because its meaning had expanded beyond the moment she first wrote it.

It was no longer just about how they showed up.

It was about what followed them when they did.

Back in her apartment, Marlie moved through her space again, her fingers brushing the edge of the table where her bag rested, her hand slipping inside with intention before retrieving the clicker, turning it between her fingers as she studied it—not as an object, but as a symbol of something controlled, something deliberate, something chosen.

Small.

Simple.

Effective.

She set it back down gently, her wrist lifting as the Dot Band caught the light again, her thumb brushing across its surface as she thought—not about the technology, but about what it allowed.

Movement.

Ease.

Forward motion.

She exhaled softly, her posture settling into something deeper than control.

The chat slowed—not because the connection weakened, but because it no longer needed constant reinforcement to exist.

Marsha: *So what we doing next?*

Mary: *We plan.*

Mia: *We breathe.*

There was a pause.

Then—

Marlie: *We move.*

And just like that, it aligned again.

Across four different homes, in four distinct spaces shaped by different rhythms, different habits, different histories, the women settled into the night in their own ways—but none of them felt removed, none of them felt disconnected, not even in the quiet.

Because what had followed them home was not just attention, not just visibility, not even the echo of the night itself.

It was something steadier.

Something that did not depend on proximity.

Something that did not require constant confirmation.

And even as the messages slowed, even as the night softened around them, even as each of them moved deeper into their own space, their own thoughts, their own stillness — the connection held.

Not louder.

Not heavier.

Just stronger.

Because what they had built was no longer contained within a moment, or a room, or even a conversation.

It had moved beyond that.

And whatever came next — would meet them already connected.

Chapter Eight: The Message That Didn't Sit Right

Night came in layers, not all at once but in a slow surrender—the light softening first, then the streets loosening their grip on urgency, then the noise shifting from demand to rhythm.

Marlie stood in her kitchen with the overhead light dimmed low, a soft jazz track moving through the room like breath—something smooth, something that didn't interrupt thought but held it gently in place.

Her phone rested on the counter, face up, alive with motion, Instagram notifications still climbing from earlier, TikTok doing what TikTok does—pushing, spinning, circulating their moment like it had somewhere to be, Facebook slower but steady, familiar names and familiar voices layering affirmation over image.

"You ladies look beautiful."

"This is what life should look like."

"I need friends like this."

Marlie didn't respond. She simply watched, her fingers resting lightly against the edge of the counter as she took it in, because something about all of this felt bigger than a post.

It felt like presence had gone public.

Across town, Mia wasn't watching anything.

She was staring.

One screen.

One thread.

Not Instagram.

Not Facebook.

WhatsApp.

The message sat there with weight, like it had been waiting longer than it admitted, the name at the top unchanged but everything beneath it different now. She tapped it open again, her thumb hesitating like the words might rearrange themselves into something easier if she gave them time.

They didn't.

She locked the phone.

Unlocked it.

Locked it again.

Then finally she stood, the movement quiet but decisive, and walked to her window, pressing her fingers lightly against the glass as the city blinked back at her.

"Why now..." she murmured, the words barely sound, more breath than voice.

Her phone buzzed again behind her.

Not the group chat.

Him.

Again.

She didn't turn back this time.

Not yet.

Marsha's house carried noise in a different way—television laughter spilling into the room, bright and exaggerated, something half-watched as she sat on her couch with her phone in hand, thumb moving in that familiar rhythm.

TikTok.

Again.

And again.

And again.

Recipes.

Dances.

Commentary.

And then—

her hand froze mid-swipe.

"Oh..."

The video.

Their video.

Not just on Mia's page anymore.

Reposted.

Remixed.

Someone else's voice layered over their moment, a younger creator speaking with conviction over their image:

"This is what I'm talking about—grown women not waiting for life to start."

Marsha sat up straighter, her eyes narrowing with interest.

"Hold on now..."

She tapped into the comments.

Thousands.

Not hundreds.

Thousands.

Her phone buzzed in her hand, the group chat lighting up before she could even process it fully.

Ebony M. Elite

Marsha: *Y'all... go on TikTok RIGHT NOW.*

Mary didn't rush.

She never did.

Her tablet rested on her lap as she sat beneath a soft lamp, reading through Facebook comments first, absorbing the longer words, the quieter affirmations, the tone of an audience that took its time. Then her phone chimed.

She glanced down, read Marsha's message, and opened TikTok with the same calm attention she brought to everything.

And then she paused.

Because it wasn't just their video anymore.

It had spread.

Different angles.

Different captions.

Different voices interpreting the same moment, reshaping it, reframing it, but always returning to the same core.

Them.

Mary adjusted her glasses slightly, her gaze steady.

"Oh... this is moving."

Back in her kitchen, Marlie finally picked up her phone, her thumb sliding across the screen as she opened TikTok.

There it was.

Their moment.

No longer contained.

No longer theirs alone.

She watched one version all the way through, then another, then a third, each one echoing something slightly different but circling the same truth—presence, confidence, ease.

A slow smile formed.

Not surprised.

Not overwhelmed.

Just… confirmed.

The group chat lit up in real time.

Mia: *I see it.*

Marsha: *No—do you SEE it?*

Mary: *This is beyond a post now.*

Marlie leaned her hip against the counter, typing with calm precision, her energy unchanged by the scale of what was happening.

Marlie: *This is momentum.*

A pause followed, subtle but felt.

Marsha: *This is a lot.*

Mia: *Yeah…*

Mary: *How does it feel?*

That question didn't rush to be answered.

It sat there.

Open.

Giving space instead of demanding it.

Mia stared at the screen before typing, her fingers slower now, more intentional.

Mia: *Good.*

A beat.

Mia: *…and something else.*

Marlie read that carefully.

Very carefully.

Because she knew that tone.

That space between what was said and what wasn't.

Her phone buzzed again.

Private.

Mia.

Marlie opened it, her posture shifting slightly as she turned the music down just enough to hear herself think.

Mia: *I need to tell you something.*

Marlie didn't respond immediately. She moved first, walking into her living room, lowering herself onto the couch, grounding her body before answering, because presence required intention.

Then she typed.

Marlie: *Okay.*

No pressure.

No urgency.

Just space.

Across town, Mia sat on the edge of her bed again.

Same place.

Different weight.

Her gaze moved between the WhatsApp thread and Marlie's message, back and forth, as if the distance between the two held the answer.

Her fingers hovered.

Then finally moved.

Mia: *He reached out.*

Marlie's expression didn't change, but something in her eyes sharpened, focused.

Marlie: *Who?*

Mia stared at the screen, then typed slower than she had all day.

Mia: *My husband.*

The room shifted.

Even miles apart—

it shifted.

Marlie leaned back slightly, not reacting, not rushing, understanding that how you respond to something like that matters.

Marlie: *Okay.*

A pause.

Intentional.

Marlie: *What did he say?*

Mia swallowed, her throat tightening as she typed, deleted, then typed again, needing the words to land exactly right.

Mia: *He saw the video.*

Back in the group chat, the energy had slowed, not gone, just waiting.

Marsha: *Why it got quiet in here...*

Mary: *Because something just shifted.*

Marsha leaned back into her couch, shaking her head slightly.

"I knew it..." she muttered, the realization settling in.

Mia's phone buzzed again.

WhatsApp.

She didn't open it.

Not yet.

Instead, she returned to Marlie.

Mia: *He said I look happy.*

Marlie closed her eyes briefly, because that line was never just that line.

Marlie: *And how did that feel?*

Mia let out a small breath, something between a laugh and a release.

Mia: *Like he noticed too late.*

Silence followed.

Heavy.

But honest.

The kind of truth that didn't need decoration.

Marlie stood, walking back into her kitchen, lifting her glass of water and taking a slow sip before responding.

Marlie: *Do you want to respond?*

Mia stared at the question, then at the message, then at the space between who she used to be and who she was becoming.

Mia: *I don't know.*

Back in the group chat, Marlie typed with quiet clarity.

Marlie: *Check on Mia.*

Marsha sat up immediately.

Mary already understood.

The messages came in without hesitation.

Marsha: *You good?*

Mary: *We're here.*

Mia looked at the chat, at the flood of presence, at the difference between this moment and the ones she used to navigate alone. Then she glanced back at WhatsApp, then back again, and something in her chest shifted—not loudly, not dramatically, but enough.

She typed.

Mia: *I'm okay.*

A pause.

Mia: *Just didn't expect my past to find me on TikTok.*

Marsha shook her head.

Marsha: *That's wild.*

Mary's voice came steady.

Mary: *Visibility changes things.*

Marlie followed without hesitation.

Marlie: *So does growth.*

Mia read that last message once.

Then again.

And for the first time since the notification came through, she didn't feel pulled backward.

She didn't feel small.

She felt… positioned.

Her phone buzzed again.

WhatsApp.

This time, she opened it.

She read the message fully, letting every word land without interruption. She didn't react. Didn't type. Didn't rush to respond.

She simply read.

Then she locked the phone, placed it beside her, and leaned back, allowing the moment to settle instead of control her.

Back in her kitchen, Marlie lifted her wrist again, the Dot Band catching the low light, smooth and controlled and forward-moving.

She tapped it lightly with her finger, not to activate it, just to feel it—a quiet reminder of where she stood, of what had shifted, of what no longer required permission.

Everything about today—from the video, to the recognition, to this moment right here—was saying the same thing.

You've moved.

And not everybody moves with you.

The group chat lit up again, the energy shifting back into something lighter, something held.

Marsha: *So what we doing this weekend?*

Mia let out a soft laugh.

Mary smiled.

Marlie didn't hesitate.

Marlie: *We're outside.*

Marsha shook her head immediately.

Marsha: *That's not a plan.*

Marlie leaned back into her space, a quiet smile settling in.

Marlie: *It is now.*

And somewhere between the past reaching forward and the present standing firm, the rhythm didn't break.

It adjusted.

Deepened.

Strengthened.

Because what followed them now wasn't just attention.

It was consequence.

And they were just beginning to understand what that meant.

Chapter Nine: Outside, On Purpose

Saturday didn't ask for permission. It arrived bright, confident, already in motion, the kind of day that didn't wait for you to catch up—it expected you to meet it where it was.

Marlie stood in front of her mirror, not rushing, not second-guessing, just adjusting the fall of her blazer with the quiet precision of someone who understood that presentation was a language.

Cream tones softened her silhouette, soft gold accents caught light without competing for it, and the clean lines of her look held everything together with intention.

On her feet, sneakers that didn't apologize—grounded, deliberate, a statement without noise. She stepped back, studying herself, tilting her head just slightly before the smallest nod of approval settled in.

Her phone buzzed.

The group chat was already alive.

Ebony M. Elite

Marsha: *What are we wearing?*

Mia: *Clothes.*

Marsha: *Be serious.*

Mary: *Intentional.*

Marlie smiled as she typed, her thumbs moving without hesitation.

Marlie: *Neutral base. Statement sneaker. Light gold or silver accents.*

A pause—then the responses landed exactly where she expected them.

Marsha: *So… money.*

Mia: *So… us.*

Mary: *So… aligned.*

Marlie slipped her phone into her bag, not lingering, not scrolling, then lifted her wrist, the Dot Band sitting secure, centered, exactly where it belonged. She tapped it lightly, a small ritual—not for function but for feeling—her reflection catching her eye one more time before she turned toward the door.

"Let's go."

Downtown carried its own rhythm—footsteps layered over traffic, sunlight bouncing off glass and steel, movement without chaos.

They didn't plan the exact moment, didn't coordinate arrival down to seconds. They understood it.

Mia arrived first this time, stepping out of her car with sunglasses already in place, her outfit catching the light with quiet confidence, the kind that didn't need validation to exist.

She checked her phone, her thumb sliding across Instagram, then TikTok, watching numbers climb, comments stack, new faces entering a space that had once felt private.

Her phone buzzed.

Not the group chat.

She paused.

Then ignored it.

Locked the screen.

Looked up.

And there was Marlie.

Walking.

Not fast. Not slow. Just steady, her movement matching the rhythm of the day like she had already synced herself to it.

Mia felt her lips curve before she even realized it and called out, *"You look like a decision."*

Marlie didn't break stride, her gaze meeting Mia's with calm certainty.

"I am."

They came together in a hug that didn't need to be exaggerated to be real—soft, grounded, present.

And then, as expected—

"Okay—y'all not about to act like I didn't understand the assignment."

Marsha's voice arrived before she did, and when they turned, there she was, stepping into the moment exactly as she intended—statement sneaker, statement energy, hair done with purpose like the destination mattered, even if the destination was simply them.

Mia clapped once, approval immediate.

"Okay Marsha."

Marsha spun just enough to let the look land.

"Don't play with me today."

Mary approached last, as always, but when she arrived, everything settled—not because she demanded attention, but because her presence aligned it.

Champagne tones wrapped around her like light had chosen her on purpose, minimal jewelry letting her energy do the work.

She looked at each of them slowly, taking them in, measuring nothing but recognizing everything.

"Yes."

That was all she said.

And it was enough.

They moved together without discussion, side by side, four women stepping into the city like it had been waiting for them. Phones came out, then disappeared, then returned—not out of need, but awareness, the difference between documenting and depending. Mia stopped mid-sidewalk, turning with instinct.

"Hold on."

She framed them, adjusting her angle as the street behind them hummed just enough to give life to the shot.

"Stand right there."

Marsha shifted her weight, adjusting her stance with playful seriousness.

"Tell me when I look expensive."

Mary exhaled softly, her tone warm but certain.

"You always do."

Mia lifted her phone, then paused, lowering it slightly as her gaze moved to Marlie.

"No—wait."

Marlie was already reaching into her bag, the clicker appearing in her hand like an extension of her thought.

"We don't do this halfway."

They positioned themselves without overthinking it—no strangers, no awkward asks, no compromise in angle or timing. Just them. Mia set the frame, stepped in, and—

Click.

The image caught movement instead of stiffness, energy instead of posing, life instead of effort. Mia glanced down at the screen, then back up, satisfaction settling in.

"Yeah… that's it."

Marsha leaned in immediately.

"Let me see."

She nodded slowly, her lips pressing together in approval.

"We're dangerous."

Mary's smile softened the word without removing its truth.

"No... we're aware."

Marlie said nothing, simply saving the photo, because she knew — this one mattered.

The rooftop lounge didn't require an announcement. They entered like they belonged, the transition from street to elevation seamless, music low, wind soft, the city stretching beneath them like a backdrop designed for their arrival. A host approached with practiced politeness.

"Do you have a reservation?"

Marlie stepped forward, calm, unbothered, her tone even.

"We do now."

The host blinked, then smiled, something about her certainty answering a question that hadn't been asked.

"Right this way."

Marsha leaned toward Mia as they followed.

"She just be saying things."

Mia whispered back, amused.

"And they work."

They were seated with a view, not because they demanded it, but because they arrived like they expected it. Menus were placed in front of them, but no one rushed to open them. Mia's phone buzzed again.

This time she picked it up, her eyes scanning the screen, holding the moment just a second longer than before, before placing it face down on the table.

Marsha noticed.

Said nothing.

Mary noticed.

Said even less.

Marlie noticed.

And shifted the moment.

"Order something you've never had before."

Marsha blinked.

"Why would I do that?"

Marlie met her gaze, steady.

"Because we're not repeating old patterns today."

Mary nodded once.

"I agree."

Mia picked up her menu, scanning it with a new kind of openness.

"Okay..."

Marsha sighed, already preparing her backup plan.

"If I don't like it, I'm ordering fries."

The server returned, and orders were placed, conversation settling into a rhythm that felt both new and familiar. Then Marlie lifted her wrist again, subtle but intentional. The server's eyes dropped, curiosity flickering.

Marlie smiled slightly.

"We'll close out now."

"Of course."

No wallet.

No phone.

Just—

Tap.

The confirmation tone was soft but final. The server paused.

"That's... convenient."

Marsha leaned back immediately.

"Convenient? That's elite."

Mia laughed, shaking her head.

Mary added quietly, her voice grounding the moment.

"That's intentional living."

Marlie rested her wrist back against the table.

"It's just knowing what works."

But the way she said it carried more than the words themselves.

Drinks arrived—light, cold, perfect—and they clinked glasses without announcing it, a quiet acknowledgment of where they were and who they were becoming. Mia's phone buzzed again, and this time it didn't feel like an interruption.

It felt like a decision waiting.

She picked it up.

Looked at the screen.

Opened the message.

Read it fully.

Then typed.

Slow.

Deliberate.

No shaking.

No hesitation.

Sent.

Marlie didn't look directly, but she felt it, that shift, that subtle release that changed the air. Mary saw it in Mia's shoulders, the tension easing. Marsha saw it in her face before she even spoke. Mia placed her phone down, exhaled, then looked up.

"Okay."

Marsha leaned forward immediately.

"Okay what?"

Mia smiled, and this time it wasn't forced, wasn't held together—it was free.

"I answered him."

A pause.

Then Marsha, unable to leave it there, pressed gently, *"And?"*

Mia lifted her glass, taking a slow sip before answering.

"And I didn't shrink."

The silence that followed wasn't heavy.

It was proud.

Marlie nodded once, slow, affirming.

"Good."

Mary's smile deepened.

"Very good."

Marsha leaned back, satisfied.

"That's what I'm talking about."

The city stretched behind them, wind moving just enough to remind them they were elevated, music rising slightly as the afternoon edged toward evening. Phones lit, dimmed, lit again—but nothing felt overwhelming anymore. Nothing felt like too much.

Because they weren't reacting.

They were choosing.

Marlie glanced down at her wrist again, the Dot Band catching sunlight, effortless, forward-moving. She tapped it lightly, then lifted her gaze to them.

"We're not visiting this version of ourselves."

A beat.

"We're staying here."

Mia held her gaze.

Mary nodded.

Marsha raised her glass with a grin that didn't hide anything.

"Well then... we outside for real."

Laughter followed, bright and unfiltered, cutting clean through the space around them. And somewhere between the skyline, the music, the messages sent and the ones left unanswered, and the quiet decisions made without announcement, they crossed another line.

Not loud.

Not dramatic.

But real.

Because being outside was never just about location.

It was about arrival.

And for the first time, none of them were wondering if they belonged there.

They knew.

Chapter Ten: When It Lands

Evening didn't fall—it arrived, soft at first, then layered with intention, gold slipping into amber, amber folding into blue while the city, always ready, lit itself like it understood it was being seen.

They stayed on the rooftop longer than planned, because leaving would have meant interrupting something still forming, something that hadn't yet said everything it came to say.

The music shifted almost without announcement, moving from background to presence, a live set unfolding as smooth R&B wrapped itself around a jazz progression, the singer's voice low and textured like every note carried memory.

Marlie leaned back in her chair, one leg crossing over the other, her wrist resting lightly against the table as the Dot Band caught the last thread of daylight before the rooftop lights took over, quiet and certain.

Mia held her phone again, not scrolling this time, not searching—waiting. Marsha was mid-story, fully in motion as always, her hands punctuating every word while her voice lifted with emphasis. *"And I'm telling you, if he would've just LISTENED the first time—"* Mary raised a finger gently, her gaze steady, her tone calm but effective.

"You're getting loud again." Marsha paused, glanced around the rooftop as if checking her volume against the atmosphere, then lowered it just enough to pretend she had adjusted.

"If he would've just listened the first time..." Mia let out a quiet laugh, the kind that didn't interrupt but acknowledged.

"There it is."

The singer's voice rose, carrying a note that didn't ask for attention but gathered it anyway, and Marlie's eyes shifted toward the stage just slightly, not fully turning, just enough to feel the pull.

Live music had a way of doing that—reminding you that your moment wasn't the only one unfolding, that something larger was always happening in parallel. Mia's phone buzzed in her hand, and this time when she looked down, there was no tightening in her chest.

That was new.

She opened the message. Read it once. Paused. Then read it again, her thumb still, her breathing even.

Marlie didn't look directly, but she felt it—the shift, subtle but present, like a current moving beneath the surface. Her voice stayed low, steady.

"You good?" Mia didn't answer right away, her eyes still on the screen, then she lifted her head slightly. *"Yeah."*

Marsha leaned forward immediately, reading tone more than words.

"That sounded like a loaded 'yeah.'"

Mary's attention sharpened, her voice softer, more precise. *"What did he say?"*

Mia exhaled slowly, turning the phone face up on the table, not hiding it, not protecting it, simply placing it where it belonged. *"He said he misses who I used to be."*

Silence followed, not awkward, not dramatic, but intentional, because that sentence carried more than it appeared to. Marsha blinked once, her reaction immediate. *"Oh."*

Mary tilted her head slightly, her thoughts already moving beneath the surface.

Marlie stayed steady, present, her voice measured when she spoke. *"And what did that mean to you?"* Mia met her gaze, holding it a second longer than usual, letting the answer settle before she gave it. *"It sounded like he misses who I was when I made him comfortable."*

That landed clean.

Sharp.

True.

Marsha leaned back slowly, absorbing it. *"Well... that's not the same thing."*

Mary nodded once, her agreement quiet but firm. *"Not even close."*

Marlie didn't rush to fill the space, didn't soften it, didn't redirect it.

She let Mia sit in what she had just said, because speaking truth and hearing it were two different experiences, and both mattered.

Behind them, the music swelled, the singer stepping deeper into her set, her voice wrapping around the table like it belonged there. Mia picked up her glass, not drinking, just holding it as if grounding herself in the moment.

"I almost felt bad for a second." Marsha leaned forward, her tone immediate. *"Almost."* Mia's lips curved slightly. *"Almost."* Mary folded her hands, her voice gentle but guiding. *"And then?"*

Mia set the glass back down, her fingers releasing it slowly. *"Then I remembered what it took for me to become this version of myself."*

A breath passed between them before she finished the thought. *"And I'm not undoing that."*

Marlie nodded once, subtle but full.

"Good."

The server approached with quiet awareness, timing the interruption with practiced ease. *"Another round?"*

Marlie didn't reach for the menu, didn't glance at anyone else for confirmation, her answer already decided. *"Yes."*

The server smiled. *"Of course."* Marsha turned toward her, eyebrows raised. *"You didn't even ask what we wanted."*

Marlie leaned back, calm, unbothered. *"I know what we're having."* Mia laughed softly, shaking her head. *"She really does this."*

Mary added, her tone warm with recognition. *"And she's usually right."*

The drinks arrived, sleek and intentional, matching the tone of everything else about the day, and Marlie lifted her wrist again without ceremony.

Tap.

Done.

The server's smile widened, curiosity turning into admiration. *"I need to look into that."*

Marsha pointed immediately, amused. *"See? She's recruiting."* Marlie's smirk was slight but undeniable. *"I'm informing."*

Mia's phone buzzed again, but this time it wasn't WhatsApp. She opened Instagram, her eyes scanning quickly before she turned the screen toward them. *"Okay... this is new."* They leaned in together, their attention narrowing.

A verified page had reposted their video, the caption sitting bold beneath it: *"THIS is what grown confidence looks like."*

Mary's brows lifted, her reaction quiet but meaningful. *"Oh."* Marsha sat up straighter, leaning closer. *"Wait—verified like... verified verified?"*

Mia nodded slowly. *"Yes."* Marlie looked at the screen, then at Mia, then back again, her expression unchanged but her awareness deepening. *"It's expanding."*

Notifications climbed faster now, the pace shifting, the energy changing. Shares multiplied, comments evolved, less casual, more intentional.

people weren't just watching anymore.

They were paying attention.

Marsha leaned back, letting the thought land fully. *"Okay... so what happens when we actually go somewhere big?"* Mia laughed lightly, gesturing around them. *"This is already big."*

Mary's gaze moved between them, her understanding settling deeper. *"No... she means something else."* Marlie's eyes shifted slightly as she thought, her voice coming with clarity when it arrived.

"The Sneaker Ball."

Marsha clutched her chest dramatically. *"Here we go."* Mia shook her head, smiling with recognition. *"You're serious about this."* Marlie didn't blink. *"Yes."*

Mary leaned forward slightly, her tone aligning with the direction. *"Then we need to be intentional."*

Marsha pointed as if she had been waiting to contribute. *"I'm already intentional. I just need food and music."*

Mia added smoothly, *"And lighting."* Mary followed, *"And space."* Marlie completed it, *"And presence."*

A pause settled over them, not empty, but full.

They all nodded.

Because they felt it.

This wasn't just an idea anymore.

It was forming.

The singer's final note stretched across the rooftop like a ribbon, pulling applause from the crowd as the city seemed to exhale beneath them.

And right there, in the middle of laughter, planning, and quiet power, Mia's phone buzzed again.

WhatsApp.

She looked at it.

Didn't flinch.

Didn't hesitate.

She opened the message, read it fully, then smiled—not soft, not uncertain, but certain. Her thumbs moved quickly this time, no hovering, no second-guessing.

Sent.

She placed the phone down.

Marsha watched her closely. *"That looked decisive."* Mia picked up her drink, finally taking a sip before answering. *"It was."*

Mary tilted her head slightly. *"What did you say?"* Mia set the glass down, her gaze steady as she looked at each of them. *"I told him I don't live there anymore."*

The silence that followed wasn't heavy.

It was powerful.

Marlie's expression softened, not with sympathy, but with respect.

"Good."

Mary's smile warmed. *"Very good."* Marsha lifted her glass, her energy bright and clear. *"To not living there anymore."*

Mia raised hers. Marlie followed. Mary joined. The glasses met with a soft, clear sound that carried more meaning than noise.

Final.

The city lights fully claimed the sky, music rising again, energy shifting as the night expanded around them.

Phones buzzed, conversations overlapped, life continued in every direction—but at their table, something had settled.

Not ended.

Not paused.

Settled.

Marlie glanced at her wrist one more time, the Dot Band catching the glow of the rooftop lights, a quiet symbol of movement, of choice, of stepping forward without looking back.

And as the night stretched wider, their laughter blending into it, the world still watching, still sharing, still responding—they didn't perform, didn't chase, didn't shrink.

They stayed.

Right there.

In the version of themselves they had fought to become.

And for the first time, nothing behind them felt louder than what was ahead.

Chapter Eleven: Seen… and Then Something Else

The night didn't end when they left the rooftop—it followed them, lingering in the soft rhythm still humming through their bodies, in the way the city lights clung to their skin, in the laughter that refused to settle all the way down.

It lived in the space between them as they walked, in the quiet understanding that this kind of night wasn't meant to be folded up and put away too quickly.

They didn't go home.

Not yet.

Because nights like this didn't ask for endings—they asked to be extended, stretched just a little further, lived in until they naturally released you.

So when they stepped into the lounge, it didn't feel like a new destination.

It felt like a continuation.

The lighting was low but deliberate, casting a soft glow across velvet seating that absorbed sound and softened movement. A DJ stood tucked into the corner, blending old-school melodies with something new—beats layered carefully over familiar rhythms so that everything felt like memory and motion at the same time.

It wasn't loud, but it was alive, and it moved through the room like something you didn't have to think about to feel.

Marlie paused just inside the entrance, her eyes sweeping the space—not searching, not adjusting—just taking it in long enough to understand it.

She didn't touch her hair, didn't smooth her outfit, didn't shift her stance.

She simply stood there, grounded, present, and then said quietly, *"This works."*

Mia followed her gaze, her eyes scanning the room with a kind of quiet precision before she nodded once.

"It does."

Beside them, Marsha let out a slow exhale, her shoulders dropping as if she had just stepped exactly where she was meant to be, a satisfied smile spreading across her face.

"Okay... now THIS is my speed."

Mary didn't say anything at all—she simply moved forward, her pace unhurried, her presence steady, and without discussion, without hesitation, the others followed her, their rhythm intact as they crossed fully into the room.

They chose their table the way they chose everything—without negotiation, without performance—just instinct. They sat, settled, arrived, and almost immediately a server appeared, as if the room itself had acknowledged them.

"Good evening, ladies."

Marlie met his eyes with calm presence, not inviting, not dismissing—just steady.

"Good evening."

He gestured slightly, attentive without being intrusive.

"Can I start you with something?"

Marsha leaned forward, her tone already playful, already engaged with the moment.

"Yes. Something that feels like a decision."

The server's smile shifted, recognizing the tone, understanding the assignment.

"I understand."

Mia let out a soft laugh, shaking her head slightly as she glanced at Marsha.

"Of course you do."

The drinks arrived cool and intentional, the glasses catching the soft light as the music lifted just enough to wrap around the room. Slowly, without announcement, the space began to fill in around them, and then—almost quietly—they were noticed.

Not all at once.

Not dramatically.

But in waves.

A glance that lingered.

A second look that confirmed.

A pause that stretched just slightly beyond casual curiosity.

The first man approached with care, stopping just outside the invisible line they carried with them. He didn't step into their space—he respected it.

"I hope I'm not interrupting."

Marsha leaned back, her expression already amused, already aware.

"You might be."

Mia smiled.

Mary watched.

And Marlie held the moment steady before answering, her tone even.

"Depends."

He nodded, accepting the rhythm they had set.

"Fair."

Then, with a small, respectful gesture toward the floor, he asked, *"Would you like to dance?"*

The pause that followed wasn't empty—it was intentional, felt, measured. Then Marlie turned her head slightly, her gaze landing on Marsha.

Marsha blinked, caught for half a second before letting out a small laugh.

"Oh—so I'm going?"

Mia's laughter slipped out easily, warm and familiar.

"You're always going."

Marsha stood, smoothing her dress with practiced ease before meeting the man's eyes.

"Don't embarrass me."

He smiled just enough to meet her tone.

"I wouldn't dare."

On the floor, the energy shifted.

Because Marsha didn't dance small.

She didn't shrink into politeness or follow out of obligation.

She moved with awareness—of the music, of her body, of herself—letting the rhythm meet her where she already was.

Not for him.

With him.

And that difference changed the way the moment held.

Back at the table, Mia leaned slightly toward Marlie, watching with quiet appreciation.

"Okay... that was smooth."

Mary nodded once, precise as ever.

"He approached correctly."

Marlie lifted her glass, her gaze still tracking the movement across the room.

"That matters."

The second man didn't hesitate when he approached. He moved with quiet intention and looked directly at Mary—not scanning, not guessing—choosing.

"May I?"

Mary studied him just long enough to understand his energy before she rose, her movement effortless.

"You may."

And just like that, she followed him into the flow of the room.

Mia watched them both for a moment before leaning back, her fingers resting lightly against her glass as she looked around.

"So... what is this?"

Marlie didn't rush to answer, letting the question settle before she turned her head slightly.

"What do you mean?"

Mia gestured subtly, her eyes moving across the room, taking in the glances, the attention that seemed to orbit without pressing.

"This... attention."

Marlie met her gaze fully now, her voice steady, grounded.

"This is what happens when you stop asking for it."

Mia held that.

Let it sit long enough to feel unfamiliar before she admitted quietly,

"That's new for me."

A small pause followed, and when Marlie responded, her voice carried a softness that wasn't pity—it was understanding.

"I know."

Mia's phone buzzed in her hand, pulling her attention downward. Instagram. Messages layered over messages, requests stacking, notifications pressing for attention. Her brows lifted slightly as she stared at the screen.

"Okay... this is getting ridiculous."

Marlie glanced briefly at it.

"That's visibility."

Mia exhaled, her thumb hovering before she locked the screen.

"It feels like noise."

Marlie shook her head slightly.

"Only if you listen to all of it."

Then, after a small pause, she added,

"You choose what matters."

The third man approached differently—no rush, no performance, just presence. He stood in front of Mia, grounded in his own space.

"Hi."

Mia blinked once, then smiled politely.

"Hi."

He didn't lean in or crowd her.

"I saw your video earlier."

Mia's brows lifted just slightly.

"Oh..."

He nodded.

"You looked... free."

That word didn't pass through her—

it landed.

She held his gaze, something shifting quietly inside her before she answered,

"I am."

He smiled—not impressed, not surprised—just acknowledging.

"Good."

A pause followed before he asked,

"Would you like to dance?"

Mia hesitated—not because of him, but because of herself. Because of what she had just walked away from. Because of what she was still learning to claim.

Marlie didn't interrupt.

Didn't nudge.

Didn't decide for her.

She simply remained there—present.

And after a slow exhale, Mia stood.

"Okay."

On the floor, the music softened, warmed, shifted into something more intentional. Mia moved carefully at first, her steps measured, her awareness sharp—but gradually, she let go.

Not completely.

But enough.

Enough to feel the moment.

Enough to exist inside it without shrinking.

Back at the table, Marlie watched—not protectively, not critically—just witnessing.

Mary returned first, easing into her seat with quiet composure.

"He was thoughtful."

Marlie nodded slightly.

"That fits you."

Mary adjusted her bracelet, her tone calm.

"He asked questions before he spoke."

After a brief pause, she added,

"I appreciated that."

Marsha returned next, her energy still bright, still lifted.

"Okay—he tried it."

Marlie raised an eyebrow slightly.

"Tried what?"

Marsha crossed one leg over the other as she sat.

"Tried to lead too much."

Mary's lips curved faintly.

"And you corrected him."

Marsha lifted her chin.

"Of course I did."

Mia returned last.

Slower.

Different.

She sat, wrapping her fingers around her glass before speaking, her voice softer now.

"Yeah... that felt good."

Marlie's smile was small but certain.

"Because it was."

Mia leaned back, her gaze moving across the room again—but this time she wasn't observing it.

She was part of it.

Her phone buzzed again—WhatsApp. She glanced at it, then turned it face down without opening it. As she settled back, her fingers lifted briefly to her temple, pressing lightly for just a second before dropping away.

Mary saw it immediately.

She always did.

"You alright?"

Mia answered too quickly, her hand already gone.

"Yeah—just a little headache."

Marsha waved it off with easy dismissal.

"That's the music."

Mia nodded.

"Probably."

Marlie didn't say anything.

But she saw it.

And this time—

she held it just a second longer.

Stored.

The night continued, folding laughter into music, music into movement, movement into memory. Glasses refilled. Phones lit and dimmed.

Moments layered without effort. And as Marlie lifted her wrist, the Dot Band caught the soft glow of the room, reflecting just enough to be noticed. She tapped it lightly, then looked at them—really looked at them.

Present.

Aligned.

Alive inside something they had created together.

"We're not slowing down."

Marsha lifted her glass, her grin wide.

"We just getting started."

Mary nodded, grounded and certain.

"There's more ahead."

Mia smiled, soft but sure.

"I can feel that."

And beneath the music…

beneath the laughter…

beneath the glow of being seen—

Something else moved.

Quiet.

Unannounced.

Unseen.

Just beginning.

And none of them knew yet—

how much everything was about to change.

Chapter Twelve: The Afterglow and the Echo

Morning didn't rush them—it lingered, stretching itself softly across the edges of the day as light slipped through curtains in quiet ribbons, settling into spaces where music had lived the night before.

The energy hadn't disappeared; it had simply changed form, softening into something more reflective, something that didn't demand attention but held it anyway.

Marlie was awake first.

Of course she was.

She stood at the window in a loosely draped robe, coffee resting warm in her hand, watching the city below reset itself with practiced indifference—cars moving, people crossing, life continuing as if nothing had shifted.

But she knew better.

Something had shifted.

Not loudly.

Not dramatically.

But real enough to feel it sitting just beneath the surface.

Behind her, her phone rested on the table—alive, waiting, aware of everything she hadn't yet looked at.

She turned slowly, picked it up, and unlocked it.

Instagram first.

Notifications stacked over notifications, messages layered, comments still arriving as if the night hadn't ended for anyone watching. She scrolled—not indulging, not reacting—just observing, letting the words pass through her with a kind of quiet assessment.

"Y'all are everything."

"This is how I want to live."

"Where was this??"

The tone was admiration.

But beneath that — something deeper.

Aspiration.

She shifted.

Then opened TikTok.

The video had moved again—further, wider, reaching people who didn't know them but somehow understood them. A woman's voice played over their clip, steady and clear:

"This is what happens when women stop shrinking."

Marlie paused the video mid-motion and let that sit, her eyes still, her expression unreadable for just a moment before something subtle moved across her face.

Then—

she smiled.

—

Across town, Mia was awake too, but she hadn't moved yet. She lay still in her bed, her phone resting against her chest, the screen dim but not fully asleep, like it was waiting for her to decide something. Her eyes traced the ceiling, but her mind wasn't there—it circled something else.

Something unresolved.

The message.

Still unopened.

Still present.

She turned her head slightly, her gaze dropping to the phone, her thumb brushing the edge of it before she flipped it over, placing it face down against her chest as if that alone could quiet it.

"Not yet."

The words barely left her lips.

They didn't need to.

—

Marsha's morning entered the day differently.

It didn't ease in — it arrived.

Music was already playing, filling her space with something upbeat and unapologetic.

Coffee brewed in the background, the scent cutting clean through the room, and her phone was already in her hand as she moved through her living space with a kind of satisfied energy.

Facebook.

She scrolled through reposts of the night, watching herself and her friends exist through other people's perspectives—clips, comments, shared moments that confirmed what she had already felt.

"Oh... okay..." she murmured, tapping into a comment thread, her eyes scanning quickly.

Women were tagging each other.

Pulling each other into the moment like it belonged to all of them.

"This is us in ten years."

"No—this is us NOW."

Marsha leaned back slightly, her smile widening as she took a slow sip of her coffee.

"Yeah... I like this."

—

Mary's morning moved at a different pace—quiet, intentional, grounded.

She sat at her table with a notebook open, her pen moving steadily but not hurried, capturing thoughts as fragments instead of full sentences.

Presence.

Visibility.

Witness.

She paused slightly before writing the next word — Consequence.

She underlined it once, slowly, deliberately, as if she wanted to feel the weight of it before moving on.

Then she reached for her phone.

Opened the group chat.

—

The thread came alive almost immediately, the rhythm of them picking up right where it had left off the night before.

Mary typed first, her tone simple, grounded.

Mary: *Good morning, ladies.*

Marsha: *Morning? I've been up.*

Mia: *Good morning.*

Marlie: *Morning.*

There was a brief pause—not empty, just settling—before Marsha added,

Marsha: *We trending.*

Mia: *We growing.*

Mary: *We shifting.*

Marlie read all three messages carefully, letting the pattern form before she responded.

Marlie: *We're being seen.*

The word sat differently.

It didn't carry the weight of attention — it carried depth.

—

Mia pushed herself up slowly, her back settling against the headboard as she reached for her phone again. This time, she opened Instagram with intention, her thumb moving more deliberately as she scrolled through the messages waiting for her—requests, invitations, conversations trying to begin.

She exhaled, the weight of it settling in.

"This is a lot..."

Her phone buzzed again.

WhatsApp.

She didn't ignore it this time.

She stared at it—long enough to decide.

Then she opened it.

Read the message fully.

Didn't flinch.

Didn't react.

She simply read.

Then typed.

One sentence.

Clear.

Finished.

She hit send without rereading, without adjusting, without questioning.

Just — sent.

—

Back in the group chat, her message landed with quiet finality.

Mia: *I'm done responding to him.*

The silence that followed wasn't confusion — it was recognition.

Marsha responded first, her tone sharpening slightly with curiosity.

Marsha: *Done… done?*

Mia: *Done.*

Mary's response came measured, thoughtful.

Mary: *How does that feel?*

Mia paused—not because she didn't know, but because she wanted to name it correctly.

Then she answered.

Mia: *Quiet.*

Marlie read that carefully before responding, her words steady, intentional.

Marlie: *That's not empty.*

Marlie: *That's peace.*

Mia leaned back, her head resting against the wall as her eyes closed briefly.

"Yeah…"

—

Marlie moved through her space slowly, setting her coffee down, adjusting nothing, existing fully inside the moment without needing to change it.

Her phone buzzed again, pulling her attention downward, and when she looked at the screen, it wasn't social this time.

An email.

Subject line simple.

Collaboration Opportunity.

She opened it, her eyes scanning quickly, her brows lifting just slightly as she read through the details.

Structured.

Intentional.

Interested.

She didn't respond.

Not yet.

—

Back in the chat, Marsha's energy pushed things forward again.

Marsha: *So what we doing today?*

Mia: *Recovering.*

Mary: *Reflecting.*

Marlie: *Planning.*

Marsha let out a small laugh, her response immediate.

Marsha: *Here she go…*

Mia smiled.

Mary did too.

—

Marlie picked up her phone again, her attention sharpening as she typed.

Marlie: *The Sneaker Ball.*

The response was immediate—three dots appearing at once.

Marsha: *You are serious.*

Mia: *Very.*

Mary: *Let's discuss.*

Marlie moved to her table and sat, her posture shifting from relaxed to focused without effort.

This wasn't dreaming.

This was building.

Marlie: *Location?*

Marsha: *Not too far.*

Mia: *But not basic.*

Mary: *Accessible.*

Marlie: *Elegant.*

The rhythm formed instantly — just like that.

—

Mia shifted slightly in her bed, her phone still in her hand as her fingers lifted again, pressing lightly against her temple. This time she held it there longer—not pain, not sharp—but present enough to notice. She frowned slightly, then shook it off, reaching for her water.

"I need coffee."

—

The chat continued to build around her.

Marsha: *Music?*

Marlie: *Live.*

Mia: *And a DJ.*

Mary: *Balanced.*

—

Marlie stood and moved toward her mirror, her reflection meeting her with quiet familiarity. She didn't study herself for approval—she checked for alignment. Then she lifted her wrist, the Dot Band catching the morning light, and tapped it lightly, the motion small but intentional.

Control.

Movement.

Forward.

—

Back in the chat, she typed again.

Marlie: *Dress code.*

Marsha: *SNEAKERS.*

Mia: *Statement.*

Mary: *Refined.*

Marlie: *Coordinated. Not matching.*

Marsha's response came with a smile behind it.

Marsha: *Of course.*

—

Mia smiled too.

Then—

winced.

Just for a second.

Her hand returned to her temple, pressing lightly again before she lowered it, dismissing it without comment.

Mary noticed the pause in her typing.

But she didn't say anything.

Not yet.

—

Marlie's phone buzzed again—the same email thread, another message added, this one carrying more urgency than the last. She read it slowly this time, her breath steady as she absorbed the tone.

Then she typed back into the group chat instead.

Marlie: *We're not just planning an event.*

A pause followed.

Then—

Marlie: *We're creating an experience.*

—

The chat went quiet.

Not uncertain.

Aligned.

Marsha responded first, her tone shifting slightly, more grounded now.

Marsha: *Well then…*

Mia: *Let's do it right.*

Mary: *We will.*

—

Marlie placed her phone down and turned back toward the window, the city now fully awake—moving, demanding, watching.

Behind her, her phone lit again.

Notifications.

Messages.

Opportunities.

Attention.

—

And in another part of the city, Mia sat still.

Quiet.

Her hand resting in her lap now, her phone beside her, screen dark.

Because for the first time in a long time — she wasn't responding.

She wasn't reacting.

She wasn't reaching back.

She was moving forward.

—

And somewhere beneath that quiet… beneath that clarity… beneath the afterglow of everything they had stepped into — the echo remained.

Soft.

Persistent.

Unnoticed by most.

—

But not gone.

—

Just waiting.

For the moment…

it would be heard.

Chapter Thirteen: Planning the Entrance

By afternoon, the day had settled into itself, not rushed, not dragging, but moving with intention—the kind of pace that allowed ideas to take shape without pressure.

Marlie's dining table no longer looked like a place to sit and eat; it had transformed into a working surface, a command center where vision was being translated into structure.

Her tablet remained open to the side, her phone within reach, and a notebook—actual paper—lay flat in front of her, filled with clean, deliberate handwriting that turned thought into direction.

The Sneaker Ball was no longer a suggestion.

It was forming.

Her phone buzzed, pulling her attention just slightly, and when she glanced down, the group chat had already come alive.

Marsha: *So we really doing this?*

Mia: *We're really doing this.*

Mary: *We need clarity.*

Marlie didn't respond immediately. She finished the line she was writing first, underlined it once with care, then reached for her phone, her posture shifting subtly as she moved from idea into declaration.

Marlie: *We're hosting.*

The pause that followed held weight, not confusion, just the natural adjustment to what that actually meant.

Marsha: *Hosting… hosting?*

Mia: *As in people coming?*

Mary: *As in responsibility?*

A slight smile curved at Marlie's mouth as she read them, her answer steady and unshaken.

Marlie: *As in all of that.*

Across town, Mia sat at her kitchen counter, her coffee finally made but still untouched, her laptop open in front of her with multiple tabs layered across the screen—venues, layouts, capacity charts, pricing structures.

She wasn't casually browsing; she was thinking, her mind moving ahead of her fingers as she scanned each option with quiet focus. A soft *"Okay…"* slipped from her as her phone buzzed again with the ongoing conversation, and when she picked it up, her answer came straight to the point.

Mia: *How many people?*

Marsha, already pacing her space with energy that refused to sit still, read the message while moving, her thoughts forming out loud before they ever made it to the screen.

She stopped mid-step, reconsidered, then typed instead, refining instinct into something usable.

Marsha: *We can't have too many people because I don't like crowds like that...*

Marsha: *But it still needs to feel full.*

Mary sat still, reading everything without interruption, allowing the conversation to build before she entered it. When she did, her words carried clarity.

Mary: *Invite list matters more than number.*

Mary: *Energy over volume.*

Marlie read all three responses, her eyes moving carefully, absorbing not just what they were saying but how they were thinking. Then she typed, her words precise.

Marlie: *Selective.*

Marlie: *Curated.*

The word settled into the space between them.

Curated.

Not open.

Not random.

Chosen.

Mia leaned forward slightly, her fingers moving with more intention now as the idea sharpened.

Mia: *So... who are we inviting?*

Marlie picked up her phone, then set it down again, then picked it back up, because this part wasn't casual.

This part mattered.

When she finally responded, her tone held definition.

Marlie: *People who understand presence.*

Marsha's response came immediately, half amused, half impatient.

Marsha: *That's not a list.*

Mia let out a soft laugh. Somewhere across the city, Mary's lips curved into a quiet smile. Marlie exhaled before refining it further.

Marlie: *People who don't need the room to validate them.*

Mary nodded to herself as she read it.

Mary: *Better.*

Marsha followed, still pushing.

Marsha: *Still vague.*

Mia added, more aligned now.

Mia: *But I get it.*

And just like that, the energy shifted—from idea into execution.

Mia opened a new tab, her fingers moving quickly as she typed *private event spaces near me*. She scrolled, paused, clicked, then clicked again, her eyes scanning faster now as options began to stack in her mind. When she typed again, it came with direction.

Mia: *I'm seeing a loft space.*

Marsha responded instantly.

Marsha: *How much?*

Mia didn't even look up from the screen.

Mia: *Relax.*

Mary leaned into the process.

Mary: *Send it.*

Links dropped into the chat one after the other, each one adding another layer to what they were building.

Marlie finally sat fully, her attention narrowing as she opened each one, studying them with intention—not casually, not passively, but critically.

Marlie: *First one is too small.*

Mia: *Agreed.*

Mary: *Second one lacks warmth.*

Marsha: *Third one looks expensive.*

Marlie didn't hesitate.

Marlie: *Third one feels right.*

Silence followed, not resistant, just acknowledging.

Then Marsha broke it with a small laugh.

Marsha: *Of course it does.*

Mia smiled. Mary nodded slowly. The decision settled into place.

Mia leaned back in her chair, her body shifting slightly as her hand lifted to her temple again, pressing lightly this time, lingering just a second longer than before. Her brows pulled together faintly before she shook it off, reaching for her water.

"I need to eat."

Back in the chat, the tone lightened again, the rhythm returning to something easy.

Marsha: *Food.*

Mia: *Important.*

Mary: *Essential.*

Marlie: *Elevated.*

Marsha's response came quickly.

Marsha: *Now you doing too much.*

Mia laughed.

Mary smiled.

Marlie stood again, walking toward her kitchen, opening the fridge and closing it just as quickly because her mind wasn't on food—it was on flow.

When she returned to the table, she picked up her pen, then her phone, and typed one word.

Marlie: *Music.*

Marsha didn't hesitate.

Marsha: *DJ.*

Mia layered onto it.

Mia: *Live band too.*

Mary refined it.

Mary: *Transition between both.*

Marlie completed it.

Marlie: *Seamless.*

The word lingered.

Because that was the goal.

Not just good.

Not just enjoyable.

Flow.

Mia's phone buzzed again, but this time it wasn't the group chat.

Instagram.

She opened it, her expression shifting slightly as she read, then murmured under her breath, *"Oh..."* Her fingers moved quickly.

Mia: *Y'all...*

The response came instantly, three dots appearing at once.

Marsha: *What?*

Mary: *What is it?*

Marlie looked up from her notebook, picked up her phone, and waited.

Mia sent the screenshot.

A message.

From a brand.

We'd love to collaborate with you and your group...

The silence that followed wasn't empty—

it was processing.

Marsha broke it first.

Marsha: *Oh we famous now?*

Mia shook her head slightly, even though they couldn't see it.

Mia: *Relax.*

Mary's tone stayed grounded.

Mary: *This is opportunity.*

Marlie read the message once, then again, her eyes narrowing slightly as she absorbed not just the words but the intention behind them. When she finally answered, it was quiet, but firm.

Marlie: *This is alignment.*

Mia blinked, a small smile pulling at her lips.

Mia: *You always say things like that…*

Marlie didn't respond to that.

Because she meant it.

Instead, she added,

Marlie: *We don't jump. We decide.*

Mary nodded to herself.

Mary: *Agreed.*

Marsha followed, practical as ever.

Marsha: *I still want to know if they paying.*

Mia laughed, the tension easing.

But then Mia shifted again, her body adjusting in her chair as her hand lifted once more to her temple. This time, she didn't pull it away immediately. Her fingers pressed lightly, her expression tightening just for a second longer than before.

Mary noticed.

Again.

Her message came gently, but direct.

Mary: *You sure you're okay?*

Mia dropped her hand quickly.

Mia: *Yeah.*

Marsha waved it off without concern.

Marsha: *Probably dehydration.*

Mia nodded.

Mia: *Yeah... probably.*

Marlie didn't speak. But her eyes stayed on Mia a moment longer than necessary.

Not dismissed.

Stored.

Back in the chat, she shifted the focus.

Marlie: *Guest list.*

Marsha responded immediately.

Marsha: *Here we go...*

Mia: *Let's start small.*

Mary: *Intentional.*

Marlie's response carried weight.

Marlie: *We don't invite people who don't understand us.*

The silence that followed this time held agreement.

Then Marsha broke it.

Marsha: *That's a short list.*

Mia laughed.

Mary smiled.

Marlie didn't.

Because she meant it.

She reached for her notebook and wrote carefully: *Experience. Not event.*

Then underlined it twice, sealing it in.

Her phone buzzed again.

She ignored it.

Because right now, she wasn't reacting.

She was building.

Across town, Mia stood slowly, her body feeling slightly off—not pain, not sharp, just a quiet pressure she couldn't quite name. She moved toward the kitchen, grabbed water, took a sip, paused, then shook it off with quiet dismissal.

"I'm fine."

Back in the chat, Marsha pushed forward again.

Marsha: *Date?*

Marlie glanced at her calendar, her mind already calculating, already aligning.

Marlie: *Soon.*

Mia responded immediately.

Mia: *That's not a date.*

Mary added,

Mary: *We need structure.*

Marlie smiled slightly, then answered with clarity.

Marlie: *Two weeks.*

The silence that followed held surprise.

Then Marsha responded.

Marsha: *Oh we moving fast.*

Mia: *We always do.*

Mary: *When it's right.*

Marlie looked at her reflection in the darkened screen of her phone, then lifted her wrist, the Dot Band catching the soft light again. She tapped it lightly, the motion small but intentional.

Control.

Movement.

Forward.

Then she typed, her words coming steady and certain.

Marlie: *We're not preparing to show up.*

Marlie: *We're preparing to arrive.*

And in three different spaces, three different women felt that, understood it, aligned with it without needing explanation.

While one—

sat quietly, her hand resting near her temple again, her expression still calm, still present, still moving forward with them.

Still smiling.

Still engaged.

And still—

not knowing.

Chapter Fourteen: The List and the Line

The difference between an idea and a moment was a list.

Names.

Energy.

Access.

By evening, The Sneaker Ball had moved beyond concept and into selection, and Marlie's table reflected the change.

It was clear now, stripped down to essentials: notebook centered, phone charged, tablet open, no clutter, no distractions—just decisions.

The room itself felt quieter, more deliberate, as if even the air understood that this was the part where vision either sharpened or fell apart.

Her phone lit up against the tabletop, and the group chat came alive before she even touched it.

Marsha: *I got my list.*

Mia: *Already?*

Marsha: *Don't question my efficiency.*

Mary: *Send it.*

A list dropped into the chat—names, notes, tiny descriptions attached to each person as if Marsha had already been rehearsing this in her head.

Mia read through it slowly, her brows lifting higher with every line until she finally let out a soft laugh.

"You really added commentary..."

Marsha didn't apologize for it.

Marsha: *Because context matters.*

Mary agreed without hesitation.

Mary: *It does.*

Marlie said nothing at first. She read every name, every note, every impression tied to every person. She didn't skim.

She weighed.

Considered.

Measured what each name would bring into the room before she finally typed:

Marlie: *Remove three.*

The chat paused.

Then Marsha came back in all caps, exactly as expected.

Marsha: *WHICH THREE?*

Mia laughed softly to herself as she read it, while Mary, somewhere in her own quiet, simply waited for Marlie to answer. When she did, her message was precise.

Marlie: *The ones who require attention to feel included.*

Silence followed again, but this time it was the silence of recognition.

Marsha leaned back wherever she was, thinking it through instead of arguing it, and after a moment she replied, slower now, more aligned.

Marsha: *Yeah... I see it.*

Three names disappeared from the list as quickly as they had entered it, and the moment felt cleaner almost immediately.

Across town, Mia sat at her counter again, laptop open, phone in hand, building a second list of her own. Not just names—categories.

She typed with more structure than emotion now, separating people into quiet columns inside her mind: Friends. Associates. Energy unknown.

Her phone buzzed again, dragging her attention sideways to Instagram, where another message waited, then another invitation, then another attempt to attach itself to what they were building.

She read just enough to understand the pattern, exhaled slowly, and closed the app.

Then she typed into the chat:

Mia: *We can't invite everybody.*

Mary answered first.

Mary: *We shouldn't.*

Marsha followed right behind her, firmer and less elegant.

Marsha: *We definitely not.*

Marlie's fingers moved more slowly when she responded, but there was nothing uncertain in the words.

Marlie: *This is not access.*

Marlie: *This is alignment.*

That word again.

Alignment.

Mary nodded to herself as she read it, the logic of it settling in her body before it reached her phone. Then she typed:

Mary: *Then we need a line.*

Mia blinked at the screen.

Mia: *A line?*

Mary answered with the patience of someone who had already finished the thought before she spoke it.

Mary: *Yes.*

Mary: *Who crosses it.*

Mary: *And who doesn't.*

Marsha sat up straighter reading that, her reaction immediate and genuine.

Marsha: *Oh… I like that.*

Marlie smiled—not big, not showy, but real—and typed back:

Marlie: *Exactly.*

She reached for her notebook and wrote the words carefully: *The Line.*

Then she underlined them.

The room around her seemed to tighten in focus after that, because this was the place where people usually got it wrong. Not the venue. Not the clothes. Not the music.

The guest list.

The line between inclusion and dilution.

The difference between a room that held and a room that leaked.

Mia leaned forward and typed again.

Mia: *What about plus ones?*

Marsha answered with instinct.

Marsha: *No.*

Mary answered with structure.

Mary: *Limited.*

Marlie read both and brought them together into something clean.

Marlie: *Invited energy only.*

The pause that followed wasn't resistance.

It was translation.

Marsha: *So no randoms.*

Mia: *No surprises.*

Mary: *No dilution.*

Marlie: *Exactly.*

Mia sat back then, but the movement didn't settle her. Her hand drifted to her temple again, pressing there longer this time, and a slight wince crossed her face before she dropped her hand too quickly, as if the speed of the motion could erase the moment.

I'm fine.

She didn't say it out loud.

But she thought it hard enough to hear.

The chat kept moving.

Marsha asked the question that had been circling the edges anyway.

Marsha: *What about the men?*

There it was.

Mia smiled slightly when she read it, because of course Marsha would say it that plainly.

Mary stayed still. Marlie read the message carefully before answering, her words arriving with the kind of clarity that ended a debate before it started.

Marlie: *They don't get invited because they're men.*

Marlie: *They get invited because they understand space.*

Mary nodded slowly and added:

Mary: *And boundaries.*

Mia followed, her message softer but no less important.

Mia: *And presence.*

Marsha leaned back with the satisfaction of somebody hearing the truth in regular language.

Marsha: *So basically... we cutting the nonsense.*

Marlie's answer came without hesitation.

Marlie: *We never invited it.*

That landed.

Mia laughed softly at that, but the laugh broke in the middle when her vision blurred for just a second. She paused, closed her eyes briefly, then opened them again and let the room reassemble around her.

"Okay..." she murmured to no one.

Then she shook it off.

Back in the chat, she redirected the moment.

Mia: *What about music guest list?*

Mary responded first, already parsing the phrase.

Mary: *Meaning?*

Mia clarified.

Mia: *The DJ and band.*

Marsha's answer came like a grin through the screen.

Marsha: *Oh we fancy now.*

Marlie corrected the tone before it could drift too far from the truth.

Marlie: *We were always.*

Mary smiled as she typed.

Mary: *We need sound that matches the room.*

Mia added:

Mia: *Not too loud.*

Marsha followed:

Marsha: *But not boring.*

And Marlie, looking down at her notes, wrote the word before she typed it.

Marlie: *Layered.*

She added it to the notebook beneath the growing architecture of the night:

Sound = Layered Experience

Her phone buzzed again—the collaboration email, another follow-up, another note of urgency pressing from the outside. She opened it, read it once, then locked her screen without answering.

Because urgency didn't move her.

Not like that.

Back in the chat, Marsha brought them to the next obvious thing.

Marsha: *Outfits.*

Mia answered with affectionate resignation.

Mia: *Here we go.*

Mary added:

Mary: *We already know.*

Marlie typed:

Marlie: *Sneakers first.*

Then, after a beat:

Marlie: *Everything else follows.*

Marsha's response came with no resistance at all.

Marsha: *I love it here.*

Mia smiled at that.

Then her hand moved again.

Temple.

This time she didn't catch it as quickly, and Mary saw it immediately because Mary always saw it. Her message appeared with unusual directness.

Mary: *Mia.*

Mia blinked, looked down at her phone as if the screen itself had called her name, and typed back:

Mia: *I'm good.*

Marsha followed with the kind of practical care that liked to disguise itself as simplicity.

Marsha: *Drink water.*

Mia answered:

Mia: *I am.*

Marlie didn't type.

Didn't interrupt.

But something in her chest shifted all the same.

Stored.

Not ignored.

The conversation moved on, because that was what the living always did, but the feeling stayed with her as she typed:

Marlie: *Date confirmed.*

A pause settled over the thread before she added:

Marlie: *Two weeks.*

Marsha's response came first, carrying both excitement and disbelief.

Marsha: *Oh we really doing this.*

Mia followed, more steady now.

Mia: *We're really doing this.*

Mary completed the thought, as she so often did.

Mary: *Then we move accordingly.*

Marlie looked down at her notebook, then up at her own reflection in the dark screen of her phone. After a moment, she lifted her wrist, the Dot Band catching the evening light that had started to settle across the room.

She tapped it once—soft, controlled, habitual now.

Control.

Movement.

Forward.

Then she typed:

Marlie: *We don't open doors for everyone.*

She let the words sit for a moment before finishing them.

Marlie: *We choose who walks through them.*

And across the city, three women felt that, accepted it, moved with it.

While one sat quietly, blinking a little slower than usual, still smiling, still typing, still present, and still not fully hearing what her body was trying to say.

Chapter Fifteen: The Test of Presence

By the next evening, the list carried weight—not just names, but decisions that had already begun shaping the room before the room even existed.

Who belonged. Who didn't. Who could enter a space and understand it without needing to be taught how to stand inside it.

Marlie stood at her mirror again, not adjusting much, because tonight wasn't about perfection.

It was about presence.

Testing the energy in real time.

A smaller outing.

Intentional.

A preview of what was coming.

Her phone buzzed against the dresser, and the group chat lit up before she reached for it.

Marsha: *What is tonight exactly?*

Mia: *A vibe check.*

Mary: *A soft launch.*

Marlie held her own reflection for a second longer before picking up her phone, her answer landing with quiet certainty.

Marlie: *A test.*

Marsha didn't miss a beat.

Marsha: *Of who?*

Marlie's reply came just as steady.

Marlie: *Everybody.*

Across town, Mia sat on the edge of her bed, dressed, ready—but still. Her phone rested in her hand, screen lit, Instagram open, but she wasn't scrolling.

She was thinking.

The messages had grown—no longer noise, but patterns. Men trying to start conversations. Women asking questions. Invitations. Interest.

Access reaching for access.

She locked the phone.

Then unlocked it again.

A quiet breath left her as she spoke softly into the stillness around her.

"Not everything is meant for me..."

She let the words sit just long enough to feel true before her phone buzzed again—WhatsApp this time. She looked at it, held it in her gaze, then turned the phone face down on the bed without opening it.

She stood.

"I'm going."

—

Marsha arrived first, of course, her energy already filling the space before anything else could.

"Okay—this better not be boring."

Her voice carried expectation like a challenge.

Marlie walked in seconds later, calm, grounded, already settled into herself.

"It won't be."

Mary followed behind them, quiet, observant, taking in more than she said.

"It doesn't need to be loud to be good."

Mia entered last.

Just slightly slower than usual.

But still present.

"Let's just... enjoy it."

—

The venue met them halfway—smaller, more intimate, the lighting dim but warm, music low enough to allow conversation but present enough to shape the room without demanding it. It didn't try too hard.

It didn't need to.

Marlie paused just inside the entrance, her eyes moving across the space, not judging, not critiquing — reading.

Measuring the flow, the people, the way the room held itself.

Then she nodded once, almost to herself.

"This works."

They moved in together without needing to discuss it. No hesitation. No confusion.

Just flow.

A few people were already there.

Not many.

But enough.

And the moment they entered, something shifted.

Heads turned—not dramatically, not exaggerated, but noticeably enough to be felt.

A woman near the bar leaned toward her friend, her voice low but not low enough.

"That's them."

Mia heard it.

Didn't react.

But she felt it.

Marsha smiled, satisfied.

"I like this already."

—

They took their table without conversation, guided by instinct rather than decision, and when the server approached, drinks were ordered—light, clean, nothing heavy enough to interrupt the night. Marlie lifted her wrist, the Dot Band catching the soft light, and tapped once.

Done.

The server blinked, surprised.

"I need that."

Marsha leaned back in her chair, amused.

"Everybody need that."

Mia laughed softly, the sound easy, natural.

Then she blinked.

Harder this time.

The room tilted—just slightly, just enough for her to notice.

She paused.

Her hand moved to the table, grounding herself in something solid.

Mary's voice came immediately, quiet but sharp with attention.

"You okay?"

Mia nodded too quickly.

"Yeah."

Marsha turned toward her, her expression shifting.

"You sure?"

Mia exhaled, slower this time.

"Yeah... just a little off."

Marlie didn't speak.

But her eyes stayed on Mia.

Longer than necessary.

Long enough to register that this wasn't nothing.

Then she shifted the moment—not dismissing it, but redirecting the energy.

"Let's stand."

Marsha blinked at her.

"Stand?"

Marlie was already moving.

"Move a little."

They followed without question, because they trusted her rhythm, and the music shifted as they stepped toward the floor, a deeper groove settling into the space. They weren't dancing.

Not yet.

They were simply present—letting the room meet them instead of chasing it.

—

A man approached.

Careful.

Measured.

"Good evening."

Marlie met his eyes, her tone even.

"Good evening."

He nodded, respectful but not overreaching.

"I've been seeing you all over my feed."

Marsha smirked, leaning into it without hesitation.

"We've been outside."

He smiled at that.

"Clearly."

Then he shifted his stance slightly, opening his attention to all of them, not just one.

"I like what you're doing."

Mary tilted her head, studying him the same way Marlie studied rooms.

"What do you think we're doing?"

He paused, considering it instead of rushing.

Then he answered,

"Living on purpose."

That landed.

Marlie nodded once.

"That's accurate."

He gestured lightly, respectful of space.

"May I join you?"

There was a pause—not rejection, not immediate acceptance.

Assessment.

Then Marlie answered,

"You may."

He stepped in carefully, not too close, not too far — just enough.

And in that moment, it became clear this wasn't just about them anymore.

People were watching.

Learning.

Responding.

—

Mia shifted again.

Her hand moved to her temple.

This time—

she didn't catch it.

Her fingers pressed slightly harder, her breathing changing in a way that didn't match the music, didn't match the room.

Mary saw it first.

She always did.

"Mia."

Mia blinked, slower now, her focus trying to settle. *"I'm fine."*

But her voice didn't land right.

Marsha stepped closer immediately, her energy tightening.

"You don't sound fine."

Mia shook her head—or tried to.

"I'm just…"

The word didn't finish.

It slipped.

Marlie stepped in instantly, not panicked but firm, her voice cutting clean through the moment.

"Sit."

Mia hesitated, just for a second.

Then she sat.

The room didn't stop.

But their space did.

Mary crouched slightly in front of her, bringing herself eye level, her voice calm but focused.

"Look at me."

Mia tried, her eyes locking in, then blinking again—harder this time, as if her body was fighting to keep up.

"I think I just need a minute."

Marsha reached for her hand, grounding her.

"You got it."

Marlie shifted her position slightly, standing just enough in front of Mia to block the room, to create a boundary without making a scene.

The man stepped back immediately, reading the shift without needing explanation.

"I'll give you a moment."

Marlie nodded once.

"Thank you."

The music continued, low, steady, unaware of the change that had just taken place.

But at that table — something had shifted.

Not broken.

Not fully understood.

But no longer ignorable.

Mia exhaled slowly, her hand still near her temple, her body trying to communicate something that didn't yet have words.

And this time— they were listening.

Even if they didn't yet understand.

And for the first time since this all began, the rhythm didn't feel completely smooth.

Chapter Sixteen: When the Energy Shifts

Morning didn't arrive gently—it entered with intention, light cutting through the blinds in clean, deliberate lines while the city found its voice earlier than usual, as if something had already begun without asking who was ready.

Marlie was up before her alarm, not restless, not anxious, but aware in a way that didn't come from noise, only from the quiet knowing that something had shifted overnight.

She stood barefoot in her kitchen, the slow brew of her coffee filling the space with a soft, steady hum while her phone rested face down on the counter, alive but not leading.

She didn't reach for it right away. Instead, she let the morning land—the light, the stillness, the grounded calm she had fought to return to—allowing herself to settle fully into it before anything else could claim her attention.

Then it buzzed.

Not once, but again, and again—persistent without being frantic, deliberate enough to be noticed.

Marlie turned her head slightly, her gaze lowering toward the phone as if she already understood this wasn't random. When she picked it up, the movement was unhurried, controlled.

Instagram opened first—notifications stacked. TikTok followed—climbing. But beneath that familiar rise of attention, there was something different this time.

A tag.

Pinned.

Featured.

She opened it and watched, her expression steady as the video unfolded—a clean edit of their rooftop moment, the walk, the laughter, the stillness, their presence captured and reassembled by someone who hadn't just seen them, but understood them. For the first time since all of this began, she wasn't just witnessing what they had done—she was seeing how far it had traveled.

The caption held its own weight:

"This is what it looks like when women stop waiting and start arriving."

Marlie exhaled slowly, not surprised, but not untouched either. *"Okay..."* she murmured under her breath, placing the phone down gently—not dismissing it, just putting it back in its place—because attention was one thing, but direction… direction was something else entirely.

—

Across town, Mia didn't ease into her morning—she sat up immediately, her phone already in her hand before her feet touched the floor.

WhatsApp opened first out of habit, the thread still there, unchanged, no new messages waiting for her. She stared at it a second longer than necessary, then locked her phone and placed it beside her.

That part was handled.

She reached for Instagram next, opened it, and paused—just long enough for the shift to register before her eyes adjusted and she blinked, sitting up straighter as her focus sharpened.

"Okay... wait." Her body followed her attention as she watched the same video Marlie had already seen, but from a different place.

Their moment—no longer theirs alone.

And the comments beneath it carried something deeper than reaction.

"I needed to see this."

"This is healing."

"Y'all don't even know what you did."

Mia's chest rose slowly, then fell as the meaning settled in. *"Yeah..."* she whispered, more to herself than anything else, because this was no longer just about them.

—

Marsha found out mid-scroll, exactly how she always did—TikTok first, then the repost, then the comments stacking until something in her posture shifted and she sat up hard, her voice breaking through her space without hesitation.

"Hold on—now WAIT a minute." She clicked into the profile, scrolled, clicked again, then moved straight into the group chat without pause.

Ebony M. Elite

Marsha: *Y'ALL UP??*

—

Mary was already awake. She always was.

Her morning unfolded slower, more intentional—tea steeping, sunlight settling across her living room in soft layers, her tablet resting neatly in her lap.

She saw the message, but didn't rush. Instead, she opened TikTok, watched the video fully, then again, and once more—not for content, but for context.

Her eyes narrowed slightly, not with concern, but recognition.

"Ah..." she said softly, placing her cup down with care. *"Here we are."*

—

Marlie's phone buzzed again.

The group chat.

She picked it up, read through it without interruption, and didn't respond immediately, allowing the moment to unfold fully before she entered it.

Marlie: *Good morning.*

Marsha came right back.

Marsha: *No don't 'good morning' me—DO YOU SEE THIS?*

Mia followed.

Mia: *I see it.*

Mary added, steady as ever.

Mary: *It's spreading.*

Marlie leaned against her counter, coffee now in her hand, her gaze steady as she read each message—not reacting, not rushing—just allowing the meaning to settle before she typed.

Marlie: *This is what happens when presence gets witnessed.*

A brief pause followed before Marsha answered in her own language.

Marsha: *This is what happens when we go viral.*

Mia let out a soft laugh.

Mia: *She's not wrong.*

Mary shifted slightly in her seat, her response grounding the moment where it could have easily lifted too far.

Mary: *Visibility always comes with responsibility.*

That landed clean.

—

Marlie read that message twice before lifting her eyes from the screen, because that was the part people didn't talk about. Attention was easy to want, but it came with weight—expectation, projection, and sometimes interruption.

Her phone buzzed again, but this time it wasn't the group chat.

A DM.

She opened it, read it once, then again, her expression unchanged, but something precise moved beneath the surface—not loud, not dramatic, just… noted.

—

Back in the chat, Marsha kept the momentum going.

Marsha: *So what we doing with this?*

Mia followed.

Mia: *Meaning?*

Marsha clarified.

Marsha: *Meaning... we just going to act regular or we stepping into it?*

Mary didn't rush.

Mary: *We define it before it defines us.*

Mia nodded to herself as she read that, the words settling into place. *"Okay..."* she murmured.

Marlie pushed off the counter then, walking slowly into her living room, grounding herself before she answered, because this wasn't loud—but it was real.

A pivot point.

She sat, then typed.

Marlie: *We don't chase it.*

Marlie: *But we don't shrink from it either.*

The silence that followed wasn't empty.

It was aligned.

—

Marsha leaned back into her couch, a slow smile forming. *"Yeah..."* she said out loud. *"That part."*

—

Mia stood, moving toward her window as the light caught her differently than it had the day before—not softer, but stronger. She typed with clarity.

Mia: *So we show up the same way.*

Mary followed, steady.

Mary: *Only more aware.*

—

Marlie glanced down at her wrist, the Dot Band resting there—simple, intentional, forward—before lifting her eyes again, looking at her phone, then the space around her, as something settled into place.

Clear.

Defined.

Ready.

—

Marlie: *The Sneaker Ball just changed.*

Marsha sat up immediately.

"See—this is what I'm talking about."

Marsha: *How?*

Mia's attention sharpened.

Mary already understood.

Marlie didn't rush the explanation. She let it land first, then gave it shape.

Marlie: *We're not just attending anymore.*

Marlie: *We're arriving.*

—

The silence that followed wasn't uncertainty.

It was recognition.

Because what had shifted wasn't the plan.

It was the scale.

—

And somewhere between a repost, a message left unanswered, a decision already made, and a room they hadn't even stepped into yet, the energy changed—not broken, not scattered, but elevated.

Because attention had found them.

But intention — was about to define what happened next.

Chapter Seventeen: When the Room Responds

Afternoon didn't settle—it expanded, stretching itself across the city in a way that felt less like time passing and more like something unfolding.

The movement outside carried a different texture now, not rushed, not chaotic, but aware, as if something unseen had shifted and the streets were adjusting in real time, people moving through light and shadow with just a little more intention than before.

Marlie felt it before she named it.

She stood in her bedroom, the soft glow from the window laying clean across her vanity while she adjusted the cuff of her blazer with slow precision, her reflection steady, unbothered, exact.

Cream layered over tone, gold catching light without asking for it, sneakers grounding everything beneath it with quiet certainty. Nothing loud, nothing forced—everything placed with intention that didn't need explanation.

Her phone rested nearby, screen dimmed but alive, not ignored, just not leading.

Her hand moved to her wrist, thumb brushing lightly over the Dot Band, the gesture now more ritual than action, less about the device and more about what it represented—control, movement, decision without hesitation. *"We're arriving."*

The words echoed back through her memory, not as something she had said, but as something she had committed to.

She picked up her bag without rushing and stepped out.

—

Downtown met them with layered sound and open light—traffic humming beneath conversation, voices rising and folding into one another, music slipping out of storefronts like the city itself refused to move quietly. The energy didn't overwhelm; it framed.

Mia was already there.

But this time, she wasn't waiting.

She was watching.

Sunglasses resting low on her nose, posture relaxed but alert, phone in her hand but not consuming her, she lifted her gaze just as Marlie approached, recognition immediate, a smile forming before she could check it.

"You feel that?" Mia asked as Marlie stepped beside her, their energy aligning without effort.

Marlie didn't look around right away. She looked at Mia first—measured, present, attentive in a way that read deeper than the surface.

"Yeah," she said quietly, her voice even. *"It's different."*

Mia nodded once, slipping her phone into her bag instead of holding onto it, a small shift but an intentional one.

"We're different," she replied.

That landed clean.

—

Marsha arrived the way she always did—voice first, presence second, energy already in motion before she reached them.

"Okay—why does it feel like something's about to happen?" she called out, adjusting her sunglasses with one hand while the other held her bag like she had somewhere else to be, even if she didn't.

Mia turned toward her, smirking slightly. *"Because you're here."*

Marsha placed a hand to her chest with mock offense. *"See? Hating already. I just got here."*

Marlie didn't interrupt. She watched, the moment unfolding exactly as it should, a small smile forming without announcing itself. Then she stepped forward, her voice calm, grounded, and precise.

"You didn't just get here." A beat. *"You entered."*

Marsha paused, the word settling in before she broke into a grin. *"See—that's what I'm talking about."*

—

Mary's arrival didn't shift the energy—it anchored it.

She stepped into their space like she had always been part of its rhythm, champagne tones catching daylight in soft reflection, her presence quiet but undeniable. Her eyes moved across each of them slowly, reading, confirming, grounding.

"Yes."

And again, it was enough.

—

They moved without a plan, which was the plan.

Side by side, four distinct energies flowing in alignment, their pace unforced, their attention shared between the world and each other.

Phones appeared when needed and disappeared just as easily, not distractions but tools—extensions of intention rather than interruptions.

Mid-block, Mia slowed, her hand lifting slightly. *"Hold on."*

They adjusted without question, turning toward her naturally, the movement of the street continuing behind them, framing rather than interrupting.

Marsha tilted her head. *"Tell me when I look expensive."*

Mary exhaled softly, almost amused. *"You always do."*

Mia lifted her phone, then paused, her eyes shifting toward Marlie instead of the screen.

Marlie was already reaching into her bag.

The clicker.

No words needed.

Just understanding.

"We don't do this halfway," Marlie said quietly, placing it into Mia's hand.

They positioned themselves—not stiff, not posed, but present, aligned in a way that didn't need direction.

Click.

The moment captured exactly as it existed—movement, breath, presence without performance.

Mia looked down at the screen, her expression softening. *"Yeah… that's it."*

Marsha leaned in, nodding slowly. *"We're dangerous."*

Mary shook her head gently. *"No… we're aware."*

Marlie didn't comment. She just saved it, because she understood something the others were still stepping into—moments like this didn't stay where they were created.

They traveled.

—

They entered the lounge without announcing it.

Not loud, not empty—curated. The music sat low enough for conversation, the lighting intentional enough to flatter without effort, the room filled with people who were present but not yet focused.

That changed.

Subtly.

Not everyone turned.

But enough did.

Eyes caught, held, lingered just long enough to register something without naming it.

A host approached, posture professional, tone polite. *"Do you have a reservation?"*

Marlie stepped forward, her movement smooth, her voice even—not requesting, but stating.

"We do now."

There was a pause, then recognition—not of name, but of presence.

The host smiled. *"Right this way."*

Marsha leaned toward Mia as they followed. *"See? She just be saying things."*

Mia's smile widened slightly. *"And they keep working."*

—

They were seated with intention, not placed but positioned, the room adjusting around them just enough to shift the balance of attention without disrupting its flow.

Menus arrived. Water poured. Time softened.

Mia's phone buzzed. She glanced down, held it for a moment, then turned it face down.

Not avoidance.

Choice.

Marsha noticed but said nothing. Mary noticed and understood. Marlie noticed—and shifted the moment before it could pull them elsewhere.

"Order something you haven't had before," she said, her tone calm but directive, her gaze moving between them.

Marsha blinked. *"Why would I do that?"*

Marlie leaned back slightly, relaxed but intentional. *"Because we're not repeating old patterns today."*

Mary nodded once. *"Agreed."*

Mia picked up her menu, thoughtful now. *"Okay..."*

Marsha sighed dramatically. *"If I don't like it, I'm ordering fries."*

Mia laughed softly. *"You're still evolving."*

—

The server returned. Orders were placed. The energy settled.

Then the shift arrived.

It didn't announce itself—it simply entered.

A woman approached their table, her presence confident but not intrusive, her smile measured, her eyes aware. *"I hope I'm not interrupting,"* she said, her tone warm but direct.

Marlie looked up first, then Mia, then Mary, then Marsha—each of them registering the same thing.

This wasn't random.

"You're not," Marlie replied.

The woman nodded slightly. *"I just wanted to say... I've seen you."* A brief pause. *"Online. And now—here."*

Mia's posture adjusted slightly—not shrinking, just recalibrating. Marsha leaned back, curiosity sharpening. Mary watched carefully.

Marlie held steady. *"And?"*

The woman smiled. *"And it's the same."*

That landed deep.

She gestured lightly. *"A lot of people... don't translate."*

Mia exhaled softly. Marsha sat a little straighter.

Mary's expression softened.

Marlie met her gaze. *"We're not performing."*

The woman nodded once, satisfied. *"I can see that."* A beat passed before she added, *"Keep going."*

And just like that, she stepped away.

—

Silence followed, not awkward, not uncertain—absorbing.

Marsha blinked. *"Okay... what just happened?"*

Mia shook her head slightly, a smile forming. *"That felt... important."*

Mary nodded. *"Because it was."*

Marlie let it settle before she answered.

"That's the room responding."

—

Their drinks arrived, cold and intentional, placed with care. Marlie lifted her wrist, the Dot Band catching the light as she tapped, the exchange seamless, almost invisible.

Marsha leaned back, shaking her head. *"I'm getting one of those."*

Mia smiled. *"You're ready now?"*

Marsha pointed. *"I'm evolving."*

Mary added quietly, *"With intention."*

—

Mia's phone buzzed again. This time, she picked it up, read the message, and without hesitation, typed her response, sent it, and placed the phone down.

Then she lifted her head.

"Okay."

Marsha leaned in. *"Okay what?"*

Mia smiled—certain, unguarded.

"I'm not negotiating with my past anymore."

—

Marlie nodded once. Mary smiled. Marsha exhaled. *"That's what I like to hear."*

—

Around them, the room continued—music rising, voices blending, glasses meeting in quiet rhythm—but the shift had already happened.

Marlie glanced at her wrist again, the band resting there like a quiet reminder, not of technology, but of movement, of control, of arrival.

She tapped it lightly, then looked at them fully.

"This doesn't stop here."

Mia held her gaze. *"It doesn't feel like it will."*

Mary nodded. *"Because it's not supposed to."*

Marsha lifted her glass slightly. *"So what's next?"*

Marlie didn't rush the answer. She let it form naturally, then spoke it clean.

"Bigger rooms."

—

And as the city continued to move outside, and the room adjusted around them inside, and the attention that had found them began to understand what it was seeing, they didn't chase it, question it, or shrink from it.

They met it.

Fully.

Exactly as they were becoming.

And for the first time—

the world didn't just notice them.

It responded.

Chapter Eighteen: When Presence Gets Chosen

Evening didn't fall over the city so much as unfold across it, slow and deliberate, like silk being drawn over glass.

Gold softened into amber, amber deepened toward blue, and every window catching the last of the light seemed to hold some private truth about who was inside and who was still on their way to becoming something more.

Marlie stood in front of her mirror without rushing, her reflection steady as her fingers smoothed the lapel of her blazer, not out of uncertainty but refinement, the final adjustment to a look that had already decided what it was doing before she ever stepped into it.

Cream rested clean against her skin, soft gold catching just enough light to whisper instead of announce, while the sneakers grounded everything beneath her with the kind of certainty that didn't ask permission to be read correctly.

Her phone rested in her hand, screen lit with a message that didn't explain itself, didn't oversell, didn't need to. An invitation. Simple. Clean. Placed.

She read it once, then again, her gaze lowering slightly as she let the energy of it settle into her body before her thumbs moved, her response exact and complete. *We'll be there.*

And when she set the phone down, she didn't question it, because she understood something most people never learned in time: the right rooms didn't require convincing.

They required arrival.

Across town, Mia sat at the edge of her bed already dressed but not fully finished, her posture upright yet still, as if she had paused mid-thought and hadn't quite returned.

Her phone buzzed softly in her hand, the group chat alive in its usual rhythm, Marsha already moving faster than the moment required while Mary shaped the edges of it into something more grounded.

Marsha's message came first, full of velocity and style even in text. Marsha: *Girl you said yes before you even asked what time.* Mary followed with her usual calibration.

Mary: *Timing matters. Presence starts before arrival.*

A slight smile touched Mia's mouth, but her fingers hovered above the screen just a fraction longer than usual, her eyes narrowing briefly as if the words in front of her needed more effort than they should have to settle into place.

Then she blinked, exhaled, and typed back. **Mia:** *What time?*

A pause followed before she added another line, quieter but more precise.

Mia: *We're arriving. Clean. Not loud.*

When she set the phone down, her hand lingered against her thigh, fingers pressing lightly as if grounding herself in something she couldn't quite name.

Marsha's energy filled her apartment before she ever stepped out of it, one sneaker on, one in her hand, her body moving through preparation like momentum itself.

She paced in front of her mirror with her voice already recording, reflection catching motion instead of stillness while she spoke straight into her phone.

Okay but are we doing statement or are we doing silent money? Because I can give both, I just need to know if we're walking in or ARRIVING arriving.

Mia's response came back quickly enough to still the room for half a second. Mia: *We're arriving.*

Marsha paused, head tilting as a slow smile spread across her face. *Say less,* she murmured, slipping on her second sneaker and grabbing her bag like the moment had finally introduced itself properly.

Mary, as always, didn't hurry anything. Her space held the same quiet order she carried into every room, every object placed with care, every choice made without spectacle. She adjusted the fall of her sleeve, the line of her outfit catching light in a way that felt less like styling and more like alignment, then reached for her phone and read through the messages once, not reacting so much as understanding.

Her response came without flourish.

Mary: *Understood.*

The word carried through the screen the way her presence did in person—calm, grounded, final.

When she stepped out, she didn't bring urgency with her. She brought presence.

The venue didn't reveal itself immediately.

It sat tucked into the city like it had no interest in being discovered by accident, its entrance understated until you crossed through it and everything changed.

Light dimmed just enough to draw attention inward. Music drifted through the air in soft R&B laid over a jazz progression that felt lived-in rather than performed.

The room itself carried a confidence that didn't need to announce exclusivity; it simply held it. Conversations didn't compete. They coexisted.

Marlie stepped in first, not claiming the space but settling into it, her movement smooth, her gaze steady, her energy adjusting the room in subtle increments as Mia followed just behind her, then Marsha, then Mary, their order unspoken but exact.

Eyes lifted. Not dramatically. Not all at once. But enough to register that something had entered which didn't ask for attention and still received it.

Okay… this is one of those rooms, Marsha murmured under her breath, her tone low but amused as her eyes moved across the space without searching.

Mia answered softly, though her voice carried the faintest delay, as if it had taken one extra step to find the surface. *Yes.* She adjusted the strap of her bag with a small, almost imperceptible shift.

From the other side, Mary's voice came gentle but directive. *Stay present.* Marlie said nothing, because she didn't need to.

Her silence held the same weight as instruction.

They hadn't reached the center of the room before the moment met them.

A man approached, not hurried, not intrusive, his presence grounded in a way that didn't require introduction to announce itself.

His suit was tailored but restrained, posture relaxed but intentional, gaze moving across them with quiet assessment before settling on Marlie.

Good evening, he said, his voice even, textured, carrying the kind of calm that came from knowing exactly where you stood.

Marlie met him without shifting. *Good evening.* He studied her for a brief second, then let a faint smile touch his mouth. *I was hoping that was you.*

Marsha's eyebrow lifted. Mia's attention sharpened. Mary's stillness deepened. Marlie tilted her head just enough to acknowledge the statement without accepting it fully. *And you are?* she asked, voice smooth, posture unchanged.

He didn't rush. *Someone who recognizes presence when it walks in.* The words didn't land like flattery. They landed like observation.

Mia's phone buzzed in her hand, the vibration small but insistent. Her fingers tightened around it for a second before she glanced down.

The screen lit. The message waited. Her thumb hovered, then pressed the side button, locking it without opening it.

When she looked back up, her expression had shifted—barely, but enough that Marlie saw it, registered it, and chose not to name it. Not yet.

There's a section upstairs, the man continued, his attention returning to the group. *I'd like you to join us.*

Marsha leaned just slightly toward Mia, her voice barely above a whisper. *See? She just be saying things and they keep working.*

Mia's lips curved, though her eyes lingered one second longer than necessary before she nodded.

Marlie held the man's gaze for one more measured beat, then stepped forward. *Lead the way.*

Upstairs, the air changed. Not heavier. Not lighter. Sharper. It was the kind of space where conversations were chosen instead of stumbled into, where attention didn't scatter so much as settle.

As they entered, a few heads turned, not in curiosity but recognition, the kind that comes from knowing something when you see it rather than needing it explained.

They were seated without hesitation, positioned with a view that framed the city beneath them like it belonged there, drinks arriving without being ordered, the rhythm of the room adjusting around them without disruption.

Mia moved with them, but just a fraction behind the pace now. Her hand brushed her bag once, then again, her brow tightening briefly before smoothing out.

Mary noticed. Marlie felt it. Neither spoke. Instead, Marlie leaned slightly forward, her voice cutting through the moment without raising itself.

Order something you've never had before. Marsha blinked, caught between confusion and amusement.

Why would I do that? Marlie leaned back, posture relaxed but intentional. *Because we're not repeating old patterns tonight.*

Mary nodded once. *Agreed.* Mia picked up her menu, eyes scanning more slowly than usual.

Okay... she said softly. Marsha exhaled dramatically. *If I don't like it, I'm ordering fries,* she muttered, though she never put the menu down.

Conversation unfolded without force.

Questions came, but not the usual ones. No one asked what they were wearing or where they had come from. The questions that arrived were about how they moved, how they thought, what they were building without announcing it.

Marlie answered without performance. Mary layered depth into the exchange without overexplaining.

Marsha balanced the table with warmth and humor.

Mia contributed too—measured, intentional, her pauses slightly longer than they should have been, her words chosen with care, as if she were stepping across them instead of speaking them.

At one point, the man's gaze returned to

Marlie and he said, *There's an event coming up. The Sneaker Ball.* Marsha straightened immediately, her eyes lighting with instant validation. *See—I knew it,* she said, pointing lightly as if confirming something she had already privately declared true.

Mia smiled, though it didn't quite reach her eyes as quickly as usual.

Mary inclined her head. *We're aware.*

Marlie's voice remained even. *We are.*

The man nodded. *You should be there. Not as guests.* He let the beat sit before finishing, *As presence.*

ia's phone buzzed again. This time, when she reached for it, her fingers moved slower. Her eyes narrowed slightly as the screen came into focus, then blurred for just a second before settling.

She blinked harder, her breath catching almost imperceptibly, then locked the phone without opening the message, her hand resting against the table before she drew it back.

Marlie's gaze flicked toward her, held for one beat, then released, her attention returning to the conversation without breaking its flow.

Okay so now we're not just going—we're making an entrance, Marsha said, leaning forward, energy rising. *An intentional one,* Mary added, steady as ever.

Mia lifted her glass, her smile softer now, quieter. *We've been doing that,* she said. Marlie met her eyes, holding them just a second longer than needed. *And we'll keep doing it.*

The city stretched beneath them, lights alive, music threading through conversation, the room fully aware of their presence now without needing confirmation.

Marlie leaned back slightly, her wrist resting on the table, the Dot Band catching ambient light as she tapped it once—not to use it, but to feel it.

Control. Movement. Forward.

She looked at them, really looked at them, and when she spoke her voice settled into the space with quiet certainty.

This is just the beginning.

Marsha smiled wide. *It better be.* Mary nodded softly. *It is.*

Mia held her glass, her gaze steady but deeper now, like something inside her was working just a little harder than it should have to keep pace with the moment. *Yeah…* she said quietly. *It is.*

And as the room adjusted around them, as invitations began taking shape and doors opened without resistance, as the night carried their presence further than it had before, something shifted—not loud, not disruptive, but real.

Because while they were being seen, while they were being chosen, while everything in front of them expanded, something beneath the surface had begun moving differently.

Not gone.

Not broken.

Just… off rhythm.

Chapter Nineteen: What Followed Them Home

The night didn't end when they left the room above the city. It followed them—into the mirrored quiet of the elevator, into the hush of the lobby where even footsteps seemed to land with more intention than before, into the black car waiting at the curb as if it had been watching for them the whole time.

Outside, the city had gone darker, but not softer. Its lights sharpened themselves against glass and steel, reflections sliding over windows while traffic moved below like blood through something still very much alive.

Marlie sat near the door, one leg crossed, her hand resting loosely over her bag while the Dot Band caught the low interior light every time the car passed beneath a streetlamp.

Across from her, Marsha was still talking—of course she was—her energy riding the last wave of the evening the way adrenaline always did after a room had answered correctly.

"I'm just saying, if we're being invited as presence, then certain people better understand this is not regular guest behavior."

Mia smiled faintly from the opposite seat, but the smile took a second longer to arrive than it should have, her fingers brushing lightly against her temple before falling back into her lap as if the motion had happened without permission.

Mary noticed. She didn't interrupt. She simply adjusted her attention, quiet and exact, the way she always did when something in the rhythm moved half a step off.

Marlie saw it too, but she didn't break the tone of the moment.

Not yet.

The city kept moving outside, and inside the car something else was building—not loud enough to name, but present enough to be felt.

Marsha leaned forward, phone already in her hand, opening the group chat even though all four of them were sitting within arm's reach.

"I need this documented while the room is still warm."

Ebony M. Elite

Marsha: *Tonight was not normal.*

All four phones vibrated within a breath of one another, the message arriving inside the car as if it needed its own echo.

Mary's lips curved softly as she looked down at her screen.

Mary: *Agreed.*

Mia glanced at the message, then at Marsha, then back at the screen before typing more slowly than the rest.

Mia: *No... tonight changed something.*

The words landed in the car with more weight than volume. Marlie read them, then lifted her eyes, meeting Mia's gaze just long enough to feel what sat underneath them.

"It did," Marlie said quietly, not typing this time, her voice low enough that it belonged to the moment instead of interrupting it. *"And we don't move from here like we don't know it."*

Marsha leaned back against the seat, one hand pressed lightly to her chest.

"See? This is why I don't like her getting too still. Every time she get quiet, she say something that sound expensive."

That earned a real laugh from Mia, though it came out softer than usual, and Mary let herself smile all the way this time.

"Because she thinks before she spends words," Mary said, her voice dry with affection.

Marlie didn't answer that. She didn't need to. The car turned, the skyline shifting in the glass, and for a second the city looked less like something they were passing through and more like something they had stepped into.

By the time the car pulled up in front of Marlie's building, the air had changed again. The night was cooler now, wind moving lightly between the buildings, carrying the faint scent of rain that hadn't yet fallen.

They didn't rush out. They gathered themselves first—bags, phones, posture, energy—because arrival still mattered even when the audience was gone.

Marlie stepped onto the sidewalk first, sneakers from this era replacing heels from another, and the others followed her beneath the low gold wash of the building lights.

A man near the corner glanced up from his phone and held the look just long enough to recognize what he was seeing.

Not youth.

Not trend.

Presence.

Inside, Marlie's apartment welcomed them the way it always did—warm, layered, curated without trying too hard.

Lamps glowed low against soft walls. Jazz rested lightly in the space like it had been waiting.

The city still lived beyond the windows, but in here the night had a different pulse.

Bags were set down. Blazers eased off shoulders. Jewelry loosened. Marsha kicked off one sneaker and then the other with a sigh that carried both relief and triumph.

"Okay. We need food or something pretty soon because elevated experiences still require substance."

"You mean snacks," Mia said, sinking gently into the couch.

Marsha glanced toward the kitchen without slowing down. *"I mean support."*

Mary set her bag beside the chair and took in the room, then Mia, then Marlie, then Mia again.

"Tea first," she said calmly. *"Then whatever Marsha is about to call survival."*

That made Mia smile, but it faded too quickly.

Her phone lit in her hand.

Not the group chat.

Not Instagram.

WhatsApp.

Her thumb hovered.

The room kept moving around her. Marsha opened cabinets with the confidence of a woman who had been there often enough to stop asking where things lived.

Marlie crossed to the kitchen island and reached for the kettle.

Mary lowered herself into the armchair, hands folded, eyes steady.

And Mia sat there in the middle of all of it, the screen casting a pale light against her face as she read something that pulled her expression tighter than it had been all night.

Marlie looked over without turning fully.

"You good?"

Mia didn't answer immediately. She locked the phone, then unlocked it again as if her body hadn't agreed with the choice the first time.

"Yeah," she said, but the word came out thinner than she intended.

Marsha looked up from the pantry.

"That was not a convincing yeah."

Mary stayed still.

"Don't rush her."

Mia exhaled slowly and lowered the phone to her lap.

"He said..." She paused, her brow drawing together like the sentence in her head wasn't arriving at her mouth the way it should.

Then she blinked, pressed her fingers lightly at her temple, and tried again. *"He said he sees who I am becoming and he... wishes he had valued it sooner."*

Silence settled into the room, not awkward, not dramatic—just honest. The kettle clicked softly as Marlie turned it on.

Marsha stared for half a second before clarity replaced irritation.

"That's a man recognizing a closing door."

Mary's gaze stayed on Mia, her tone level.

"And what did that feel like to you?"

Mia looked down at the screen again, then set the phone face down on the couch beside her as if she needed it further away to hear herself think.

"Complicated," she said. *"Not because I want to go back. I don't."* She swallowed, her eyes narrowing slightly. *"But because there was a time I would've waited for a message like that and called it healing."*

Marlie turned from the stove and leaned one hand against the counter, her gaze steady on Mia.

"And now?"

Mia let the question sit. The room breathed around her. Jazz moved low beneath the silence.

Wind brushed lightly against the windows.

"Now it feels like timing trying to pretend it's love."

That landed deep.

Marsha closed the pantry door with more force than necessary.

"See? That's what I don't like. Men always want revelation once the labor is done."

Mary's lips tightened slightly in agreement.

"They often admire in hindsight what they mishandled in real time."

Marlie looked at Mia for one more beat.

"And what do you want to do with it?"

Mia reached for her phone again, but slower this time, her fingers not as certain. The screen lit.

The message waited. Her thumb moved once, then stopped. She frowned—not at the words, but at her own hand, as if it wasn't obeying the pace in her mind.

"I know what I want to say," she murmured, almost to herself, her voice tightening into concentration.

Marsha straightened from the counter.

"Then say it."

Mia glanced up, and for one brief second frustration flashed across her face—not sharp, not loud, but real.

"I'm trying."

The room stilled.

Mary moved first, though gently.

"No pressure."

Marlie crossed the space and lowered herself onto the edge of the coffee table in front of Mia, close enough to ground her, far enough not to crowd her.

"Take your time."

Mia inhaled, then looked back down at the screen. Her fingers moved again. Stopped. Moved. She shook her head once, small and irritated with herself.

"That's weird."

Marsha's tone softened immediately.

"What is?"

Mia pressed two fingers to her temple, this time longer than before.

"Nothing. I'm tired."

But even as she said it, she didn't sound convinced.

The kettle began to hum louder. Marlie held Mia's gaze a second longer, then stood and returned to the kitchen without breaking the line of the room.

"Tea first," she said quietly. *"Then messages."*

No one argued.

The next few minutes unfolded in small movements—the kind that told the truth better than speech.

Marsha arranged snacks onto plates like she needed the act of doing something tangible.

Mary poured honey into mugs with measured precision.

Marlie moved between counter and table, her body steady even as her thoughts sharpened.

And Mia sat on the couch beneath the low lamp, her phone beside her now, both hands wrapped around nothing, her eyes following the room as if she were trying to stay inside it through intention alone.

By the time the tea was in their hands and the night had deepened fully beyond the windows, the group chat lit up again even though they were all still together. Marsha looked down at her phone and laughed softly.

"I know we're in the same room, but some things belong in the archive."

Ebony M. Elite

Marsha: *Tonight confirmed something.*

Mary's screen glowed next.

Mary: *That we are no longer entering rooms as possibility.*

Mia looked at the messages, then slowly lifted her phone and typed.

Mia: *We enter as fact.*

Marlie read that and something in her expression eased—not because everything was fine, but because Mia was still here, still with them, still naming the truth in her own voice. She typed back from where she stood near the window.

Marlie: *Exactly.*

Marsha looked up from her screen.

"See? This is why I don't let y'all leave without processing. Things get said."

That made them all smile, and for a moment the room held exactly what it had been building toward all along—not performance, not image, but depth.

The kind that didn't disappear when phones went dark.

Mia reached for her phone again. Opened WhatsApp. Read the thread one more time. Then, very slowly, she typed. Her thumb hesitated twice, and once her expression tightened like the letters on the screen were fighting her for order, but she stayed with it.

Marlie watched without staring. Mary noticed without intruding. Marsha held her breath without meaning to.

Then Mia hit send.

She set the phone down.

Looked up.

Mary's voice came softly. *"What did you say?"*

Mia let out a small breath, not quite a laugh, not quite relief.

"I told him gratitude and regret are not the same thing."

Marsha sat back, satisfaction and heartbreak moving through her at once.

"That's cold."

"No," Mary said quietly, looking at Mia with full understanding. *"That's clear."*

Marlie nodded once.

"And clarity is mercy when it's honest."

Mia smiled then, but it was tired around the edges.

"I'm done for tonight."

"Then be done," Marlie said.

No one pushed. No one asked for one more revelation. The night had already said enough.

Later, after Marsha finally left with half the snacks she claimed were being wasted, after Mary gathered her bag but lingered just long enough to make sure the room had resettled, after the apartment quieted back down to its own breathing, Marlie stood by the window once more with her phone in one hand and her tea in the other.

Behind her, Mia had gone still on the couch—not asleep yet, but close, one arm across her middle, her face softer now that she wasn't forcing herself to keep pace.

Marlie glanced down at the group chat one last time before the night closed.

Mary: *Check on her tomorrow.*

Marsha: *Already planning to.*

Marlie: *I know.*

She locked the phone and looked out at the city, its lights stretched wide and indifferent and beautiful. The room behind her held warmth.

The night ahead held consequence. And somewhere inside the stillness, beneath the rise and the rooms and the invitations and the attention that kept finding them, something else was pressing closer.

Not enough yet to stop anything.

Not enough yet to name.

But enough — that when the chat went quiet again,

the silence didn't feel empty.

It felt like listening.

Chapter Twenty: The Day After Arrival

Morning came with more shape than softness, light cutting clean across Marlie's bedroom in long, deliberate bands, laying itself over the chair by the window, the edge of her mirror, the blazer she hadn't hung up because the night had followed her home in pieces and she hadn't yet been ready to fold it away.

Outside, the city was already moving—delivery trucks backing into alleys, someone somewhere leaning too hard on a horn, the low mechanical hum of life beginning again without asking who had slept well and who had not.

Marlie stood barefoot in her kitchen with the kettle warming and her phone in her hand, not scrolling yet, not fully entering the day, just holding the quiet for one more minute before the world reached in.

It reached in quickly.

Instagram first.

The rooftop clip had continued overnight, comments layering beneath comments, strangers turning a moment into language and language into meaning.

"This is elegance without apology." "They don't even know how much this healed me." "Grown women moving like they know the room and themselves."

Marlie read without reacting outwardly, but something in her posture sharpened, not from vanity and not from surprise, but from recognition.

Attention was no longer arriving as novelty.

It was settling in as pattern.

Then the group chat lit.

Ebony M. Elite

Marsha: *Please tell me y'all are awake because we need to discuss the fact that we are apparently a movement now.*

Marlie smiled before she meant to, the expression small but real, and leaned her hip against the counter while the kettle hummed louder behind her.

Marlie: *Good morning.*

Mary followed a beat later, steady as ever.

Mary: *Good morning. Movements still require hydration.*

Marsha came back instantly.

Marsha: *Mary, if you don't let me be dramatic before breakfast…*

Mia's name appeared in the typing bubbles, disappeared, then appeared again before finally settling into a message.

Morning.

Short.

Present.

But slower.

Marlie read it once, then again, her thumb hovering before she answered.

Marlie: *How are you feeling?*

There was a pause—longer than it should have been for such a simple question—and when Mia's reply came through, it landed flat in a way that didn't belong to her.

Mia: *Tired. But okay.*

Mary saw it too.

Of course she did.

Mary: *Rest if you need to.*

Marsha, without missing the emotional shift entirely, still refused to let the room collapse under it.

Marsha: *Rest, yes. But after we acknowledge that verified people are looking at us like we got a publicist.*

That softened something.

Not erased.

Just softened.

Marlie finally moved, reaching for the kettle as it clicked off, pouring water into her mug with slow precision while steam rose between her and the phone.

The morning held itself together in layers—tea, light, city noise, conversation, all of it familiar enough to feel safe, all of it just different enough to require attention.

Across town, Mia was still sitting on the edge of her bed in the same oversized sleep shirt she had meant to change out of ten minutes ago.

Her phone rested in both hands, but her grip wasn't relaxed. She read the chat, read it again, blinked, then pressed her fingers lightly to her temple before lowering her hand as if the motion had embarrassed her.

On the nightstand beside her, a glass of water sat half-finished.

Her room looked lived in but paused—curtains half-open, one shoe lying on its side near the closet, the air still holding last night's perfume and whatever hadn't quite settled inside her body.

Her phone buzzed again.

A private message.

Marlie.

Marlie: *You don't sound like yourself.*

Mia stared at it, her eyes narrowing slightly, not at the words but at the effort it suddenly took to focus on them. She closed one eye, then opened it again, then sighed.

Mia: *I'm just tired.*

The response came back almost immediately.

Marlie: *Okay. Then be tired honestly.*

That made Mia smile despite herself, though it came slow and faint around the edges.

Mia: *That's annoying.*

Marlie's answer arrived with no hesitation.

Marlie: *And true.*

Mia looked at the message longer than she needed to.

Then she set the phone down beside her and stood, slower than usual, her body resisting the clean transition from stillness to motion. She crossed to the bathroom, one hand brushing the wall lightly as she passed, and caught her reflection under the white light over the mirror. For a second she just looked.

Not alarmed.

Not exactly.

But aware.

"Get it together," she murmured to herself, reaching for her toothbrush like routine alone could put the day back into order.

At Marsha's house, routine had no such elegance. Her kitchen already looked like intention and interruption had gotten into a light argument.

Toast half-buttered. Coffee too hot. Phone propped against a paper towel holder while she walked in and out of frame talking to the group chat like they were physically sitting on her counter.

Marsha: *I'm just saying, if people are already watching, then The Sneaker Ball better not look like some rushed community center misunderstanding.*

She took a sip, winced because it was too hot, and kept going.

Marsha: *No. We need shape. We need music. We need entry. We need the room to understand before we even sit down.*

Mary, seated by her window with tea and a notebook already open, read Marsha's message with the kind of expression that suggested she agreed but refused to reward the volume. She typed slowly.

Mary: *Then we plan it properly.*

Marsha's dots came up instantly.

Marsha: *Thank you. Finally. Somebody respecting my vision.*

Marlie set her mug down and glanced out at the city before typing.

Marlie: *Tonight. My place. We map it out.*

That sharpened the thread immediately.

Marsha: *Now we're talking.*

Mary: *What time?*

Marlie: *Seven.*

There was another pause before Mia answered.

Mia: *I'll be there.*

Again, Marlie read it twice.

The words were right.

The rhythm wasn't.

She didn't call it out in the chat.

She stored it.

The day moved, not in big scenes, but in small proofs.

Marlie spent the afternoon moving through errands that felt less like tasks and more like calibration—fabric swatches, a stop at a small stationery shop where paper still mattered, a quiet walk through a boutique where she didn't buy anything but saw enough to confirm she was already thinking ahead of the room she intended to create.

She answered two DMs and ignored seven. She saved one message from a man whose tone had been respectful enough to survive the first cut. She let another sit unanswered because interest without substance was still just noise.

When she returned home, the apartment had shifted back into receiving mode. Lamps were set low. The table was cleared. A notepad, pens, tablet, charger, and a bowl of fruit sat in place as if arrangement itself could make clarity easier to reach. By the time the buzzer sounded, she was ready.

Marsha arrived first, naturally, carrying both her energy and a bakery box she announced before she was fully inside.

"I brought lemon cake because strategy requires sugar."

She stepped into the apartment already dressed like she expected someone important to see her on the stairs—neutral set, statement sneaker, gold hoops catching the light every time she moved her head. Marlie closed the door behind her and took the box with a glance that was half appreciation, half inevitability.

"You brought support," Marlie said.

Marsha slipped out of her jacket and looked around with satisfaction.

"I brought solutions." Her eyes moved across the room once, taking it in. *"Okay. This feels like planning with consequences. I like it."*

Mary arrived next, quiet enough that the room settled when she entered. She wore warm champagne tones and carried a leather notebook tucked under one arm, her presence immediate without being invasive. She greeted Marlie softly, nodded at Marsha, and looked once around the room as if taking attendance beyond bodies.

Marsha dropped into a chair and glanced toward the door. *"We're missing the loudest quiet person."*

Mary looked at her.

"That sentence shouldn't make sense."

Marsha uncrossed and recrossed her legs. *"And yet."*

They waited.

Not long enough to call it concern.

Long enough to feel it.

Marlie looked at the time once, then placed her phone face up on the table instead of reaching for it. The room held its breath in small ways—the shift of Mary's fingers on her notebook, the way Marsha recrossed her legs twice, the low jazz moving through the apartment like a hand trying to keep everyone calm without announcing that anything needed calming.

Then Mia texted.

Mia: *Parking.*

Marsha exhaled immediately.

"See? Fine."

But when the knock finally came and Marlie opened the door, the first thing she noticed wasn't the outfit.

It was the delay in Mia's face catching up to her smile.

She looked beautiful.

Of course she did.

Soft taupe layered cleanly, hair smooth, makeup light enough to feel like skin, sneakers immaculate, bag resting against her shoulder like it belonged there. But her eyes were a little tired around the edges, and when she stepped in, her movement carried a fraction less certainty than usual.

Marlie moved aside.

"Come in."

Mia smiled.

"You say that like I was uncertain."

From inside, Marsha called out, *"You were late."*

"I said parking," Mia answered, but the line came out slower than the thought behind it, as if her words had to cross something before they reached the room.

Mary's eyes lifted.

Marlie heard it.

So did Marsha.

The silence that followed was microscopic.

Then Marsha, bless her, broke it on purpose.

"Sit down before I make your plate look judgmental."

That got a real laugh out of Mia, and for a second the room breathed again.

They settled around the table, not in formal positions but in familiar ones, and the planning began the way their best moments always did—not with structure first, but with rhythm.

"The Sneaker Ball," Marlie said, opening her tablet and letting the words sit in the center of the table like a match waiting to be struck. *"Not as trend. Not as gimmick. As arrival."*

Mary uncapped her pen.

"Then the room has to understand that before the first track plays."

Marsha nodded with immediate approval, already cutting into the lemon cake like momentum needed dessert.

"Exactly. No confusion. No cheap lighting. No somebody's-cousin-on-the-AUX energy."

Mia smiled at that, but her hand had gone to her temple again, fingers pressing lightly, briefly, before she dropped it and reached for tea instead.

Marlie watched without looking like she was watching.

"Music first," she said, redirecting the room while still holding Mia in the edge of her attention.

"Live at the beginning," Mary answered.

"Then a DJ once people loosen up," Marsha added.

"And no dead air between the two," Mia said, finally sounding like herself again, and the room brightened around it.

"Exactly," Marlie said. *"Seamless."*

They moved from music into lighting, from lighting into layout, from layout into guest energy.

Men were mentioned—not as targets, not as trophies, but as presences that would either understand the room or not be invited into it. The language stayed grown. Intentional. No one in the room had patience for spectacle without substance anymore.

Marsha leaned back, cake on her fork and judgment already in place. *"And if a man enters like he thinks the room owes him something?"*

Mary didn't look up from her notes.

"He leaves with less than he came for."

That pleased Marsha more than it should have.

Mia laughed again, softer this time, then winced almost invisibly as she lowered her head.

Marlie caught it.

This time she didn't let it pass.

"Mia."

The room stilled.

Mia looked up.

"What?"

Marlie kept her voice even.

"How bad is the headache?"

For a second, irritation flashed across Mia's face—not at Marlie, but at being read too well.

"It's not a headache," she said, then paused and corrected herself. *"It's just pressure."*

Mary put her pen down.

Marsha stopped moving entirely.

Marlie leaned forward, forearms resting lightly on the table.

"Since when?"

Mia looked from one face to another, suddenly aware she had become the center of the room without meaning to.

"A few days," she said. *"Maybe a week. It comes and goes."*

Marsha stared.

"And you didn't think that was worth mentioning?"

Mia exhaled, tired now in a way that went beyond the body.

"It didn't feel serious."

Mary's voice came calm, but lower than before.

"Pressure where?"

Mia touched her temple.

"Mostly here."

Marlie held her gaze.

"Vision?"

Mia hesitated.

"Sometimes weird."

That shifted everything without breaking the room.

Not panic.

Not yet.

But gravity.

Marsha sat back slowly, all the performance gone from her face.

"No. We're not doing that."

Mia frowned.

"Doing what?"

Marsha's eyes didn't leave her.

"Ignoring something just because it arrived quietly."

The words landed harder than she intended, mostly because they were true.

Mary reached for her cup but didn't drink.

"You need to get checked."

Mia opened her mouth to resist, then closed it again, her eyes lowering to the table as if that single sentence had pulled more weight than argument would.

Marlie didn't crowd her. Didn't dramatize the moment. She simply nodded once.

"Tomorrow."

Mia looked up.

"I'm fine."

Marlie's face didn't change.

"Tomorrow."

A beat passed. Then another.

And finally Mia looked away, exhausted by the resistance before it had fully formed.

"Okay."

The room breathed again, but differently now.

More carefully.

More honestly.

Marsha, still staring at Mia like irritation and love were wrestling for first place, muttered under her breath, *"I knew something felt off."*

Mary resumed holding her pen but didn't write.

Marlie reached for the teapot and refilled Mia's cup before her own.

The planning continued after that, because that was who they were—they didn't collapse under what needed to be handled.

But the energy had changed. The night was still warm. The apartment was still beautiful.

The Sneaker Ball was still taking shape. Yet beneath all of it, a quieter current had entered the room and settled into the spaces between words.

By the time they stood to leave, no one mentioned it again directly.

Marsha hugged Mia first and longer than usual, trying to make it look casual and failing.

Mary held her face for a second after their embrace, eyes steady behind her glasses. Marlie walked her to the door.

In the hallway light, Mia looked suddenly softer, less composed by force, more honest by accident.

"I'm okay," she said, almost as if she needed Marlie to agree.

Marlie adjusted the strap of Mia's bag where it had slipped against her shoulder.

"Then tomorrow makes that easier to prove."

Mia looked at her, then laughed under her breath because there was no arguing with that kind of love.

"You're annoying too."

"I know."

Mia smiled for real then, and this time the expression met her face on time.

But when the door closed and the apartment quieted around her, Marlie stood with her hand still on the knob for one second longer than necessary.

The jazz had ended. The city outside kept moving.

And inside, all the beautiful plans they had just made still sat on the table in notes and crumbs and teacups and light.

She looked at Mia's untouched second slice of cake.

Then at the group chat as it lit again with small, safe things.

Marsha: *Tomorrow means tomorrow.*

Mary: *Agreed.*

Marlie: *I know.*

And in that moment, beneath the style, the rooms, the rise, the invitations, and the future they were building with so much intention, something deeper took its place at the center.

Not fear.

Not yet.

Just the quiet, unmistakable sound of real friendship turning toward what mattered.

Chapter Twenty-One: The Thing They Couldn't Laugh Away

Sunday morning arrived too bright. Not cruel, just clear—the kind of brightness that left nowhere for anything to hide, not the dust in the corners, not the crease in a bedsheet, not the quiet thing sitting at the center of a room pretending it wasn't there.

Light moved clean across Marlie's bedroom wall and found her already awake, one arm folded beneath her head, the other resting over the phone on her chest like she had slept with responsibility instead of rest.

Outside, the city was slower than usual, church traffic beginning, buses moving in long patient sighs, someone somewhere dragging a cart across concrete with a sound that made the morning feel more real than gentle.

She didn't check the time first.

She checked the chat.

Tap.

Unlock.

Ebony M. Elite 💬

Nothing new.

Marlie stared at the screen a second longer than necessary, the silence between the last messages still holding shape from the night before. *Tomorrow means tomorrow.*

Marsha had written it like a warning wrapped in humor. *Agreed.* Mary had followed with the kind of finality that didn't need decoration. And Marlie had closed the thread with the only answer that fit.

I know.

She sat up slowly, the phone still in her hand, and moved barefoot toward the kitchen, letting the hardwood remind her where she was before the day could start deciding anything on its own.

Coffee came first out of habit, but she reached for tea instead. The shift was small.

The body notices before the mind admits.

Her phone buzzed before the kettle had fully warmed.

Marsha.

Private.

Marsha: *You up?*

Marlie didn't answer immediately. She filled the kettle, set it on the stove, then leaned one hip against the counter and typed.

Marlie: *I'm up.*

The reply came instantly.

Marsha: *I barely slept and I'm annoyed with all of us.*

That made Marlie smile despite herself, but only for a second.

Marlie: *Come over after church if you want.*

Marsha: *I want before church.*

Marlie looked at the message, then out the window, then back again.

Marlie: *Come.*

Across town, Mia was sitting at the edge of her bed in silence dense enough to feel upholstered.

One curtain was open, one still drawn. Her room looked divided in small ways she would normally have corrected by now.

The water glass from the night before sat on the dresser untouched.

One earring rested beside it, the other still in her jewelry tray because she hadn't finished the thought of putting both away.

Her phone lay in her lap, unlocked but unread, and her hand rested lightly against her temple, not pressing this time, just there, like her body had made the motion permanent in some small unconscious corner of itself.

She blinked.

Then again.

The room tilted so slightly it could have been imagined.

Could have been.

She waited for it to pass.

It did.

Mostly.

Her phone buzzed.

Marlie.

Marlie: *Good morning. Be honest.*

Mia stared at the words longer than she meant to. She knew what Marlie was asking. She also knew that honesty was becoming more expensive than she had planned for. Her thumbs hovered once, lowered, then rose again.

Mia: *Morning.*

Mia: *I'm okay. Just off.*

That was truer.

Not complete.

But truer.

The three dots appeared almost immediately, disappeared, then came back.

Marlie: *I'm coming with you today.*

Mia exhaled through her nose, her head lowering slightly.

Mia: *You don't have to.*

Marlie: *I know.*

There was no arguing with that kind of love.

Mia locked the phone, then unlocked it again, then typed one more line before she could stop herself.

Mia: *Okay.*

Marsha arrived at Marlie's apartment still buttoning the sleeve of her denim shirt, sunglasses pushed up into her hair like she had come prepared for both sunlight and battle.

She held a large iced coffee in one hand and a paper bag in the other, and when Marlie opened the door, she stepped inside already mid-sentence.

"I brought muffins because concern burns calories and because if we walk into a waiting room hungry, somebody going to get corrected."

Marlie took the bag from her without argument, the warmth of it soft in her hand.

"Good morning to you too."

Marsha kept moving, energy already pacing ahead of her body.

"It's not a good morning until somebody tells me this woman is fine."

Mary arrived ten minutes later with a tote bag over one shoulder and a quiet steadiness that changed the temperature of the room on contact.

She didn't rush a greeting. She entered, took Marlie in with one look, Marsha with the next, and then placed her bag down like she was setting more than leather onto a chair.

"Has she responded?"

Marlie nodded once.

"She said she feels off."

Marsha crossed her arms.

"Off is not a diagnosis."

Mary's eyes lifted gently.

"No. But it is information."

The three of them stood inside the kitchen for a moment with the muffins unopened, the tea steeping, the city alive beyond the windows, and none of them saying the word that kept circling the room because once certain words were spoken, they changed the architecture of the day.

Marlie picked up her phone and typed.

Marlie: *I'm leaving in twenty. We'll meet you downstairs.*

This time Mia didn't answer immediately.

That wasn't new.

But it felt different now.

They gave her time.

Too much time.

Then finally—

Mia: *Okay.*

No punctuation.

No softness.

Just the word.

The drive to Mia's building carried a quiet they respected instead of filling.

Marsha tried twice to turn on the radio and turned it back off both times before the first full chorus landed.

Mary sat in the back with her hands folded over her bag, her gaze moving between the window and the phone in her lap.

Marlie drove with both hands steady on the wheel, her eyes forward, her mind elsewhere and everywhere at once.

Sunday moved around them in pieces—families dressed for church, corner stores raising grates, men washing cars they loved more than they admitted.

The city was still being itself.

That was the strangest part.

How ordinary everything remained while one small center of the world shifted.

Mia was waiting outside when they pulled up, but *waiting* was too strong a word.

She was standing.

That was closer.

One hand hooked through her bag strap, the other resting against the side of her face for a second before dropping. Her outfit was clean and intentional in the way hers always were—soft neutral knit, dark leggings, statement sneakers, hoops small enough not to fight the day—but something in her body looked assembled rather than settled.

Marsha was out of the car first.

"You look nice," she said, then frowned. *"And tired."*

Mia tried to smile.

It arrived late.

"Good morning to you too."

Mary stepped closer, her eyes scanning Mia's face without making her feel examined.

"How long has it been since you ate?"

Mia blinked.

"I had tea."

Marsha closed her eyes briefly.

"That's not food."

Marlie came around the front of the car, her expression calm enough to keep the ground from breaking beneath them.

"Get in," she said softly.

Mia did.

The clinic sat in New Jersey in one of those medical complexes that all looked like they had been designed by people who thought beige was reassuring.

The lobby held that same careful neutrality—muted artwork, low voices, rows of chairs no one ever chose unless they had to.

The receptionist smiled professionally, asked questions that felt both routine and too intimate, and slid a clipboard across the counter with the quiet brutality of process.

Mia reached for the pen.

Paused.

Looked down at the form.

Then blinked hard once before beginning to write.

The first line came out slow.

The second slower.

She frowned.

Not at the content.

At her own hand.

Marsha saw it first. Of course she did.

"You okay?"

Mia nodded too quickly.

"Yeah."

But the word dragged slightly across her mouth, the edge of it softer than it should have been.

Mary took one step closer.

"Mia."

Mia pressed the pen harder to the paper as if force could fix fluidity. Her name came out wrong on the line. One letter missing. Then another. She stopped. Looked at it. Looked again.

"That's not—"

Her voice thinned.

Marlie leaned down beside her, close enough to ground but not crowd.

"Breathe."

Mia inhaled.

Then tried again.

The room tilted more this time.

Not the floor.

Her.

She reached for the edge of the chair and missed it on the first try.

Everything that happened after that unfolded both fast and impossibly slow.

The receptionist stood.

Someone behind the desk called for a nurse.

Marsha's voice changed shape entirely.

"No, no, no—look at me. Mia. Look at me."

Mary was already at her side, one hand at Mia's shoulder, the other taking the clipboard before it fell.

Marlie crouched directly in front of her, both hands gently on Mia's knees, forcing the moment to narrow.

"Stay with me."

Mia was trying.

That was the heartbreak.

She was trying so hard.

Her mouth opened. Nothing came out right.

Her eyes filled first with confusion, then anger at the confusion, then something worse when she realized she knew exactly what she wanted to say and her body was no longer treating that as relevant.

The nurse was there now. Then another.

Then a wheelchair. Questions came fast and practiced.

"Can you lift both arms?"

Mia did.

One slower.

"Smile for me."

She tried.

Marsha turned away for one second, not because she couldn't handle it, but because if she watched that request happen she might break something with her bare hands.

Mary didn't move.

Marlie didn't either.

"How long has this been going on?" the nurse asked.

No one answered immediately.

Because suddenly time had become accusation.

Mia tried to speak again.

The sound hurt to hear.

Not because it was loud.

Because it wasn't.

Her own frustration flashed across her face so quickly and so nakedly that all three women around her felt it like impact.

"It's okay," Marlie said, and her voice held so steady it could have convinced a less truthful room. *"You don't have to fight us right now."*

But Mia was already fighting.

Not them.

The distance between her mind and her mouth.

They moved her quickly after that. Triage.

Blood pressure. Questions. Light in her eyes. A doctor who arrived too calm to be comforting.

Words like *neurology* and *imaging* and *possible event* moved through the room with the smooth cruelty of language used every day by people who could afford for it not to be personal.

Marsha sat only when Mary physically touched her shoulder and pushed gently downward.

"Sit."

"I don't want to sit."

"Sit anyway."

So she did.

For one minute.

Then stood again.

Marlie handled calls with a voice so even it almost sounded detached, except Mary knew her well enough to hear the steel underneath. Insurance.

Contact information. What hospital. Which floor. How long. The questions multiplied because bureaucracy loved pain and believed it should be itemized.

By the time the scan was done and the doctor returned, the light outside had changed. Sunday had moved past midday without their permission.

Everything in the room had taken on the strange flattening quality of time spent under fluorescent truth.

The doctor stood in front of them with one hand tucked into his coat pocket and said the words carefully, like care could soften them.

"She has had a stroke."

The room did not explode.

It emptied.

Not of people.

Of oxygen.

Marsha sat down hard this time, one hand flying to her chest as if the words had crossed the room and struck her physically.

Mary closed her eyes once, then opened them and looked directly at the doctor the way she looked at anything she intended to survive.

Marlie didn't move for a full second.

Then she did what she always did when something unraveled without permission.

She organized.

"What now?"

The doctor answered in steps. Observation.

Stabilization. Speech impact. Follow-up.

Rehabilitation likely. They nodded as if understanding in order could keep the grief from spilling.

It couldn't.

But it gave their hands somewhere to go.

When they were finally allowed back in to see her, Mia looked both exactly like herself and unlike anyone they had ever known. Her face was still her face. Her hands still wore the rings she had chosen that morning.

Her hair still lay smooth against the pillow. But the woman who had corrected rooms with a glance and threaded truth through a group chat in six words or less now looked at them like she was trapped behind clear glass.

She saw everything.

That was the cruelty.

She saw.

Marsha lost the first tear and turned it into anger before it could become pity.

"Don't you dare look at me like I'm supposed to fall apart first," she whispered, coming to the side of the bed and taking Mia's hand. *"That's not how this works."*

Mia's mouth tried to move around something that wouldn't come.

Nothing clean emerged.

Her eyes closed.

Opened.

Filled.

Mary came to the other side, both hands around the rail before one rose and rested lightly over Mia's forearm.

"We are here."

Marlie stood at the foot of the bed for one second, taking in the machines, the wires, the angle of the blanket, the impossible indignity of hospital stillness wrapped around a woman who had been arriving everywhere on purpose just hours ago.

Then she moved to her.

Close enough for Mia to see there was no distance in her face.

"You are not alone in this room," Marlie said quietly.

Mia looked at her and tried again to speak.

The sound broke apart.

Marsha looked up at the ceiling.

Mary lowered her head.

Marlie reached for the notepad on the tray table beside the bed.

"Then write."

Mia took the pen.

Her hand trembled.

Not wildly.

Just enough.

She pressed it to paper.

Made one mark.

Stopped.

Looked at the page like betrayal had become visible.

Tried again.

The letters wouldn't obey.

Whatever she meant to say remained in her eyes—furious and trapped and fully alive.

Marsha turned her face away and cried properly then, silent at first and then not.

Mary put one hand over her own mouth, breath shuddering once before she mastered it.

Marlie took the pen gently from Mia's hand and placed it back on the tray.

"Then don't write today."

Mia looked at her.

Looked at all of them.

And what passed between the four women in that hospital room was not speech, not style, not visibility, not any of the things the world had recently begun rewarding them for.

It was something older.

Stronger.

Uncurated.

The kind of love that doesn't ask whether it looks graceful while it is breaking.

Outside, the city continued as if Sunday had held no emergency at all. People ate. Prayed. Slept. Scrolled. Laughed at videos. Commented on confidence. Planned events. Bought sneakers. But inside that room, time had changed species.

By evening, when the first wave of visitors had ended and hospital staff had begun speaking in lower tones, the three women gathered in the hallway with paper cups of coffee none of them really wanted.

The air smelled like sanitizer and something underneath it that every hospital held—fear made practical.

Marsha wiped her face with the heel of her hand and stared at the floor.

"I knew something was wrong."

Mary nodded once.

"So did we."

Marlie looked back through the glass at Mia's room, where her friend lay awake under thin white light, eyes open, body still fighting a war none of them could join for her.

"Now we know what the pause was saying," she said.

Neither of them answered.

They didn't need to.

Because the story had turned.

And from this point forward, everything beautiful they had built was going to have to prove it knew how to stay.

Chapter Twenty-Two: The Room That Didn't Close

Night did not fall the same way anymore. It didn't soften, didn't blur the edges—it clarified.

The hospital carried its own version of time, measured not in hours but in beeps, footsteps, doors opening and closing with controlled urgency, voices lowered not out of calm but out of habit.

Fluorescent light replaced sunset, monitors replaced music, and still, within all of it, the four of them remained exactly what they had always been—present, aligned, unwilling to let the room define the story without shaping it back into something that still belonged to them.

Marlie stood near the window of Mia's room, though the glass offered nothing but a reflection of the interior—her own silhouette layered over machines, over stillness, over the quiet rise and fall of Mia's chest beneath a thin hospital blanket.

Her arms folded lightly, not defensive, just enough to hold herself steady while her mind worked through what came next, because something always came next and she had built her life on meeting it without hesitation.

Across the room, Marsha had claimed the chair nearest the bed like it belonged to her now, one leg crossed, one foot tapping before she forced it still, her hands resting over the blanket with her fingers splayed as if contact alone could anchor Mia in place.

Every few seconds her eyes lifted, studying Mia's face with a focus that refused to soften into pity, refused to let this become something fragile when everything in her demanded it be fought.

Mary stood slightly back, not distant—never distant—but positioned where she could see everything at once. The machines. The posture. The breath. The subtle shifts most people would miss.

Her hands rested loosely in front of her, fingers interlaced, her gaze steady and deeply attentive, absorbing without reacting prematurely, holding the room in quiet discipline the way she held everything that mattered.

And Mia — Mia was awake.

That mattered.

Her eyes moved between them slowly, not unfocused, not lost—aware, present—but there was a delay now, a fraction of a second between intention and execution, between thought and expression, as if her body had introduced a small, stubborn distance she had not agreed to.

Marlie turned from the window and stepped closer, her movement smooth, controlled, her presence filling the space without overwhelming it as she leaned slightly toward Mia, her voice low and even, giving her room to meet it without pressure. *"How are you feeling?"*

Mia blinked once, then again, her gaze settling on Marlie's face as her lips parted, forming the beginning of a word that didn't quite land the way she intended. *"...fine."* The word arrived uneven—not broken, but not hers.

Marsha's jaw tightened for a second before she softened it, her hand pressing lightly against Mia's arm as she leaned in, her tone gentler than her eyes. *"You don't have to be fine today. You can just be here."*

Mia looked at her, something flickering behind her eyes—recognition, frustration, agreement layered together—and gave the smallest nod.

Mary stepped forward then, just enough to enter the circle without shifting its balance, her voice grounded, not soft for comfort but steady with truth. *"The doctor said the speech will come back with time. We work with what's here, not what we fear."*

Marlie's gaze flickered toward Mary, a quiet alignment passing between them before she reached for the tray beside the bed and adjusted it slightly, creating space where there hadn't been enough, because space mattered—even now.

Mia's hand moved against the blanket, her fingers curling as if reaching for something not yet there.

Marlie saw it.

Of course she did.

She picked up the pen and placed it gently in Mia's hand, not forcing, only offering as she met her eyes. *"Try when you want."*

Mia looked down at the pen, her grip uncertain at first, then firmer as she steadied herself, bringing it toward the paper with slow, deliberate focus.

The first line dragged—not clean, not smooth, but there. She stopped, studied it, then tried again. A shape formed. Then another. Not a word—but intention.

Marsha leaned in slightly, her voice lowering as if she were guarding the moment. *"That's it… don't rush it."*

Mary watched the movement, her attention on the effort more than the result, her voice quiet but precise. *"Repetition will rebuild the pathway."*

Marlie said nothing, her hand resting lightly on the edge of the bed, grounding the moment without interrupting it.

The room held—not tense, not fragile—just focused.

Outside, the world had not slowed down for them. Phones buzzed. Notifications stacked. The moments they had created continued moving without their supervision, carrying their image, their presence, their energy forward whether they were there to witness it or not.

Marsha's phone lit first, the vibration sharp against the table beside her chair. She glanced at it, then again, then reached for it with a quiet exhale, her brow tightening before she turned the screen toward them, her voice edged with something caught between disbelief and recognition.

"Y'all..."

Marlie looked up. Mary shifted her gaze. Mia's eyes followed the movement.

The TikTok had grown.

Not incrementally.

Exponentially.

Thousands had become tens of thousands, comments layering over comments, voices stacking in admiration, curiosity, projection.

"This is what I want my future to look like."

"They look like they've lived and still chose joy."

"Who ARE they??"

Marsha shook her head slowly, her thumb hovering over the screen. *"This thing didn't stop."*

Marlie's expression didn't change, but her eyes sharpened, her voice steady, certain. *"It won't."*

Mary stepped closer, her gaze moving across the screen, not impressed by the numbers but by the pattern forming beneath them. *"Visibility doesn't pause because life does."*

That landed.

Deep.

Because it was true.

Mia watched the screen longer than expected, her eyes narrowing slightly—not in confusion, but recognition. That was them. Out there. Moving. Smiling. Entering rooms. While she—

Her hand tightened around the pen.

The room felt it.

Marlie stepped in before the thought could root itself too deeply, her voice calm but firm, her presence closing the gap between perception and truth. *"That's still yours. None of this changes what you built with us."*

Mia looked at her, held her gaze, and for a moment the frustration softened into something steadier.

Understanding.

The door opened quietly then, a nurse stepping in followed by a doctor whose calm carried the weight of repetition, not detachment. *"Good evening,"* he said, his eyes moving across the room, taking in not just a patient but a unit, something structured, something aligned. *"How are we doing?"*

Marlie answered naturally, stepping into the space without overstepping it, her voice composed, clear. *"She's responsive. Alert. Working."*

The doctor nodded, stepping closer to Mia, his tone shifting as he addressed her directly. *"That's good. That's exactly what we want."*

He moved through the checks—measured, practiced, revealing more than they appeared to.

"Lift your hand."

Mia did—slower, but controlled.

"Good."

"Smile."

She tried.

It came.

Not perfectly.

But present.

Marsha turned her head slightly, blinking once before steadying herself again. Mary remained still. Marlie watched everything, every detail, every shift, studying the room until it made sense because that was what she did—she organized what others felt.

Later, when the doctor stepped out and the nurse followed, the room settled again into something quieter—not empty, not heavy—just real.

Marsha leaned back finally, exhaling long, her voice softer now, less guarded but no less certain. *"Okay... we're going to handle this."*

Mary nodded once. *"We already are."*

Marlie looked at Mia, her expression unchanged but deeper now, layered with commitment that had moved beyond control. *"One step at a time."*

Mia blinked.

Then nodded.

Hours passed without announcement. The city dimmed outside. The hospital lights did not. Marsha dozed briefly, her head tilting back before she caught herself, refusing full rest.

Mary stepped out and returned with tea no one had asked for but everyone accepted.

Marlie remained steady, her presence constant until she finally stepped into the hallway, her phone in her hand, the quiet there stretching long and heavy if you let it.

She opened Instagram—not to scroll, but to see.

The messages had multiplied. Requests. Invitations. Questions. A different kind of room opening.

She read one slowly.

"We're hosting a private event next week. Your energy would be perfect in that space."

Marlie stared at it for a moment, then locked her phone.

Not now.

Because some doors opened at the same time others required your full attention, and knowing which one to walk through—that mattered.

When she stepped back into the room, nothing had changed.

And everything had.

Mia was still there. Marsha still watching. Mary still steady.

But the air — The air had settled into something new.

Not fear.

Not uncertainty.

But a quiet, undeniable shift.

The kind that didn't ask permission.

The kind that didn't announce itself.

The kind that simply arrived and said — Now we see what this really is.

Marlie moved back to her place near the bed, her hand resting lightly against the rail as she looked at Mia, her voice low enough to belong only to the four of them, steady and sure.

"We're still moving."

Mia looked at her.

And this time — There was no delay in her understanding.

Only in her words.

And even that—

Would not last forever.

Chapter Twenty-Three: The Shape of Staying

Morning came to the hospital without tenderness. It did not soften for grief, did not filter itself into anything gentle, arriving instead through blinds that laid pale, deliberate stripes across the floor, the wall, the side of Mia's bed, and the plastic chair where Marsha had finally lost her battle with sleep sometime before dawn.

The room carried that over-clean scent hospitals wore like a second skin—sanitizer, paper, linen, machine heat—and beneath it, something more human had settled overnight, something lived-in and unpolished. Fatigue. Fear. Loyalty. The kind of love that had been up too long to pretend it was anything other than what it was.

Marlie was the only one fully awake.

Of course she was.

She stood at the small sink rinsing out a paper cup she had no intention of reusing, the motion giving her hands something quiet to do while her mind stayed several steps ahead of the room. The soft scrape of plastic against porcelain marked time without disturbing anyone, a rhythm she controlled while everything else waited to be named.

Behind her, Marsha slept crooked in the chair, one arm folded tightly across her middle, the other hanging halfway off the armrest, her face set even in rest like she was still arguing with the entire medical system somewhere inside a dream.

Mary sat near the window with her coat still on, not asleep, not quite—resting with intention, her posture composed even in stillness, the morning light catching the edge of her glasses and the leather spine of the notebook open in her lap to a page she had not yet written on.

Mia was awake.

Marlie knew it before she turned.

There was a difference between stillness and presence, and Mia—even now—had presence.

She turned just as Mia's eyes shifted to meet hers. No panic. No performance. Just the quiet acknowledgment of someone who had woken inside a life that had changed shape overnight and was still locating its edges without asking permission to collapse.

Marlie dried her hands slowly, deliberately, then stepped toward the bed, her voice low enough to belong only to the space between them. *"Morning."*

Mia held her gaze for a moment before answering, the word moving slower than the thought behind it, softer than her intention. *"...morning."*

It wasn't clean.

But it was there.

Marlie didn't flinch. She rested her hand lightly along the bed rail and nodded once, accepting the word as whole, as sufficient, as hers. *"Good."*

Marsha woke to that.

Not fully at first—just enough for her head to lift sharply, her eyes clearing before the rest of her body caught up. She looked at Mia, then at the light, then at Marlie, scanning for damage, for change, for anything she might have missed in the minutes she had allowed herself to fall under.

"I was awake," she muttered, though no one had accused her of anything.

Mary's mouth shifted just enough to register a smile as she adjusted her glasses. *"You were snoring with intention."*

Marsha turned her head slowly. *"I do everything with intention."*

The smallest lift touched Mia's mouth—not quite a smile, more the memory of one—and it moved through the room like something sacred.

It mattered.

The nurse entered shortly after, efficient without being cold, her badge swinging lightly against her scrub top as she moved through the routine with practiced ease—checking monitors, noting numbers, adjusting a line—before greeting Mia directly, never speaking around her, never reducing her to the bed she occupied.

"Good morning, Ms. Ellis. Did you rest at all?"

Mia tried to answer, her lips forming the beginning of something that stalled halfway to sound. Frustration flashed across her face so quickly it could have been missed by someone who didn't know her.

But they knew her.

Mary rose first—not in alarm, but in quiet reinforcement, stepping into the moment without taking it over, her tone steady, respectful. *"She did, in pieces."*

The nurse accepted that without redirecting Mia, without diminishing her. *"That's normal. The speech team will come by later this morning. Physical therapy too. The doctor will go over next steps."*

Marlie caught that immediately.

Next steps.

She didn't ask.

She stored it.

Because timing mattered.

The nurse smiled at Mia again as she finished checking her pulse. *"You're doing well."*

Mia looked back at her with eyes too aware to be comforted by easy phrasing.

She understood more than she could return.

When the nurse left, the room did not return to its previous quiet. This one had direction in it. The day had opened, and it was going somewhere whether they were ready or not.

Marsha pushed herself up from the chair, stretching the stiffness out of her back with a controlled grimace. *"I need coffee before somebody says one more professional thing to me with a calm face."*

Marlie reached for her bag without hesitation. *"Bring food too. Real food. Not waiting-room crackers pretending to be useful."*

Marsha pointed at her as she moved toward the door. *"See? That's leadership I can respect."*

Mary stood, smoothing her coat with a small, habitual motion before turning toward Mia, her voice grounded and certain. *"We're stepping out for a few minutes. We'll be right back."*

Mia blinked once.

Then nodded.

The hallway outside was too bright, too ordinary, too full of people whose lives had not been rearranged by a sentence spoken in a quiet voice.

Marlie stood still for a moment, looking down its length, her phone finally in her hand.

It had been buzzing all morning.

She had ignored it on purpose.

Now she unlocked it.

Instagram. TikTok. Messages. Tags. Requests.

A private invite from a boutique collective in Manhattan. A feature request from a woman-run lifestyle page. A sneaker brand rep asking about their styling. An event host asking whether they were attending The Sneaker Ball or *"gracing it."*

Marsha leaned in over her shoulder and let out a low breath. *"The internet really does not care that we are in a hospital."*

Mary walked beside them, her tone steady, unbothered by the contrast. *"The internet responds to image. Life responds to truth."*

Marlie locked the screen.

"Then we deal with truth first."

The cafeteria coffee was terrible, but it was hot, and that was enough. Marsha returned carrying more than necessary—three coffees, a fruit cup nobody wanted, two muffins, a yogurt, and a banana she held like it carried authority.

They walked back in with posture—intentional, controlled, held together on purpose.

Mia was still awake.

Still watching.

Still trying.

Marlie set the coffee down. Marsha unpacked the bag with more force than necessary. Mary moved the tray table closer, adjusting the space until it made sense again.

"We brought options," Marsha said, lifting the banana slightly. *"Don't make me negotiate with you this early."*

Mia looked at it, then at Marsha, and slowly rolled her eyes.

Small.

Precise.

Alive.

Marsha pressed her hand to her chest. *"Oh, so sarcasm survived? Good. We got a chance."*

Mia tried to laugh. It caught halfway, uneven, but present, and Mary looked down immediately to steady herself before her eyes gave her away.

Then the speech therapist arrived.

She introduced herself to Mia first, then the room, then placed a small stack of cards on the tray—simple images carrying the weight of everything that would have to be rebuilt.

She sat at eye level, her voice patient without being patronizing. *"We're going to start where your brain still feels strongest. Not where today feels weakest."*

Mia nodded.

The therapist held up a card.

"Tell me what this is."

Mia saw it.

Everyone could tell she saw it.

But the word didn't come.

Her lips moved around it, searching, failing, beginning again. Frustration sharpened across her face—not at the therapist, not at the room, but at the betrayal of clarity without access.

The therapist adjusted without hesitation. *"Okay. Point."*

Mia pointed.

"Good. Again."

They worked like that, time folding in on itself—twenty minutes stretching long and collapsing short at the same time. Pointing. Trying. Missing. Landing one word cleanly and losing the next entirely.

Effort sat visibly across Mia's face by the end, and when the therapist offered to stop, Mia shook her head once.

No.

Not yet.

Marlie looked down at her hands, steadying herself through stillness. Mary held the room with quiet discipline.

Marsha remained seated only because Mia had looked at her once—direct, firm—and told her without words not to fall apart here.

When the therapist left, she left with a plan, a packet, and a promise to return.

Then the doctor came.

This time he sat.

That was how they knew.

He explained the scan again, less clinical now, more final. Progress. Timing. Response. Rehabilitation. Intensive. Structured.

Then — New Jersey.

Marlie's body stilled before her expression did.

Mary leaned forward slightly.

Marsha's head snapped up.

"New Jersey?" Marlie asked, her tone even.

The doctor nodded. *"There's a facility with an excellent stroke recovery unit. She's a strong candidate. We'd like to transfer her once she's medically cleared."*

Mary's gaze moved immediately to Marlie, logistics already forming between them.

Marsha didn't hesitate. *"Good. Bring her closer to us."*

Mia looked from face to face, absorbing more than words—the shift, the movement, the next room already forming around her. Her hand gathered the blanket lightly, grounding herself in something she could still control.

Marlie stepped closer and placed her hand gently over Mia's. *"You heard him."*

Mia looked at her.

"Closer."

The word took effort.

But it made it out.

Marsha's face broke for a second before she caught it. *"Exactly. Closer. Which means you're stuck with us dressing this whole experience up."*

Mia's mouth moved again—almost a smile.

Almost.

The afternoon stretched into logistics. Calls. Forms. Queens. Clothing. Transfers. The practical world arrived without apology, as it always did.

And they did what women like them did.

They built beauty around it.

Not denial.

Not distraction.

Dignity.

Mary started the list—essentials, structure, care. Marsha added everything that made it human—lotion, socks, satin, softness. Marlie shaped it into motion—today, tomorrow, next week, after.

Mia watched them.

Every piece of it.

Her eyes moving from one to the next, following the shape of their loyalty as it filled the room more completely than any machine.

Marsha stepped close and adjusted Mia's scarf where it had shifted. *"We are not about to let you be in here looking like circumstances won."*

Mia's eyes closed briefly.

Opened again.

Wet.

Mary turned away under the quiet excuse of her notebook.

Marlie stood at the window, one hand on the rail, letting the grief move through her without changing her posture.

Outside, the world kept moving.

Inside, something stronger had taken hold.

By evening, the group chat returned—but differently.

Ebony M. Elite

Marsha: *"She's coming to Jersey."*

Mary: *"We plan around that immediately."*

Marlie looked at the thread, then at Mia, then typed.

Marlie: *"We stay visible in this too."*

The typing bubble came quickly.

Marsha: *"Meaning?"*

Marlie stepped closer to Mia, adjusting the blanket where it had folded wrong, then looked down at her phone again.

Marlie: *"Meaning we don't abandon who we are because life got hard."*

Mary: *"Agreed."*

Marsha: *"Then we visit right. Every time."*

Marlie turned the screen toward Mia.

Mia read.

Then looked up.

The tears didn't fall.

But the gratitude did.

And in that room, under hospital light, with plans forming around pain that had barely finished naming itself, the story shifted again—not away from them, but deeper into them.

Because what came next was not just recovery.

It was witness.

It was style refusing to collapse under sorrow.

It was friendship learning how to speak when language failed.

And not one of them—not one—was going to let Mia walk into that next room alone.

Chapter Twenty-Four: The Hours Between Visits

Transfer days did not feel like progress. They felt like interruption, like a sentence being moved to another page before it had finished saying what it meant.

The ambulance doors closed with that hollow, official sound that made everything inside them real in a different way, and the city beyond the glass—loud, familiar, always in motion—slid past without any visible understanding that something inside that vehicle had shifted permanently.

Mia lay still for most of the ride, not because stillness was what she wanted, but because focusing straight ahead required less negotiation than looking out. The ceiling was simpler than consequence.

Marlie sat closest, her hand resting lightly against the rail, not gripping, not hovering—just there, present in the exact way Mia needed. Her phone lay silent in her lap, though notifications continued stacking against the darkened screen like people knocking on a door she had no intention of opening right now.

Across from her, Marsha was quieter than usual, her eyes moving between Mia and everything else—the equipment, the route, the passing mile markers—as if she could calculate control out of observation alone.

Mary followed behind in her own car, because someone had to think ahead, someone had to meet the next room before they entered it and remove as much randomness from it as possible.

The rehabilitation center did not smell like the hospital. It smelled like effort—soap, rubber soles, faint disinfectant, and something underneath all of it that felt like repetition, the kind of place where people did the same hard thing every day until it stopped feeling like impossibility and started answering to another name.

Mia's room was smaller, simpler, less machine and more space. A bed. A chair. A narrow wardrobe. A window that actually showed outside instead of throwing the room back at itself. Across the hall, voices moved in and out of hearing—counting, encouragement, instructions repeated in calm tones that held both patience and expectation.

Mary was already there when they wheeled Mia in, standing near the foot of the bed with a small bag half-unpacked, the contents arranged not randomly but deliberately.

A scarf folded neatly. A framed photo. A soft throw draped over the chair as if beauty itself had been invited in before the patient arrived.

She looked up as they entered and said, with the kind of certainty that was less hope than decision, *"It's quieter here."*

Marlie nodded once, taking in the room, the light, the available surfaces, the possibilities. *"Good."*

Marsha looked around with hands braced at her hips, measuring the place the way she measured people. *"Alright,"* she muttered, *"we can work with this."*

Mia's eyes moved slowly through the room, taking it in piece by piece—the new walls, the new light, the new sounds, the unfamiliar order of another beginning.

Her hand tightened slightly against the sheet, not out of fear, but adjustment.

The intake process was smoother than the hospital, but no less structured. Papers. Questions. Assessments.

A therapist who introduced himself with calm authority and eyes that did not underestimate her.

He crouched slightly to meet her at eye level and said, *"We're going to rebuild what you already know. Nothing here is new. It's just waiting for you to reconnect to it."*

Mia looked at him, listened carefully, then gave the smallest nod, because she understood that even if she could not yet send the understanding back through language cleanly.

It was not until later—after the paperwork, after the first round of orientation, after the room had been adjusted enough to feel less temporary—that the part no one wanted but everyone expected arrived.

A staff member stepped into the doorway, polite but practiced, her tone warm enough not to bruise but firm enough not to invite negotiation.

"We do have to go over visiting guidelines," she said, looking between them. *"To allow patients to rest and focus on therapy, visits are limited to specific hours. Two visitors at a time. Evenings are shorter. And we do encourage some independent recovery time."*

The silence that followed was not resistance at first. It was reality landing.

Marsha crossed her arms slowly. *"Two?"* she asked, her voice controlled but edged.

The staff member nodded gently. *"At a time."*

Marlie stepped in before the energy tipped in the wrong direction, her voice smooth and composed, carrying acceptance without surrender. *"We understand. We'll work within it."*

Marsha looked at her, then at Mia, then back toward the doorway before exhaling through her nose. *"We'll rotate,"* she said. *"Fine."*

Mary was already reorganizing the future in her mind. *"We create a schedule."*

Marlie nodded once, because structure was how they survived things like this. Not by denying limitation, but by designing around it.

When the staff member left, the room returned to them in a different shape. The four women stood in a circle quieter than before, the air changed not by fear but by the introduction of limits.

Mia looked from face to face, her eyes sharper than her voice could match. She understood what had just been taken—access, presence, unrestricted time.

Marsha moved first, stepping closer and resting one hand gently against Mia's shoulder. *"Don't look at it like that,"* she said softly. *"We're still here. Just... in shifts."*

Mia blinked, then nodded once. Mary stepped in next and adjusted Mia's scarf where it had shifted. *"Consistency matters more than quantity,"* she said. *"You'll see us every day. Just not all at once."*

Marlie waited until last, then leaned slightly closer, her voice lower than the others, meant only for Mia. *"We don't disappear. We adjust."* Mia held her gaze, and something in her shoulders released just enough to be seen.

That night felt different, not because of the room, but because of the absence already waiting beyond it.

Marsha left first and hated it, looking back twice before the door closed behind her.

Mary stayed longer, writing something in her notebook before placing it in the drawer beside Mia's bed with the kind of quiet care that made objects feel less alone.

Marlie stayed until the last allowable minute, then stood still for one second before stepping back. Not rushed. Not dramatic. Measured. *"We'll be back in the morning,"* she said.

Mia tried to answer. The word took longer this time. *"...okay."* Marlie nodded once, then left.

The hallway felt longer on the way out. Quieter. Each of them moving back toward lives that had not paused even though something inside them had.

Marsha drove home with the radio off, her hands tighter on the wheel than usual.

Mary stopped at a store before heading back, picking up items she had already added to her mental list.

Marlie sat in her car for a moment longer than necessary, her phone lighting up in her hand again. This time she looked. Messages layered across the screen.

Opportunities still knocking. Rooms still opening. A life still moving forward whether she acknowledged it or not.

She exhaled slowly, then opened the group chat.

Ebony M. Elite

Marlie: *We need a rotation. Mornings, afternoons, evenings.*

Mary answered first. *I'll take mornings when I can.*

Marsha followed. *Evenings for me. After work.*

Marlie read both, then added what all three of them already knew.

Marlie: *I'll fill the gaps.*

Marsha's typing bubble appeared almost immediately. *You always do.*

Marlie did not answer that. She did not need to.

The days after that began to take shape in the only way hard seasons ever could when handled by women like them—structured, divided, intentional.

Mornings belonged to quiet. To Mary sitting beside Mia with a calm presence, reading softly, guiding her through simple exercises, helping her write the same word three times until it began to resemble itself again. Afternoons carried effort.

Therapy rooms. Measured steps. Words attempted. Muscles relearning. Frustration rising and falling like breath.

Evenings belonged to Marsha, who brought energy back into the room by force if necessary—stories, commentary, small laughter pushed in until it stopped being pushed.

One evening, as she adjusted Mia's blanket with exaggerated care, she said, *"You're not about to turn into somebody quiet on me. We didn't survive everything just for you to get soft-spoken now."*

Mia tried to laugh, and this time it came out clearer. Not perfect. But closer.

And in between all of it, there was Marlie.

Filling the spaces.

Arriving early. Leaving late. Managing calls in hallways. Answering messages without stepping away from the room entirely. Balancing because she had to. Because they all did. One afternoon, standing just outside the therapy room while Mia worked through a set of exercises inside, Marlie finally answered one of the messages that had been waiting in her inbox.

We'd love to host you at a private event next week...

She stared at it for a second, then typed carefully.

I'll confirm availability.

Not yes.

Not no.

Because life required a different kind of timing now.

That evening, back in Mia's room, the group chat lit again.

Ebony M. Elite

Mary: *She wrote her name today.*

There was a pause.

Marsha: *Say that again.*

Mary answered with a photo.

Not Mia's face.

The paper.

Uneven. Shaky. But there.

Mia.

Marlie stared at it longer than she expected to, the simple truth of those four letters carrying more force than half the rooms they had walked into lately. Then she typed.

Marlie: *We're moving.*

Marsha answered immediately. *We never stopped.*

Mia watched the screen from the bed as Marlie angled the phone just enough for her to see it. She read the message, then looked up. Her eyes were clearer now than they had been that morning.

Her hand moved slowly toward the tray, toward the pen. And this time, when she wrote, it was not just effort.

It was intention beginning to return.

Outside, the world still moved. Events still happened. Music still played. Rooms still opened.

But inside that smaller, quieter space in New Jersey, something else was building—something not loud, not quick, but steady. The kind of progress that did not announce itself and yet changed everything anyway.

Chapter Twenty-Five: What They Brought Into the Room

The rhythm of the rehabilitation center announced itself differently than the hospital ever had. It did not beep so much as repeat.

Doors opened on schedule. Soft-soled shoes crossed polished floors in patterns that eventually began to feel like music. Voices rose in encouragement, fell into correction, then rose again.

Somewhere down the hall, someone counted backward from ten. Somewhere else, a therapist said *again* with the kind of patience that had learned not to break under resistance.

The place smelled like effort—clean linen, hand soap, coffee from a staff lounge that stayed brewing too long—and beneath all of it, the faint electric scent of people trying to get themselves back.

By the end of the first full week, the women had learned the center's shape almost as intimately as they had learned the shape of one another's moods.

They knew which hallway caught the best afternoon light, which vending machine always jammed on the second row, which nurse liked her scrub tops bright enough to challenge the walls, and which chair in Mia's room punished your back if you sat in it longer than thirty minutes.

They knew, too, that the posted visiting policy was not a suggestion and that staff enforced it with the same calm firmness they used for medication times and therapy schedules.

Two visitors at a time.

Limited hours.

No exceptions because love was loud.

Reality had arrived wearing a badge and comfortable shoes, and they had done what grown women with obligations always did when life refused to bend.

They adjusted.

The rotation held—not perfectly, not romantically, but honestly. Mary took mornings when she could, stepping into Mia's room with tea in a thermal cup and a tote bag full of practical mercy: lotion that actually worked, a satin scarf softer than the pillowcase, hand cream, lip balm, socks that did not insult the feet.

Marsha came after work most evenings with stories, snacks, and enough personality to interrupt despair when it tried to settle too hard.

Marlie filled the spaces in between—the midday gaps, the callbacks, the errands, the forms, the moments that did not fit neatly into anyone else's schedule.

And outside all of it, their lives continued to insist on being lived. Bills still came. Jobs still expected attendance.

Laundry still multiplied. Calls still needed returning. Visibility still moved without asking whether their private grief had room for it.

That morning, Mary arrived first.

The center's lobby was quieter than usual, early light pale against the glass doors, the receptionist still on her first cup of coffee, her greeting warm but abbreviated in the way people in care work learned to master.

Mary signed in, clipped the visitor badge to her coat, and moved through the hallway with the same composed pace she brought to everything.

Her shoes made almost no sound. Her notebook rested beneath her arm. By the time she reached Mia's room, she had already noticed the breakfast tray still half-full and the blinds slightly misaligned, one side letting in more light than the other.

Mia was sitting up.

That alone had become its own form of progress.

A small pillow supported her lower back. Her hair had been loosely wrapped overnight and had begun to slip at the edges, curls and softness breaking free around her face in ways she once would have corrected immediately. Now she noticed, but not fast enough to act on it before someone else did.

A workbook sat open across the tray table, one page marked with uneven attempts at letters that had improved since the beginning, though not enough to satisfy her.

Mary paused in the doorway for a second, taking all of that in before she smiled.

"Good morning."

Mia looked up, and the effort of answering still showed in her face before it reached her mouth.

"Morn…ing."

It came more clearly than it had a week ago.

Not fluid.

But not lost.

Mary walked in, set the tea on the side table, and adjusted the slipping scarf with gentle fingers that asked permission without requiring it.

"That counts," she said quietly.

Mia's eyes shifted toward the workbook. Her hand moved, slow but more certain than before, and she pointed to the line she had been practicing.

Mary lowered herself into the chair and leaned in. The word on the page was *home*. Not clean. Not graceful. But legible. Entire. Earned.

Her throat tightened before she allowed herself to smile.

"Yes," she said softly. *"That is exactly what that says."*

Something in Mia's mouth moved toward relief, then veered into irritation because relief sat too close to needing praise. Mary understood the difference.

"You're allowed to be proud and annoyed in the same hour."

That pulled the faintest almost-laugh out of Mia, one that caught halfway and turned into breath.

They worked for forty minutes before speech therapy arrived. Naming objects. Matching sounds. Repeating syllables until language felt less like betrayal and more like a pathway under reconstruction.

Mary sat slightly off to the side during the session, hands folded in her lap, resisting the instinct to rescue.

Mia did not need saving from effort. She needed witnesses who could endure it with her without trying to perform competence on her behalf.

That was the real labor.

To stay.

To watch someone intelligent get trapped behind the mechanics of speech and not fill in every blank too quickly just because you loved them.

When the therapist finally ended the session, Mia looked exhausted in a way that made the room itself seem tired. Her shoulders had dropped. Her breath came shallower. One hand rested limp against the blanket, the other still curled around the pen as if she had forgotten she was holding it.

Mary stood.

"Rest," she said, gathering the workbook but leaving it within reach. *"I'll be back tomorrow."*

Mia looked at her and blinked once, then tapped two fingers gently against the blanket—their new shorthand for *I heard you.*

By noon, Marlie had already answered eight messages she did not care about, ignored twelve that did not deserve acknowledgment, confirmed one invoice, shifted one fitting, and returned one call from a woman who wanted to *partner* without yet explaining what that actually meant.

She walked into the rehab center carrying a garment bag, a cosmetic case, and the kind of calm that only looked effortless to people who did not know how much it cost.

She signed in.

Entered.

Adjusted.

The staff had gotten used to her now—the poised woman who always looked assembled even when tired, who asked efficient questions without becoming rude, who remembered names, who did not waste anyone's time, and who somehow managed to make a patient room feel like a temporary suite instead of an institutional pause.

Today she had brought clothes. Not because Mia needed fashion to survive, but because identity mattered, and facility wear had already taken enough.

When Marlie entered the room, Mia was asleep.

Not deeply.

Just enough.

Her face had softened in sleep, losing some of the visible effort daylight now demanded from it.

Marlie set the garment bag over the chair, placed the cosmetic case on the side table, and moved quietly through the room, replacing the water pitcher with a fresh one from the hall, straightening the folded blanket, adjusting the frame Mary had brought earlier so it faced the bed more directly.

Then Mia's eyes opened.

Not startled.

Just aware.

Marlie turned at once, the movement smooth.

"I didn't mean to wake you."

Mia looked at the garment bag. Then at Marlie. Then back again.

Her brow lifted slightly.

Marlie understood immediately.

"No," she said. *"You are not spending the next week looking like recovery took your standards."*

A breath of laughter left Mia, uneven but real.

Marlie unzipped the bag and held up the first choice—soft knit, beautiful line, easy structure, a color that would warm her without trying to brighten her into false cheer.

"Comfort with dignity," she said. *"That is today's agenda."*

Mia looked at the piece, then at Marlie's face, and for a second her eyes filled too quickly for either of them to pretend not to notice.

Marlie did not make the mistake of softening into pity.

Instead, she laid the outfit across the foot of the bed and opened the cosmetic case.

Brush.

Moisturizer.

A silk scarf.

Two lip colors.

Hand cream.

A nail buffer.

A soft hair tie.

Small things.

Powerful things.

The tools of continuity.

"We'll do your hair after you rest," she said. *"And before you argue, no one asked your permission to look cared for."*

That got a stronger response—a look half offense, half gratitude, fully Mia.

Marlie pulled up the chair.

"The center called about the updated visiting schedule."

Mia's eyes shifted.

The reality of it still hurt.

Marlie nodded once.

"I know."

Then she reached into her bag and pulled out her phone.

"So we made our own system."

The group chat was already open.

Ebony M. Elite

Mary: *Morning session complete. She got 'home' onto the page.*

Marsha: *Well now I'm emotional in traffic and I blame everybody.*

Marlie: *Bring that energy in after five. And pick up food that deserves to be eaten.*

Marsha: *Already handled. Also I found a nail color called Rich Auntie.*

There it was.

Life.

Still itself.

Still ridiculous enough to keep grief from becoming the only language in the room.

Mia looked at the screen longer than she had been looking at most things lately. Then her hand moved, and she reached for the phone.

Marlie gave it to her.

Carefully.

Mia typed with one finger now when tired, the motion slower than before, but steadier than the week had begun. The first attempt came out wrong.

She deleted it. Tried again.

Mi…a: *Rich a…*

She stopped.

Frowned.

Marlie waited.

No correction.

No rescue.

Mia tried again.

Rich Auntie is ugly.

It took time.

It took concentration.

But when Marlie read it, she laughed out loud—full enough that the nurse passing the doorway smiled without even knowing why.

"You're rude," Marlie said, still grinning as she sent it.

The chat reacted instantly.

Marsha: *SHE'S BACK.*

Mary: *That was unnecessarily specific.*

Marlie: *And entirely on brand.*

Mia watched the screen and smiled—small, tired, but on time.

That mattered more than anyone said.

The afternoon passed in pieces. Rest. PT. A hallway walk measured in careful, stubborn steps.

One therapist encouraging. Another correcting. Mia hating both of them equally, and that, too, feeling like progress. By the time evening arrived, the room had shifted again, warm light replacing institutional glare, shadows settling into the corners in a way that made everything feel more human.

And then Marsha arrived.

She came in carrying food, noise, a rolling tote, and the kind of energy that suggested if the center had tried to deny her entry, she would have negotiated it into a spiritual problem for them.

Her workday still clung lightly to her—perfume softened by hours, earrings swapped for simpler ones, irritation at traffic not yet fully burned off—but her presence entered the room a full ten seconds before her body crossed the threshold.

"Okay," she announced softly enough not to violate policy but firmly enough to override despair, *"I brought soup, roasted chicken, mashed sweet potatoes, and that lip balm you like that costs too much to be disappearing this fast."*

Mia looked at the bags, then at Marsha, then lifted one brow.

"Too... much," she said, the words imperfect but clear enough.

Marsha set the containers down and pointed at her.

"And yet appreciated."

She unpacked everything with swift practicality, then pulled the nail polish from her bag like a magician revealing the final trick.

"Now," she said, holding up the bottle, *"this is the Rich Auntie shade. And I brought a second option in case you still want to be wrong."*

Mia laughed again.

This time there was almost no snag.

Mary, who had stayed later than planned, looked down to hide her smile.

Marlie, standing near the sink and washing out another cup, saw all of it reflected faintly in the window and held it there in her mind like a photograph.

This was the work.

Not just the rehab.

Not just the appointments.

This.

The bringing.

The sitting.

The ordinary tenderness arranged around extraordinary interruption.

Eventually, as realism always insisted, the staff knocked gently and reminded them of evening policy. Two visitors at a time had become one this late.

The room had to quiet. Patients needed rest. Rehab demanded limits as much as love demanded presence.

Marsha's mouth tightened before she smoothed it.

"See? This is what I mean. I understand order, but I don't care for it."

Mary rose first, collecting her things with the grace of someone who knew how to leave without making departure feel like abandonment.

"We'll be back tomorrow," she said.

Mia looked between them, then down at her hands, then back again.

The old instinct—to reassure everyone else that she was fine—still flashed in her eyes before it could become language.

Marlie stepped closer.

"You don't have to make us comfortable."

The sentence landed deep enough that Mia's eyes filled again.

Marsha moved in before the tears could take over the room and kissed her forehead with the rough tenderness only she could get away with.

"Sleep. Recover. Try not to become unbearable once your mouth catches back up, but honestly that may be asking too much."

Mia's smile was there before the words.

Then Marsha left.

Then Mary.

Then eventually Marlie, after adjusting the blanket, setting tomorrow's outfit where Mia could see it from the bed, and placing the lip balm within reach.

When the door finally closed and the room quieted around her, Mia lay back beneath the soft hum of the vent and the low light above the sink.

Outside the window, New Jersey moved through its own evening without consulting her.

Somewhere, people were dressing for dinner. Somewhere, music had already started. Somewhere, a room was opening.

Her phone buzzed.

The group chat.

She looked.

Ebony M. Elite

Marsha: *Tomorrow I'm bringing the good hand cream.*

Mary: *And I'll bring the silk scarf from your top drawer.*

Marlie: *And I'm bringing the black sneakers. The good ones.*

A long pause.

Then Mia typed.

Slowly.

Carefully.

No one to witness the effort except the room itself.

Okay.

Sent.

Another pause.

Then:

Love y…

Her hand stalled.

She frowned.

Tried again.

Love you.

This time it stayed.

And in three different homes, three different women stopped what they were doing long enough to feel exactly what that cost.

Because progress was not glamorous.

It was not smooth.

It did not arrive dressed for admiration.

It came shaky.

Late.

Half-finished.

Beautiful anyway.

And while the world outside still responded to the image of who they had been before all this happened, inside the smaller, slower truth of the rehab center, something even more powerful was being built.

Not just presence.

Not just influence.

Endurance.

And all of them—every last one—were learning the shape of staying.

Chapter Twenty-Six: The Version That Stayed

By the second week, the rehabilitation center had stopped feeling temporary and started feeling specific.

Not home—never that—but no longer foreign either. The halls had their own sound now: rubber soles crossing waxed floors, the low rattle of meal carts, therapists calling out encouragement in measured tones that made effort sound almost ordinary.

Morning light found the same windows at the same angle every day, sliding across doorframes, wheelchairs, tray tables, settling on whatever it could reach with equal indifference.

The place had been built for repetition, for the kind of progress that refused spectacle, and that was perhaps the hardest part of all. Nothing about healing here announced itself dramatically.

It arrived in inches, in clearer syllables, in a stronger grip, in one more step taken without assistance than the day before.

Mia hated that.

Not the work.

The pace.

She had always been a woman whose mind arrived before the room did, whose wit could cut clean through a moment before anyone else had fully named it. Now she lived in a body that kept requiring her to wait for it. Her thoughts still moved like lightning.

Her mouth, her hands, her balance—those had become weather. Some mornings they cooperated. Some mornings they did not. The inconsistency irritated her more than the limits themselves, because there was no elegance in not trusting your own timing.

That morning began better than the last one had, and Marlie could hear it in Mia's voice before she saw it in her face.

She arrived just after nine, work tote on one shoulder, garment bag in one hand, coffee in the other, the rhythm of her own life still clinging lightly to her in the form of unread emails, one rescheduled fitting, and a missed call from a woman she had every intention of returning later.

The front desk receptionist looked up, recognized her now, and smiled with the easy familiarity repetition made possible.

"Good morning, Ms. Bennett."

"Morning," Marlie answered, signing in, clipping the visitor badge to her blazer, and adjusting the garment bag before heading down the hall.

The center had already begun its day. A man in physical therapy practiced stairs three doors down while his therapist counted in calm increments.

Somewhere near the nurses' station, someone laughed hard enough to surprise themselves. The ordinary persistence of the place moved around her as she stepped into Mia's room without knocking.

Mia was sitting up in bed, already dressed from the waist up in a soft charcoal knit top instead of the center-issued gown, her scarf tied low and neat, one hoop earring in place and the other resting on the tray table beside a cup of untouched applesauce.

The morning light caught her face at a forgiving angle, and for one suspended second she looked so much like herself that the difference hurt more than it helped.

She looked up when Marlie entered.

"You're... late," she said, and though the sentence came slower than she would have liked, the words were clean enough to make Marlie stop in the doorway and smile.

"I'm seven minutes behind schedule," Marlie corrected, setting the coffee down. *"That is not late. That is life."*

Mia rolled her eyes.

It was small.

But perfect.

Marlie exhaled through a smile, the closest she had come all week to relief that actually reached her body. She hung the garment bag over the back of the chair, then moved toward the tray table and picked up the abandoned earring.

"You left her behind?"

Mia reached for it, missed slightly on the first try, then caught it on the second with visible annoyance.

"She was... slippery."

Marlie did not pretend not to hear the effort in that sentence, but she also did not pause over it. She simply stepped closer and held the mirror compact open while Mia fixed the earring herself.

That mattered.

Self still mattered.

When the earring finally clicked into place, Mia looked at her reflection for a beat longer than vanity required. Her mouth set. Her chin lifted slightly.

"Better."

"Obviously," Marlie said, then unzipped the garment bag. *"And I brought options for after therapy."*

Mia glanced over.

"Why?"

Marlie lifted one brow.

"Because recovery is not a reason to start dressing like surrender."

That landed exactly where it was supposed to. Mia's lips parted around the beginning of a smile, and the look she gave Marlie held the old mixture of gratitude and offense that had defined their friendship for years.

"You are... very dramatic."

"No," Marlie replied, laying the first outfit across the chair. *"I am consistent."*

The phone in her tote buzzed then, low but insistent. She ignored it. The room came first. It had to.

By the time speech therapy ended and occupational therapy began, Mary had joined them, carrying one of her large leather totes and the kind of calm that altered the atmosphere simply by existing inside it.

She brought two things every time: something practical Mia needed and something Mia had not yet realized she needed. Today it was a better pen—weighted, easier to grip—and a narrow notebook with thick cream pages that would not bleed ink when words came out heavier than intended.

Mary placed both on the tray table without ceremony.

"Try these later."

Mia touched the pen first, then the notebook, then looked up.

"You shop... like prayer."

The sentence cost effort, but it arrived beautifully enough that Mary's face softened before she could stop it.

"That may be the nicest thing anyone has ever said about my tote bag," she replied as she settled into the chair.

Marlie watched them from near the window, her phone finally in hand. The unread messages had multiplied.

One from the lifestyle page again. One from the event host.

One from a man whose approach remained respectfully paced enough not to irritate her.

Another from a woman in Brooklyn asking whether the Ebony M. Elite would consider speaking at a women's brunch.

The world outside continued responding to a version of them suspended in video and captions—elegant, viral, untouched by IV lines and therapist instructions.

It would have been easy to resent that split, to feel something bitter at how the internet kept clapping while real life sat in a rehab room relearning verbs.

But Marlie did not resent it.

She studied it.

Because attention, even now, was still information.

She typed one message back to the brunch host.

I'll let you know what is possible.

Then she locked the phone and slipped it back into her bag.

Possible had become a different word now.

At noon, the center enforced its policy without apology. Morning visitors out. Rest period. Staff only unless otherwise approved. Mary rose first, smoothing the front of her coat the way she always did before leaving any room she cared about.

"I'll come back tomorrow before work."

Mia nodded, then looked at the weighted pen on the tray table as if she already understood the assignment hidden inside the promise.

Marlie stayed a minute longer, adjusting the blanket where it had folded wrong.

"I have two calls this afternoon and one appointment I can't move," she said, keeping her voice level—not guilty, just honest. *"Marsha's coming after."*

Mia looked at her, and something quiet passed through her eyes—understanding mixed with the faintest trace of mourning for all the ways life did not stop just because pain had become the center of the story.

"Go."

That one word came cleaner than most.

Marlie held her gaze.

"I'm still coming back tonight."

Mia nodded once.

"I know."

Outside the room, the hallway felt louder than it had an hour earlier. Phones rang at desks. A therapist guided an older man through seated leg lifts with infinite patience.

Someone down the hall argued gently with a nurse about salt intake. The world of maintenance and care kept moving, and inside it Marlie finally answered the call she had missed twice that morning.

The event host's voice was warm and entirely too enthusiastic for a hallway outside a rehab room.

"Marlie, I'm so glad I caught you. We'd love to lock in a date. People are really responding to you and the ladies—"

Marlie stepped toward the window at the end of the hall, lowering her voice automatically.

"I appreciate that," she said. *"But my availability has changed."*

There was a brief pause on the other end—the sound of a person recalibrating around reality.

"Of course. Is everything alright?"

Marlie looked back down the hall toward Mia's room, where the door stood closed now, and chose the truth without the details.

"Everything important is requiring attention."

The host softened immediately.

"Understood."

That, more than anything, almost undid her. Not pity.

Understanding.

"I'll be in touch when I can commit properly," Marlie said.

"Take your time."

When the call ended, she stood there for a second longer than necessary, watching sunlight move across the parking lot, the ordinary afternoon carrying on in parked cars and people leaving with coffee.

Then she straightened, adjusted the strap of her tote, and left the building to go tend the parts of life that still insisted on being fed.

Marsha arrived after five like she had punched a time clock in her soul and then sprinted through traffic on principle.

Her heels were lower than usual, her work tote replaced by a weekender-style bag full of nonsense and necessity, and she entered the room already talking.

"Okay, first of all, if one more person at my job asks me if I'm 'holding up,' I'm going to start billing for emotional labor."

Mia looked up from the notebook in her lap, and the expression that crossed her face was unmistakably amused.

"Bill... them."

Marsha stopped cold.

Then pointed at her like she had just been vindicated by scripture.

"See? This is why I come here. The wisdom is returning."

She set the bag down and began unpacking with efficient flair. A container of soup. Hand cream. A compact mirror. A different scarf. A small speaker. A bottle of nail polish in a color so rich it looked expensive in silence.

"And before you start, yes, I know this shade is extra. That is the point."

Mia looked at the bottle.

Then at Marsha.

"No... it's good."

Marsha's expression softened for one quick second before she covered it with bravado.

"Well obviously."

The rehab aide assigned to that wing knocked lightly at the door sometime after six and gave them the same reminder as always: one visitor for the remainder of evening hours.

Quiet down after seven. Lights out considerations. Rest mattered. Recovery demanded routine. Marsha nodded like she was cooperating entirely out of personal generosity.

"We know the rules," she muttered after the aide left. *"I just don't like them."*

Mia's fingers moved to the edge of the notebook.

"Me... either."

That was when Marsha saw the page.

Not the old practice sheets.

The new writing.

Uneven but legible.

A list.

Three words.

water

walk

again

Marsha stared.

Then sat down more slowly than before.

"You wrote this?"

Mia looked down, suddenly shy in a way that felt almost cruel after everything else this body had forced on her.

Then she nodded.

Marsha blinked rapidly once, then reached for the hand cream because it was either that or cry, and she had already decided on principle not to do the second thing first.

"Alright," she said, unscrewing the cap. *"Then tonight we moisturize like women with goals."*

By the time Marlie returned just before the end of visiting hours, the room had changed shape again. The speaker played low jazz from the corner.

Mia's nails had been shaped and polished one hand at a time with the gravity of sacred work.

Her scarf had been retied. Her lips had been touched lightly with balm. There was color in the room now that had not been there at noon.

Not denial.

Not dress-up over despair.

Continuity.

Marlie stopped in the doorway and took it in.

Marsha looked up first.

"Don't say it. I already know I saved the whole atmosphere."

Marlie's mouth curved.

"You did."

Mia lifted one hand slightly, the polish catching the lamplight.

"Rich... auntie."

The words came broken over the edges, but recognizable, and all three women laughed hard enough that the room itself seemed to soften around them.

Later, after Marsha left and the lights lowered, the group chat lit again from three different homes and one rehab bed.

Ebony M. Elite

Marsha: *Hand reveal was elite.*

Mary: *How tired is she?*

Marlie sat in her car outside the center, not ready to drive yet, and typed with both hands resting on the steering wheel.

Marlie: *Tired, but clearer.*

A pause.

Then, from Mia:

Mia: *Still… here.*

Three dots appeared from Marsha immediately, disappeared, then came back.

Marsha: *That's all we need right now.*

Mary answered next.

Mary: *No. It's more than that.*

Marlie read both, then looked up through her windshield at the windows of the rehab wing.

One of them, somewhere up there, held Mia.

Held effort. Held rage. Held progress. Held the version of their lives no one would have chosen, but all of them were learning to stand inside without flinching.

She typed.

Marlie: *It's enough for tonight.*

And because honesty mattered more now than inspiration, no one tried to improve that sentence after it arrived.

Inside her room, Mia read the thread with the notebook still open beside her and the expensive polish drying fully at last.

Her hand ached. Her head felt thick around the edges.

Her body had become a place where every small victory demanded payment. But the room still smelled faintly of the hand cream Marsha had rubbed into her skin, the scarf at her neck still held the warmth of Marlie's fingers, and the pen Mary brought had made the word *again* possible.

That counted.

That all counted.

She typed one more line, slowly, carefully, letting each letter arrive in its own time.

Mia: *See y'all… tomorrow.*

When the message landed, it did what all the best truths did.

It made three women in three different places go still long enough to feel exactly how much love could fit inside something ordinary.

And in the quiet that followed, nothing disappeared.

It simply stayed.

Chapter Twenty-Seven: The Lives They Kept Carrying

By the third week, the rhythm had become less shocking and more exhausting, which in some ways was harder.

Crisis had a shape you could brace against. Routine did not. Routine asked you to keep loving with your calendar open, to keep showing up with laundry still undone, meetings still scheduled, phone calls still waiting, dishes still in the sink, bills still due, and your own body still expecting sleep.

The rehabilitation center continued its work with the same measured confidence it had carried from the beginning—therapy at nine, speech after lunch, walking practice in the afternoon, medication delivered with quiet efficiency, visiting hours enforced by staff who did not care how much love was waiting in the parking lot.

Life outside the building never paused. It simply learned to circle this new center of gravity.

Marlie felt that more than she admitted.

That morning began in motion. Her apartment still held the soft remains of the night before—one mug in the sink, a scarf draped over the back of a chair, a blazer hanging where she had dropped it instead of where it belonged—but she was already dressed, already moving between coffee, emails, and a quick review of the day she had no choice but to execute.

One fitting had to happen. One invoice had to be approved. One call with a potential event host could no longer be avoided. And in between all of it, there was New Jersey. There was Mia. There was the schedule they had built not because it was ideal, but because it was possible.

Her phone lit up while she was pinning an earring.

Ebony M. Elite

Mary: *She has physical therapy at ten. Speech moved to one-thirty.*

Marlie read the message while fastening the earring, her reflection steady, her face more composed than rested.

Marsha: *I can get there after work, but traffic better respect somebody's suffering today.*

The line made her smile in spite of herself.

Then Mia appeared. The typing bubbles came, disappeared, came back. Finally, the message landed.

Mia: *Woke up mad.*

Marlie stared at that a second longer than necessary, not because it worried her, but because it sounded like Mia.

And that, now, mattered.

She typed back immediately.

Marlie: *Good. That means your standards survived.*

Mary followed almost at once.

Mary: *Anger is often energy looking for direction.*

Marsha: *Well tell her to direct some of that toward walking past these people and showing out in therapy.*

Marlie slipped the phone into her bag and picked up her keys. The day had already started answering back.

At the center, Mary had reached Mia first. She sat near the window in the now-familiar chair, coat folded neatly over the back, notebook open in her lap, reading the room with the same patience she brought to everything.

Mia was dressed already, though the process had clearly taken more from her than she wanted anyone to know.

Her scarf was tied properly but tighter than usual, one side slightly off. Her lips were moisturized, but she had missed a bit near the corner. Her sneakers were on, but one lace had been redone twice, the bow larger than the other.

Small things.

Frustration leaves fingerprints.

Mary had noticed all of it without making the mistake of calling attention to any of it.

"Good morning," she said, not too brightly, not too softly.

Mia looked up from where she had been staring at the tray table and answered with enough clarity to show the work was taking hold, even if slowly.

"Morning."

Then, after a pause and a glance toward the laces that had apparently offended her on principle, she added, *"I'm irritated."*

Mary nodded once, as if this were useful data and not a mood she needed to fix.

"With what specifically?"

Mia let out a breath through her nose and looked toward the hallway, where a therapist's voice counted someone through leg lifts.

"Everything."

That answer might have sounded general from someone else.

From Mia, it was precision disguised as fatigue.

Mary closed the notebook.

"Good," she said.

Mia turned her head slowly.

"Good?"

Mary's face remained composed, but her voice held the slightest thread of dry warmth.

"Yes. Specifics can come later. But I prefer 'everything' to pretending."

That almost earned a smile.

Almost.

The therapist came for Mia at ten with her usual blend of patience and firmness, and by then Marlie had joined them, her tote bag set neatly against the wall, her phone finally face down on the side table.

She had made one call from the parking lot and postponed another from the elevator. She stood now with one shoulder against the wall, arms folded loosely, watching Mia step from bed to walker to hallway in increments so small they would have looked meaningless to anyone not invested in the cost.

Mia hated the walker.

Not privately.

Openly.

Her dislike for it had become one of the few things she could communicate without friction.

"Temporary," the therapist said, not for the first time, as Mia's grip tightened around the handles.

Mia shot her a look that, even now, carried old authority.

"It should... pray."

The therapist blinked. Marlie looked down quickly, but not fast enough to hide the laugh that escaped.

Mary covered her mouth. Then the therapist laughed too, the sound honest and surprised.

"It should pray?"

Mia, breathing harder now from the effort of standing, nodded once.

"That I... leave it."

This time all three women laughed with her, not at her, and the hallway itself seemed to loosen.

That mattered too.

The walk itself was hard, hard in the humiliating, incremental way recovery often is. Mia could think the entire hallway in one second. Her body still needed three cautious minutes to travel it.

Her right foot lagged when she was tired. Her balance shifted half a beat late on turns. Once, when the therapist asked her to stop and reset her posture, the look on Mia's face held such pure, exhausted contempt that Marlie had to glance out the window to steady herself.

"I know," the therapist said softly, not patronizing, just truthful. *"But do it again."*

Mia did.

Because that was who she had always been beneath the style and wit and curated entrance.

Someone who did the hard thing again.

By the time they returned to the room, Mia was spent. The anger from earlier had burned down into fatigue, and fatigue looked different on her now—quieter, heavier around the eyes, slower in the hands.

Marlie adjusted the pillow behind her back and lifted the water cup toward her without comment.

Mia took two sips, then let her head fall back.

"Hate this," she murmured.

Marlie sat at the edge of the chair, one leg crossed, her blazer still smooth despite the day.

"I know."

Mia turned her face slightly.

"You don't… have to say 'you know' to everything."

That came out more cleanly than she expected, and the irritation in it sounded so normal that Marlie smiled.

"True," she said. *"But in this case, I do know."*

Mary stepped closer, her tote already open.

"And in this case, so do I."

Mia looked at both of them, then at the ceiling.

"Annoying."

"Also true," Marlie said.

The room softened around that.

Around noon, reality returned wearing practical shoes.

Marlie's phone buzzed. She ignored it once.

Then again. The third time, she stood and stepped into the hallway, closing the door most of the way behind her.

The event host was still calling. The lifestyle page wanted dates. The boutique collaboration wanted confirmation.

A man whose number she had not saved but recognized by rhythm had sent a message that, under other circumstances, would have earned a response.

Thinking of you ladies. Hoping your friend is improving. No pressure to answer.

That one made her stop.

Not because of romance.

Because of tone.

Respect had become rarer than attention.

She typed back from the hallway with one hand while the other held the phone tighter than necessary.

Thank you. She is working. We are too.

Then she returned the event host's call and did what women like her had been doing quietly for decades—held one part of life in one hand and another in the other without dropping either, even when both had edges.

By evening, Marsha took over. She always announced herself before the door fully opened, but tonight the volume came with visible fatigue.

Her work shoes were in her hand, not on her feet. Her hair was still neat, but one strand near her temple had escaped whatever polish had held the rest of the day together.

She carried a takeout bag, a tote, and the weariness of someone who had been expected to be productive all day while half her mind remained in another state.

"I want it noted," she said, kicking the door closed gently behind her, *"that I have been fake-listening to people for nine hours and none of them deserved the performance."*

Mia, lying back with her notebook beside her, looked at her and managed a laugh that caught less than it would have last week.

"You fake... listen well."

Marsha stopped in the middle of unpacking.

"See?" she said, looking toward Mary, who had stayed later than planned again. *"This is why I come. Validation."*

Mary looked up from the notebook she had been helping Mia with.

"That was not validation. That was diagnosis."

Mia smiled.

This time it arrived on time.

The room had that feeling now—not light, not heavy, but lived-in. The rehab center had done something none of them wanted and all of them needed: it had forced intimacy to become practical.

They no longer spoke only in declarations and emotional peaks. They talked about what had happened at work. About parking costs. About whether the soup downstairs was worse today than yesterday. About whether Mia wanted the lavender scarf or the black one tomorrow.

About how unfair it was that healing still required paperwork. About whether Marsha was allowed to threaten the vending machine spiritually if it ate her dollar again.

They also talked about the stroke.

Not every second.

But honestly.

That night, after the aide reminded them—again—that one visitor needed to leave by seven-thirty and the room had to quiet after eight, Mary gathered her bag and stood.

"I have an early meeting," she said, looking toward Mia. *"And if I'm late to it, I will resent strangers before breakfast."*

Mia nodded.

"Go."

Mary stepped closer and adjusted the blanket where it had slipped near Mia's shoulder.

"I'll be back Saturday morning."

Mia's eyes lifted.

"You always... say when."

Mary's hand paused against the blanket.

"Because absence lands harder when it has no shape."

That stayed in the room after she left.

Marlie had work to return to as well. She stood near the bed, one hand on the strap of her bag, the other lightly touching the side rail.

"I've got a call at eight," she said. *"I'm taking it from home. If it runs short, I'll call before you sleep."*

Mia nodded once.

Then frowned slightly.

"You don't have to... do all of this."

Marsha, sitting in the chair with one sneaker back on and one still off, looked up sharply.

"We absolutely do."

Mia turned her head toward her.

"That's not... what I mean."

Marlie understood before the rest of the sentence had a chance to struggle itself into shape.

She moved closer.

"I know."

Mia looked down at her hands.

"I don't want... to become a job."

There it was.

The real fear.

Not the walker.

Not the words.

Not the weakness.

Burden.

Marsha's face changed first, all the humor leaving it without making the room cold.

"Don't do that," she said quietly.

Mia's eyes filled before she could stop them.

"I had a whole life," she said, the words slower now because emotion made everything harder. *"And now y'all... have to fit me into yours."*

The room did not rush to contradict her.

Because part of it was true.

Their lives had changed.

They had adjusted work, sleep, distance, schedules, attention.

Real friendship did that.

But truth required precision.

Marlie sat on the edge of the bed—not enough to jostle her, just enough to close the space.

"Listen to me."

Mia looked up.

Held her gaze.

"You are not a job," Marlie said, each word clean, grounded, undeniable. *"You are part of our life. That is different."*

Marsha leaned forward, elbows on her knees, voice lower now.

"My job is people I don't like asking me dumb questions before coffee. This?" She gestured around the room. *"This is mine to do."*

Mia's mouth moved.

Stopped.

Mary, still at the door because she had not yet fully left, added the final line the moment needed.

"Love is not inconvenience simply because it costs something."

Silence followed.

Not empty.

Full.

Mia blinked hard and looked away toward the window, where evening was gathering beyond the glass in slow blue layers.

"Still hate this," she whispered.

Marlie nodded.

"You can hate it."

Marsha picked up the hand cream again, because apparently that had become part of the emotional architecture of the room.

"And still let us be here."

That got Mia through the moment.

Not out of it.

Through it.

Later, after Marlie left for her call and Mary finally drove home with the heater on because her bones were tired, Marsha stayed until the last allowable minute.

They talked less then, realistically, like people at the end of long days who had run out of energy for performance.

Marsha sat with one leg tucked under her, scrolling half-heartedly through the group chat, through work messages she planned to ignore until morning, through comments still arriving under old videos as if the world had not understood that the women in those clips were now divided across boroughs and counties by visiting policies, rehab schedules, and the blunt logistics of caregiving.

"People keep saying we look effortless,"

Marsha murmured, turning her phone so Mia could see one of the comments.

Mia looked.

Then gave a tired little snort.

"Lies."

Marsha laughed.

"Exactly."

Mia's eyes stayed on the screen a second longer.

Then she looked at Marsha.

"You ever… get mad?"

Marsha's thumb stopped moving.

"At what?"

Mia looked toward the ceiling.

Toward the room.

Toward her own hand lying still against the blanket.

"All of it."

Marsha sat back.

Did not rush.

Did not tidy the answer.

"Yes."

Mia turned her head.

Marsha held her gaze.

"I get mad that this happened. I get mad that you're in here. I get mad that people say stupid things when they mean well. I get mad that I have to leave every night because of policy. I get mad that my regular life keeps asking me to care about nonsense while this is happening." She paused, then exhaled. *"But being mad doesn't mean I want to be somewhere else."*

That stayed with Mia.

You could see it staying.

She closed her eyes for a second, then opened them.

"Okay."

By the time Marsha left, the room had gone quiet again, but not lonely.

Mia reached for her phone after the door shut. The group chat was still there, alive in small, safe ways.

Mary: *Home.*

Marlie: *Call done. You still awake?*

Marsha: *Don't start no emotional nonsense after I leave. I need sleep.*

Mia smiled. The work of typing at night always cost more. Her hand was tired. Her head pulsed faintly behind her eyes. Even so, she opened the thread and pressed through it.

Slowly. Carefully.

Mia: *Still here.*

Sent.

A beat later, Marlie responded.

Marlie: *I know.*

Mary: *We do.*

And then, because Marsha could never let sincerity remain unsupervised for too long:

Marsha: *Good. Then continue.*

Mia laughed again, softer now, the sound barely making it fully into the air but real enough to count.

Outside the rehab center, lives continued.

Cars passed. Events were planned.

Invitations waited. Men with good manners and proper timing remained somewhere on the edge of the story. The world still recognized the women they had been in those videos—the elegant, visible, untouchable versions moving through light. But inside these rooms, in the hours between work and visiting limits and real exhaustion, a different version of them was taking shape.

Less polished. More permanent.

The kind that did not disappear when the room got hard.

The kind that stayed.

Chapter Twenty-Eight: The Kind of Grace That Learns New Shoes

By the fourth week, progress had stopped looking like miracles and started looking like practice, which made it harder for outsiders to admire and easier for the women who loved Mia to understand exactly what it cost.

The rehabilitation center had settled into their bones now—not as home, never that, but as a place they could navigate without asking where anything was.

They knew the smell of the morning shift before they reached the second hallway.

They knew which elevator took too long and which vending machine still refused to release the good crackers without a small act of faith.

They knew the schedule taped to Mia's wall by sight, knew when speech therapy ended by the way her shoulders dropped afterward, knew when physical therapy had gone well because she looked angry instead of defeated.

Anger had become one of the better signs.

That morning the sky over New Jersey hung low and silver, the kind of weather that made everything look more honest than glamorous.

Rain had come in the night and left the parking lot damp, shining dull beneath the weak daylight.

Marlie noticed it as she crossed from her car to the building entrance, coat belted, umbrella closed but still dripping, her tote bag heavier than usual because she had packed both her laptop and two changes of clothes she had no intention of leaving in the wrong place.

Her day had already begun before the sun had fully committed to arriving—one phone call with a printer, one message from a woman at a community center who wanted to *talk possibilities*, one reply to a man who had finally learned the art of checking in without leaning too hard.

She had handled all of it in the spaces between coffee and keys and traffic, because that was what life looked like now.

Not paused.

Layered.

At the front desk, the receptionist glanced up and smiled with the familiarity repetition creates. *"Morning, Ms. James."*

"Morning." Marlie signed in, clipped the badge to her coat, and moved down the hall with the same steady pace she brought into every room she intended to improve. The rehab center was already awake.

A therapist's voice carried from somewhere around the corner, counting out steps in calm increments. A television played too loudly in one common area until a nurse lowered it without looking up from her chart.

Down the corridor, someone laughed mid-sentence and then coughed from laughing too hard. Recovery, like grief, had textures no one talked about enough.

When Marlie entered Mia's room, the first thing she noticed was not Mia.

It was the shoes.

They sat beside the chair instead of on the floor where Mia usually kicked them off, both neatly aligned, laces tucked in, one slightly more loosened than the other. It was a small thing.

A meaningful thing. The kind of detail women who knew one another well enough could read like weather.

Then she saw Mia.

She was sitting in the chair near the window instead of in bed, one leg crossed loosely at the ankle, her scarf tied in a softer knot today, the color warmer against her skin than the ones she had worn earlier in the week.

A tray with breakfast sat half-finished beside her. The notebook Mary had brought lay open on her lap, and her pen rested between her fingers with a grip that looked less combative than it had before.

That was new too. Her face still carried effort in small places—around the mouth, behind the eyes—but there was less confusion in it now, less of that private rage that had flared every time her body betrayed her timing.

She looked up when Marlie walked in.

"You're... early."

The words came slower than they once would have, but they arrived with more confidence, the pauses now feeling more like stepping stones than broken ground.

Marlie closed the door behind her and let the compliment stand. *"You sound better."*

Mia rolled one shoulder in a small shrug that failed to hide her pleasure. *"I sounded... annoyed yesterday."*

"That too," Marlie said, slipping out of her coat. *"The two are not mutually exclusive."*

That earned a real smile. Small. Quick. But hers.

Marlie set her bag down and crossed to the tray table, glancing at the notebook only after she had set the umbrella aside.

Three lines had been written there already. Not quotes. Not exercises. A list.

call bank

wash hair

walk farther

Marlie read it without comment for a second. Then she looked up.

"You're making plans."

Mia's eyes followed hers to the notebook, then back again. *"Trying to."*

The distinction mattered.

Marlie nodded once. *"Same difference for now."*

She reached for the cup on the tray and sniffed it. *"This coffee is disrespectful."*

Mia let out a laugh that almost doubled back into itself but didn't. *"It's bad."*

"I brought better."

Of course she had.

She unpacked with her usual efficiency—real coffee in a thermal cup, a soft cardigan because rehab centers were always either too warm or not warm enough, a small pouch with Mia's favorite hand cream, lip balm, a satin head wrap in deep plum, and the black sneakers she had promised in the chat three nights ago.

Mia looked at the shoes first.

Then at Marlie.

Then back again.

The expression on her face shifted slowly enough to be seen becoming something else.

"Those are... my good ones."

"Exactly." Marlie set them beside the chair. *"And today looks like a good enough day to deserve them."*

Mia's hand moved toward the shoes as if to check that they were real. Her fingers brushed the leather lightly.

"I can't wear those… for therapy."

"No," Marlie agreed. *"You wear them after."*

There it was again—that insistence on a later, on a version of the day that existed beyond effort, beyond the center-issued routine, beyond being only a patient.

Marlie brought that into the room every time she entered it, and Mia, even when tired enough to resent hope on principle, still responded to it.

A knock sounded at the door before either of them could say more.

Mary entered with a smaller bag than usual and the centered energy of someone who had already spent an hour in the world and refused to let it cling to her.

Her coat was damp at the hem from the weather, but everything else about her looked assembled, aligned, intact.

"I passed Marsha in the parking lot," she said, setting the bag on the chair. *"She was arguing with her phone."*

Mia's mouth twitched. *"About what?"*

Mary unwrapped her scarf and folded it neatly. *"I believe the phrase was, 'No, because if y'all think I'm setting up another school fundraiser while my friend is in rehab, you have lost the plot entirely.'"*

That one made both women laugh.

Then Marlie's phone buzzed.

Then Mary's.

Then Mia's.

The synchronized vibration of the group chat felt so familiar now that it almost counted as a fifth presence in the room.

Ebony M. Elite

Marsha: *I need it noted that I am still employable despite wanting to throw my phone into traffic.*

Mary looked down and typed first.

Mary: *A strong opening statement.*

Marlie followed.

Marlie: *Try not to lose your income before noon.*

Mia took longer, one thumb moving more carefully than it once had, but when her message landed, it carried the old bite of her humor clean enough to make Marlie look up.

Mia: *Bills... are repetitive trauma.*

The three dots that followed from Marsha appeared so quickly they felt like a cackle.

Marsha: *SEE? This is why I love her.*

Mia read it.

Then read it again.

The room did not need to speak the truth out loud. Her words were returning. Not all at once. Not beautifully. But undeniably.

Therapy took most of the morning. The physical therapist came first, a woman with patient eyes and no tolerance for self-pity dressed up as sarcasm.

She guided Mia through standing exercises, weight shifts, balance work, the gait corrections that made each hallway trip feel like a negotiation between past and present.

Mia hated being corrected in front of people.

That too remained consistent.

"Left foot first," the therapist reminded her gently.

Mia frowned. *"I know."*

"Then show me."

Mia did.

Not smoothly.

Not yet.

But with enough irritation to fuel the attempt.

Marlie stood by the door with her arms folded, saying nothing, because she knew there were moments when encouragement helped and moments when it only got in the way of pride doing the heavy lifting.

Mary sat in the chair near the bed, notebook closed, eyes following each step with the concentration of someone learning a second language she had no choice but to master.

By the time speech therapy arrived, Mia was tired enough that the effort showed at the corners of everything.

Her vowels thinned.

Her focus drifted half a beat longer before returning. Once, when the therapist asked her to repeat a sentence about tomorrow's weather, Mia closed her eyes and whispered, *"I don't care... about tomorrow's weather."*

The therapist did not laugh.

Marlie did.

Softly.

Because the sentence had come out almost entirely right, and because there she was again—the woman who had never had time for pointless exercises unless someone could explain their purpose properly.

"Use that," the therapist said, not missing a beat. *"Tell me what you care about."*

Mia opened her eyes.

Looked at her.

Then at Marlie.

Then down at her own hand.

"Walking... better."

It was imperfect.

It was slow.

It was completely clear.

Mary's fingers tightened around the notebook in her lap.

Marlie looked away for one second—not because she could not handle the moment, but because she could feel it too fully and refused to let the room become about their relief instead of Mia's labor.

After therapy, the room emptied for rest.

Policy required it. The center had rules, and love, however committed, still had to wear a visitor's badge and leave on schedule.

This was one of the harder truths they had accepted: devotion does not cancel institutional policy, and real women with real obligations do not get to abandon everything in order to prove what they feel. So they rotated. Adjusted. Took calls in hallways. Replied to work emails from parking lots. Brought life with them in bags and left it waiting on car seats while they sat with Mia through one more hour, one more practice page, one more walk.

At lunch, Marlie stepped outside under the covered entrance and finally returned a call she had delayed twice that week. The woman on the line was warm, polished, clearly used to getting yeses faster than this.

"We'd love to feature the Ebony M. Elite next month. A panel, maybe a conversation about visibility, reinvention, second chapters—"

Rain tapped lightly against the concrete lip of the overhang. Cars hissed through the damp lot. Somewhere inside, an aide called for transport to imaging.

Marlie listened.

Then chose the truth with the same precision she used everywhere else.

"That may be possible," she said, *"but not in the way I would have said yes before."*

A pause met her.

Not resistance.

Recalibration.

"Meaning?"

Marlie looked through the glass doors toward the hallway that led back to Mia's room.

"Meaning if we do it, we do it honestly."

The woman on the line softened in a way that told Marlie she had expected polish and gotten substance instead.

"I'd still like that conversation."

Marlie believed her.

"Then I'll call you when I can bring the right version of it."

When she returned upstairs, the room was quieter. Mary had left for work. Mia was resting with one hand over her stomach and the blanket folded lower than it should have been.

The black sneakers sat waiting by the chair, their presence almost ridiculous in the middle of a rehab room and all the more necessary for that.

Marsha came just after five with rain still clinging to the shoulders of her coat and a look on her face that said her day had offered several people the chance to disappoint her and at least two of them had succeeded.

"I brought food, I brought lip gloss, and I brought enough irritation to power the whole wing," she announced, setting her tote down with controlled force.

Mia opened one eye.

"You look... dramatic."

Marsha froze.

Then put one hand to her chest.

"Say it again. Slower. I want to remember the miracle."

This time Mia laughed first.

A real laugh.

Uneven at the end, but real enough to make the room brighten.

Marsha unpacked dinner while talking through her day in pieces—not every detail, just the important ones, the way women tell stories when they have earned the right not to perform.

Somebody at work had said the wrong thing with the right intention. A stranger had complimented her coat in the pharmacy. The group's old video had surfaced again on another platform.

Someone had commented, *"I want friends like these women."* That one had annoyed her for reasons she could not fully explain.

"People always say that," she muttered, opening the soup container. *"Like friendship is just matching aesthetics and one good brunch picture."*

Mia looked at her.

Then at the room.

Then at the therapy bands draped over the chair and the weighted pen on the tray and the cardigan Marlie had left folded by the bed.

"It's work," she said.

The words came slow, but they came.

Marsha looked up sharply.

Mary, who had just texted to say she would call later, lit the phone at that exact moment as if summoned.

Marlie, standing by the sink washing out a cup, turned and held Mia's gaze.

"Yes," she said quietly. *"It is."*

The sentence stayed in the room.

Because that was the thing people outside did not understand. Friendship at this age, at this level, in this season—it was not just loyalty in feeling. It was labor. Time. Rearrangement. Gas money. Missed calls. Reheated dinners.

Honest exhaustion. Showing up dressed because dignity mattered. Showing up tired because presence mattered more.

Later, after the food and the laughter and the hand cream and the small evening rituals that had now become their own kind of liturgy, Marsha helped Mia into the black sneakers.

It took time.

More than it should have.

Enough to make Mia angry with her own fingers.

Enough to make her close her eyes once and inhale too sharply.

Marsha stayed down on one knee without turning the moment into tragedy.

"Don't start fighting the laces like they insulted your family," she said quietly.

Mia looked down at her.

"They did."

Marsha snorted.

"Better."

When the shoes were finally on, Mia sat still for a second, feet on the floor, hands resting on the edge of the bed.

Then she stood.

Not for therapy.

Not because anyone asked.

Just stood.

The black sneakers held.

The room watched.

Marsha rose slowly, as if any sudden movement might break the spell of something simple and hard-won.

Mia looked down at the shoes.

Then up.

"Good," she said.

No one improved that sentence.

No one needed to.

That night, after policy narrowed the room down to one last visitor and then none, after Marsha had left with promises to bring the good satin pillowcase tomorrow, after the hallway lights dimmed slightly and the wing settled into its nighttime sounds, the group chat lit again.

Ebony M. Elite

Mary: *How did today end?*

Marlie had already driven home and changed into softer clothes, but she still carried the day in her shoulders as she sat at her kitchen counter with tea gone cold beside her.

Marlie: *She stood in the black sneakers.*

Three dots appeared from Mary.

Mary: *That is not small.*

Marsha followed immediately.

Marsha: *I know. I almost lost my mind respectfully.*

Mia's typing bubble came slower.

Stayed.

Disappeared.

Returned.

Then finally—

Mia: *They fit.*

Marlie read it twice, smiling before she meant to.

Marlie: *Of course they do.*

Another pause.

Then Mia again.

Mia: *I still hate… this place.*

Mary answered first.

Mary: *You are not required to love the room to honor what it is doing.*

Marsha followed.

Marsha: *Exactly. Hate the room. Beat the room. Same difference.*

Marlie looked at the thread, then out at the rain darkening the window beyond her kitchen.

Marlie: *Just don't let it convince you it's the whole story.*

This time it took Mia longer to answer.

When it came, the line was simple enough to hurt.

Mia: *Trying not to.*

And in three different homes, three women sat with that sentence, each of them tired in her own way, each of them still holding lives that required attention, each of them still choosing—again and again—to carry one another forward without pretending that love made the carrying light.

Outside, the world continued to respond to the image of them.

Inside, they were living the truth of it.

And both mattered now.

Chapter Twenty-Nine: The Parts of Life That Didn't Pause

By the fifth week, everybody had stopped asking whether life was going to settle and started negotiating with the fact that it wasn't.

The rehab center still ran on its own unyielding choreography—breakfast trays at the same hour, therapy blocks stacked like appointments with reality, visiting rules enforced with a calm that never once apologized for itself—but outside those walls, their personal lives kept arriving with full entitlement.

Work still called. Rent still existed. Deadlines still moved toward them with no reverence for grief. Laundry still multiplied. Invitations still came. Men still noticed.

Opportunities still circled. The world had not paused because one beloved woman had been interrupted, and there was something almost offensive about that until they admitted the harder truth: this was exactly what grown life looked like.

Not one thing at a time.

Everything at once.

Marlie felt that most in the morning.

Her apartment held the evidence of a life in motion—one shoe near the sofa where she had kicked it off the night before, two open garment bags draped over the dining chair, receipts trapped beneath a pen, a charger trailing off the counter, and on the kitchen island, her phone glowing with the layered demands of both visibility and ordinary obligation.

An event host needed a decision. A customer wanted a rush adjustment to a hemline that should never have been cut that way in the first place.

The brunch organizer had circled back again. A man with a grounded voice and enough sense to never over-message had sent a simple line—*thinking of your friend today*—that sat differently than the rest.

Marlie stood barefoot in front of the coffee maker, one hand around a mug, the other scrolling through a life that still expected her to remain herself while carrying more than before.

The group chat lit before she answered anything else.

Ebony M. Elite

Marsha: *I need everybody to know I almost wore two different shoes to work yesterday and no one gets to judge me because my spirit is overbooked.*

Marlie smiled into her coffee before she could stop herself and typed back with one hand.

Marlie: *Your spirit has always been overbooked.*

Mary answered next, exactly on brand and right on time.

Mary: *This is why we lay things out the night before.*

The typing bubble from Mia took longer, disappeared once, then came back.

Mia: *Two different shoes… could have been fashion.*

The sentence was imperfect in pacing but sharp in thought, and all three women on the other side of it felt the old Mia press through the newer version like light through curtains.

Marsha: *See? This is the support I need.*

Marlie didn't linger in the thread, but the warmth of it followed her as she got dressed. Neutral knit. Gold at the ear. Clean sneaker.

The Dot Band secure at her wrist. Even now—especially now—she dressed like a woman who understood that being put together was not denial.

It was discipline. A way of refusing surrender in small visible ways.

At the rehab center, mornings carried a familiar seriousness. The hall outside Mia's room always sounded slightly busier before ten—wheelchairs moving, speech therapists calling names, nurses trading updates at the station, the hum of fluorescent lights doing their own form of labor overhead.

Mary had already been there and gone by the time Marlie arrived, leaving behind a folded note in her slanted, composed handwriting beside the weighted pen and cream-paper notebook.

She was tired this morning but steady. Ate half her eggs. Got through naming exercises without shutting down. Don't let her skip water. —Mary

Marlie picked up the note, read it once, and slipped it into her coat pocket like it belonged there.

Mia was by the window instead of in bed, seated in the straight-backed chair with one leg crossed at the ankle, the black sneakers back on, the scarf tied lower today in a shade of warm smoke that softened her face without trying to brighten it falsely.

Her workbook rested open on her lap. The pages had begun to change over the last week. Less isolated words.

More small phrases. Fragments of thought struggling toward full return.

Progress had become visible enough that it no longer felt imaginary, though not yet kind enough to feel easy.

When she looked up and saw Marlie, her first expression was annoyance.

Which, in this season, often meant she was stronger than yesterday.

"You look like… errands," Mia said.

The line came out delayed at the edges, but clear enough to sting and amuse in equal measure.

Marlie closed the door behind her. *"That's because I have them."*

Mia exhaled through her nose, not quite a laugh.

"Rude."

"Truthful," Marlie corrected, setting her tote and garment bag down. Then she studied Mia more closely. *"How are you?"*

Mia's eyes moved toward the workbook before they came back.

"Tired. Mad. Better."

Marlie nodded once.

"Excellent order."

That made Mia smile. Small. Real. On time.

The morning session was harder than the day before.

That happened too, and realism had taught all of them to stop treating every difficult day like a betrayal of progress. Some mornings the words came cleaner. Some mornings the body felt heavier.

Some mornings the fatigue arrived before breakfast and sat over everything like weather. By the time physical therapy began, Mia's patience was already thin.

Her right foot dragged once on the turn. The therapist corrected her posture twice. On the third reminder, Mia stopped, stared at the woman with exhausted fury, and said, *"I heard you... the first two times."*

The therapist didn't take offense.

Good therapists rarely did.

"Then I know you can do it the third time correctly."

Marlie looked down to hide her smile. Mary would have called it redirection. Marsha would have called it nerve. Mia called it annoying, but she did the turn again.

And better.

After therapy, while Mia rested and the nurse adjusted something at the side of the bed, Marlie stepped into the hallway to take a call she could no longer ignore. The brunch organizer's voice arrived warm and polished, the kind of woman who had spent years making opportunity sound like invitation rather than transaction.

"Marlie, I know your schedule is full, but I keep thinking about what you and the ladies represent right now. We'd love to host a conversation—reinvention, friendship, later-in-life visibility..."

Marlie listened, her gaze drifting through the narrow window at the end of the hall where damp New Jersey trees stood still beneath a pale sky.

"You keep saying 'represent,'" she said calmly. *"What do you think we represent?"*

The woman paused.

Not offended.

Thinking.

"Women who didn't disappear just because the world expected them to."

That answer gave Marlie pause. Not because it was perfect.

Because it was close.

"I can't promise anything yet," she said. *"But if we say yes to something, it has to be true to where we actually are. Not just to what people saw online."*

The woman's response came softer this time.

"Then when you're ready, I'd rather have the truth."

When the call ended, Marlie stood alone in the hallway for one extra breath, phone still in her hand, feeling the split as sharply as ever.

Outside, attention kept growing. Inside, recovery kept asking for slowness.

She had not yet figured out how to hold both without dropping one, but she was beginning to understand that maybe the point was not choosing between them.

Maybe the point was letting one deepen the other.

By late afternoon, work came calling harder.

A customer texted twice. A venue manager emailed back. A man whose name she had not saved but whose tone remained measured sent another message—*No need to answer. Just hoping today was kind to you.* She looked at that one longer than she should have, then slipped the phone back into her bag and returned to the room.

Mia had moved from the bed back into the chair. The notebook was open again. Three lines had been attempted. One scratched out. One abandoned halfway. One legible enough to feel like a victory.

need more time

Marlie read it.

Then looked at Mia.

Mia looked away first.

Not in shame.

In irritation.

"I know," Marlie said quietly.

Mia's jaw tightened. *"Everybody says... be patient."*

"Because everybody isn't the one living inside the wait."

That landed deep enough that Mia's eyes came back to her face slowly.

"You understand... too much."

"That," Marlie said, *"is one of my more expensive qualities."*

Mia laughed at that. The laugh caught on the back end, but not enough to ruin it.

When Marsha arrived after work, she carried all the evidence of a day lived too fast—a wrinkled cardigan, lipstick faded at the edges, one earring switched to the wrong side because she had clearly redressed herself in a car mirror and decided the world would survive imperfection.

She dumped her tote into the visitor chair and let out a long breath before speaking.

"I need it noted that I am one unreasonable email away from becoming a legend in the wrong way."

Mia looked at her and, without missing the emotional cue beneath the humor, asked more cleanly than either of them expected, *"What happened?"*

The question stopped Marsha in place.

Her face changed.

Not because she was shocked to be asked.

Because she felt seen.

"Oh," she said softly, then sat down. *"That's new."*

Mia blinked, half-annoyed with being turned into a milestone.

"Answer."

And so Marsha did. She talked about work—not every useless detail, just enough to tell the truth like real women do when they are no longer interested in pretending their lives outside caregiving have politely gone silent.

Somebody junior had made a mistake and dressed it in confidence. Her supervisor had used the phrase *circling back* so many times she considered violence.

Her bus ride had smelled like wet umbrellas and bad choices. None of it was tragic. All of it was real.

Mia listened.

Actually listened.

Then shook her head slowly.

"You need... a raise."

Marsha pressed one hand to her chest and looked toward the ceiling like gratitude had finally become visible enough to praise.

"See? This right here? Worth the tolls."

The room eased.

That was the thing now—not constant heaviness, but constant adjustment. They laughed. They complained. They passed lotion. They discussed therapy and shoes and bank calls and dinner and whether Mia was going to let Marsha redo the scarf because *this knot is emotionally unfinished.*

They also discussed the unfortunate event exactly the way real women do when something terrible has already happened and survival has made space for analysis.

That evening, after the nurse had checked blood pressure and reminded them about one visitor at a time after seven, after Marlie had left to return two calls from the parking lot and Mary had texted that she was home but still reviewing the speech exercise sheet Mia hated, Marsha sat in the fading light of the room and finally said what all of them had been circling.

"I keep thinking about how close we came to not catching this when we did."

Mia didn't answer right away.

Her eyes moved toward the window, where the sky had gone from gray to ink without anyone really noticing.

"I know."

Marsha leaned forward, elbows on knees, hands clasped tightly.

"And I hate that. I hate that you were in pain and still trying to be agreeable in the chat. I hate that we thought 'off' just meant off. I hate—"

She stopped, exhaled hard, then started again more quietly. *"I hate that real life doesn't come with a louder warning sound."*

Mia looked down at her own hands.

Then at the notebook.

Then back at Marsha.

"I didn't know."

"I know you didn't."

That was the only answer.

No blame.

No false ease.

Just the truth sitting between them.

Mia's fingers moved toward the edge of the blanket.

"I keep remembering… trying to answer. In the chat. Like if I could just… sound normal…"

The sentence fractured there, not from damage this time, but emotion. Marsha saw it and softened immediately.

"You don't have to sound normal to us."

Mia looked at her.

Really looked.

Then glanced toward the phone lying face down on the tray table.

"I know that now."

By the time Marlie returned, the room had quieted into something almost sacred. Marsha had one hand wrapped around Mia's, the television in the corner muted, rain beginning to tap lightly against the window.

Marlie stepped in without breaking the mood, set down the takeout container she had picked up on the way back, and looked from one woman to the other before speaking.

"What did I miss?"

Marsha looked up.

"Honesty."

Marlie nodded as if that made perfect sense.

"Good. We should keep doing that."

They stayed until policy pushed them out—not harshly, but firmly enough to remind them that love was still on a schedule there.

Marsha left first tonight, work dragging tomorrow behind her whether she liked it or not.

Marlie lingered. She always did when she could.

Mia looked more tired than she had that morning, but also more settled. Sometimes the room needed tears in it before it could hold sleep properly.

On the side table, the phone buzzed.

Then again.

Marlie glanced at it.

Instagram. A repost. A new message request. A tagged clip from an old video with thousands more views than yesterday.

Mia followed her eyes.

"Still happening?"

Marlie smiled without humor.

"Yes."

Mia studied that for a second, her face harder to read now than it had been before the stroke. Not because she was more closed.

Because effort had made every visible emotion more costly.

"Weird."

"Very."

Another silence.

Then Mia looked at her.

"Don't stop... everything."

Marlie's gaze sharpened.

"What do you mean?"

Mia took a breath, steadied herself, and pushed the sentence through carefully. *"The events. The people. The things coming."* She paused, annoyed with the pace of her own mouth, then tried again. *"Don't make my... hard thing... your whole life."*

There it was.

Again.

That fear of becoming the center too completely.

Marlie moved closer to the bed and sat without rush, one hand resting on the blanket near Mia's knee.

"You are part of my life," she said. *"Not an eraser of it."*

Mia listened.

Marlie continued.

"And because you are part of it, I'm not going to turn into a martyr just to prove love. That would insult both of us."

The corners of Mia's mouth shifted.

Almost.

"That was... very you."

"Exactly."

This time the almost-smile arrived fully.

Later, when Marlie was back in her apartment and the city had gone dark enough to reflect itself in the windows, the group chat came alive again.

Ebony M. Elite

Mary: *Did she settle?*

Marlie sat at the counter with one heel off, one still on, tea untouched beside her.

Marlie: *Eventually. We talked.*

Marsha: *I knew y'all did. My spirit could feel the seriousness.*

Marlie smiled.

Then typed:

Marlie: *She told me not to stop everything.*

That landed.

Even digitally.

Mary answered first.

Mary: *She would say that.*

Marsha followed.

Marsha: *And she would be right. But I'm still bringing hand cream tomorrow.*

Then the typing bubble from Mia came. Slower. More deliberate.

Mia: *Bring the good one.*

The three women who loved her enough to understand the sentence all smiled in three different rooms for three different reasons.

And because life insisted on itself, Marlie answered two messages after that. One to the brunch host. One to the respectful man whose timing remained almost annoyingly good.

Mary set out her clothes for the next morning's visit before bed.

Marsha finally answered the email she had been threatening all evening, but with less violence than promised.

And in the rehab room, Mia placed the phone down beside the notebook and let the quiet settle over her without fighting it.

Outside, the world still wanted the visible version of them.

Inside, they were learning how to keep carrying the truth of it.

Both mattered now.

And none of them were the same women they had been when the chat first paused.

Chapter Thirty: The Things They Carried Back Out

By the sixth week, the center had begun to reveal itself in two versions.

There was the version visitors saw first—the clean floors, the practiced smiles, the soft authority in every posted schedule, the way the staff moved through the building as if routine itself were a form of medicine.

Then there was the version the women had learned to recognize because they had spent enough hours inside it for the truth to rise.

The tiredness under the fluorescent lights by late afternoon. The way effort collected in the corners of a room after therapy left.

The silence that sat differently after a hard day than after a good one. The way recovery, for all its noble language, could still make a grown woman feel like her own body had put her on hold.

That morning the rain had finally broken. Sun came hard and bright across New Jersey, leaving the sidewalks wet but shining, the kind of light that made everything look newly exposed.

Marlie noticed it the moment she stepped out of her car and reached automatically for her sunglasses, her phone caught between her shoulder and ear, her tote bag heavier than usual because she had not yet had time to drop off a folder from work.

The call itself was brief, practical, unnecessary in the way only *quick check-ins* from people with no real sense of timing ever are.

"Yes, I saw the message." She listened, jaw set not with anger but with precision. *"No, not this morning. Send me the revised numbers and I'll look at them tonight."*

Another pause followed, and then she said, more clearly this time, *"I said tonight."*

She ended the call before the apology fully finished, slid the phone into her bag, and exhaled once before looking up at the building.

was no resentment in her face. Just adjustment. That had become the shape of things now. Not less life. More of it, stacked unevenly, all demanding to be carried at once.

Inside the center, the air felt warmer than usual, sunlight pressing itself against the windows hard enough to make the halls look almost cheerful if you didn't know better. A volunteer was arranging puzzle books in the common room.

Someone down the hall was practicing the names of the months in a slow, stubborn sequence.

A physical therapist laughed at something one of her patients had said, and the laugh sounded so ordinary it almost hurt.

Marlie signed in and moved through the hallway with familiar purpose, her visitor badge clipped neatly against her blazer, her sneakers making almost no sound on the waxed floor.

When she reached Mia's room, she paused just long enough at the doorway to take it in.

Mia was standing.

No walker.

Not alone—the therapist stood close enough to catch what needed catching—but still, standing.

One hand rested lightly against the parallel bar set up near the wall, the other hovered in the air as if she didn't fully trust the room not to tilt without warning.

Her body looked focused in a way that made all softness feel expensive. Concentration had tightened her face. One sneaker was half a step ahead of the other. The scarf at her neck had slipped slightly left. Her jaw was set.

Marlie did not interrupt.

She leaned one shoulder against the doorframe and watched.

"Again," the therapist said gently.

Mia looked at her the way only a woman already over the day could look at another adult using the word *again* like it was harmless.

Then she shifted her weight and tried once more.

The step came small, uneven, but hers.

Not graceful.

Not pretty.

Not filmed.

Real.

The kind of progress no one online ever clapped for because it did not know how to perform itself attractively.

That, more than anything, brought heat behind Marlie's eyes.

She blinked once and kept still.

When the therapist finally noticed her, she smiled but did not stop the session. *"Good timing. She's determined today."*

Mia turned her head slightly and saw Marlie in the doorway. Her expression changed—not softened exactly, but widened, as if seeing someone who knew her before this made the effort mean something different.

"Don't..." she started, the word catching before finding shape. She tried again, cleaner this time. *"Don't make that face."*

Marlie straightened. *"What face?"*

Mia's mouth twitched.

"The... emotional rich friend face."

That pulled a short laugh out of the therapist and a deeper one out of Marlie, enough to break the tension around the moment without disrespecting it.

"You are standing in a room after everything that happened," Marlie said as she crossed the threshold. *"I'm allowed one face."*

Mia looked at her.

Then, after the tiniest pause, nodded once.

"One."

By the time the session ended, Mia was breathing harder than she wanted anyone to notice.

Sweat had gathered lightly at her hairline. Her right hand looked more tired than the rest of her, fingers curling and uncurling with a stiffness she clearly resented.

Marlie handed her water before anyone had to ask, and Mia took it with the impatience of someone who still wanted to remain independent but had also grown too honest to reject what helped.

"I hate... how long everything takes," she muttered after a sip, lowering herself carefully into the chair.

Marlie sat across from her, setting her own bag down by the wall. *"I know."*

Mia looked at her over the rim of the cup. *"You do say that... a lot."*

"Because you keep being right in recognizable ways."

That got a better smile out of her. Still small. But easier.

The morning moved forward in pieces. A nurse came in to check blood pressure. A speech therapist stopped by to confirm the afternoon slot.

Mary texted that she would be late because a meeting at work had grown teeth.

Marsha sent a photo of two shoe options with the caption already underneath it in her usual mix of crisis and theater.

Ebony M. Elite

Marsha: *Help me decide whether I'm dressing for resilience or revenge.*

Mia read it twice, then typed with one finger, slow but sure enough to get the point across.

Mia: *Both.*

Marsha replied in under ten seconds.

Marsha: *Exactly why I trust you.*

The room settled around that the way it always did now—not because humor erased the heaviness, but because it gave everyone somewhere humane to stand inside it.

Around noon, Marlie finally opened the message she had been avoiding all morning. The respectful man again. He was becoming a pattern. Not because he pushed.

Because he didn't.

Heard you all might be doing a speaking engagement. If that happens, I'd like a ticket before it becomes impossible to get one.

Marlie read it once, then slipped the phone back into her bag without answering. Not dismissive. Not indulgent. Filed. There had been a time in her life when attention from a composed man would have moved much more quickly to the front of her day. Now it had to wait behind what mattered, and somehow that made the attention feel more useful, not less.

Mary arrived just after one with apology in her posture and none in her voice.

"I was detained by people who love meetings because they are not acquainted with purpose."

Mia looked up from the notebook. *"You should... invoice them."*

Mary stopped mid-step, then lowered her bag slowly. *"That,"* she said, *"is Marsha's influence."*

Mia's lips lifted. *"Unfortunately."*

The workbook came next. Naming exercises. Short written responses. One breathing drill that made Mia visibly irritated before it made her compliant. Mary sat beside her, not assisting until asked, the weighted pen resting near Mia's hand like a promise she was still making peace with. On the page, the therapist had written a sentence starter in thick, careful print.

Today I feel ______. Mia stared at it too long. Mary waited.

Mia picked up the pen, adjusted it once, frowned, adjusted it again, then wrote slowly.

heavy

better

still mad

She stopped.

Read it.

Then underlined the last one.

Mary's face softened in a way she did not let turn into pity. *"That sounds accurate."*

Mia pointed to the paper with the pen.

"All true."

The sentence came out rougher than the words on the page looked, but the clarity of it was its own milestone.

By late afternoon, visiting policy did what it always did—it reminded all of them that love, however relentless, still had to live inside someone else's rules.

Marlie had to leave for a fitting she could not cancel again without losing more than money. Mary had to go home, change clothes, and host a virtual call she had already moved twice. Marsha would come after work, but not until traffic permitted. The center gave them its schedule. Life gave them another. Grown women did not always get to choose which one hurt more.

Marlie stood by the bed, retying the end of Mia's scarf where it had loosened. *"I'll be back tomorrow morning."*

Mia looked at her. *"And tonight?"*

It was not accusation. Just accounting.

Marlie's hand stilled at the scarf. *"No."* She did not soften it with explanations she did not owe. *"I have to handle something tonight."*

Mia's eyes dropped once, then rose back up.

The old version of her would have hidden the disappointment behind immediate grace. This version had less energy for performance.

"Okay."

Marlie heard the difference.

So she answered the real thing.

"I know."

Mia held her gaze for a second longer than usual.

Then nodded. *"Go... handle it."*

That was how they loved each other now.

Not only in showing up. In naming when they couldn't.

When Marsha finally arrived, the room changed the way it always did when she brought the outside world in with her. She came through the door smelling faintly of rain-dried perfume and office air, her tote bag stuffed too full, her earrings changed since morning, one of her bangles missing because she had likely taken it off mid-email and forgotten to put it back on.

"I'm here, I'm irritated, and I bought two different kinds of soup because apparently my spirit likes options."

Mia looked up from the chair, one foot bare because she had been rubbing the ache out of it with absent-minded annoyance. *"You look... overworked."*

Marsha put the soup down and pointed at her. *"And still attractive. Keep both truths together."*

That made Mia laugh harder than expected, enough that she had to catch her breath afterward, enough that the tension sitting in her shoulders finally loosened.

Marsha unpacked while talking through the shape of her day. A woman at work had cried over something that should have been an email. S Somebody else had called Marsha *strong* in a tone that made it sound like a sentence instead of a compliment. The video had resurfaced again on another account, this time with music layered over it that made the four women look almost mythic.

"I'm starting to think we're haunting people with maturity," Marsha said, stirring the soup once before handing the spoon over.

Mia took it, then paused. *"Did you answer... anybody?"*

Marsha blinked. *"Anybody who?"*

Mia's expression shifted slowly, intentionally, as if placing each part of the thought where it belonged. *"The invitations. The people. The... things asking."*

There it was.

Not jealousy.

Not distance.

Awareness.

Marsha sat back and watched her for a second. *"Some,"* she said. *"Not all."*

Mia took a sip, swallowed, then looked down into the cup.

"Good."

Marsha narrowed one eye. *"Good because?"*

Mia tapped the spoon gently against the edge of the container, searching for the sentence rather than pretending she already had it.

"Because the world... didn't stop."

The line settled in the room with the kind of weight that made even Marsha go still.

"No," she said quietly. *"It didn't."*

Mia looked up. *"And it shouldn't."*

That one hurt more, because it was generous, because it was true, because all of them had been afraid of the opposite.

Marsha leaned forward, elbows on knees.

"It didn't stop," she said carefully, *"but it changed speed."*

Mia listened.

Marsha kept going. *"Everything still moves. Work. Money. Men. Invitations. Social media. Stupid people. But none of it moves the same way now. Not for us."*

Mia's eyes narrowed slightly. *"How?"*

Marsha looked around the room—at the notebook, the weighted pen, the cardigan folded on the chair, the black sneakers by the bed, the soup balanced on the tray, the rehab schedule taped to the wall.

Then she answered with more honesty than flourish.

"Because now we know what matters when all the extra gets stripped off."

That stayed.

Long enough that even the sound from the television in the common room outside seemed far away.

Later, when policy narrowed the room down again and Marsha had to gather herself to leave, she stood in front of Mia with her bag over one shoulder and one hand still resting on the bed rail.

"I'm not coming tomorrow," she said.

She said it directly.

No apology wrapped around it.

No performance of guilt.

"I have to work late and then go see about my mother."

Mia looked at her, absorbing not just the information but the way it was given.

"Okay."

Marsha's mouth tightened. *"You sure?"*

Mia nodded once, then again as if to steady the motion. *"Yes. You have... a life."*

Marsha exhaled slowly. *"I do."*

Then she bent and kissed Mia's forehead. *"And so do you. This is still your life too, even from in here."*

When she left, the room did not feel abandoned.

It felt honest.

That night, Marlie's fitting ran long, Mary's virtual meeting went later than expected, and the group chat slowed into the new realistic rhythm it had learned since the stroke—not constant, not playful for the sake of reassurance, but alive enough to keep everyone tethered.

Ebony M. Elite

Mary: *Home at last.*

Marsha: *Same. My bra is off. I am no longer available for nonsense.*

Marlie, still in the back of a car crossing toward the city, looked out at the lights and typed with one thumb.

Marlie: *How was she when you left?*

Marsha answered first.

Marsha: *Tired. Clear. Thinking too much.*

There was a pause.

Then the typing bubble from Mia appeared.

Stopped.

Started again.

Mia: *I'm still... here.*

Three women read that in three different places and felt the same thing move through them—a mix of ache, pride, and the strange exhausted gratitude that comes when someone you love keeps finding ways to remain visible to you through effort.

Marlie answered first.

Marlie: *I know.*

Mary followed.

Mary: *And you are not here alone.*

Marsha, predictably, closed it her way.

Marsha: *Exactly. Now go to sleep before I come back and supervise your rest myself.*

This time the laugh Mia let out was private. Quiet. But enough to count.

She placed the phone down beside the notebook and stared at the ceiling for a while after that, listening to the low sounds of the center settling into night. Someone coughed down the hall.

A cart squeaked once and was corrected by a hand that knew exactly where to press. The lights in the parking lot threw pale bars across the floor.

The world had not stopped.

That was true.

But neither had she.

And maybe, just maybe, that was the beginning of a different kind of grace—the kind that did not require your old shoes to fit exactly the same way in order to keep walking forward.

Chapter Thirty-One: The First Laugh That Didn't Hurt

The message came through the way so many of their moments did now—without ceremony, without buildup, just a quiet offering placed inside the space they had always shared, waiting to see who would reach for it first.

Marsha's name lit up the group chat with her usual urgency, her words carrying that familiar blend of impatience, exhaustion, and self-preservation that had become its own dialect over the years.

Ebony M. Elite 💬

Marsha: *I'm leaving work early before I curse somebody out and lose my pension. Anybody available for something quick that involves food and minding our business?*

For a moment, the message simply sat there—not ignored, not avoided, just held. Because what it represented was not merely a meal, not merely an hour carved out of a crowded day. It was the first time they would choose to step back into the world without Mia physically beside them. Not leaving her. Not replacing her. Not acting as though anything had been restored to normal. Continuing.

And continuation, when grief had already rearranged the furniture of your life, asked for a different kind of courage than crisis ever did.

Mary saw it first. She was seated at her desk with her glasses lowered slightly on her nose, laptop open, one tab full of meeting notes, another full of a spreadsheet she had already spent too much of her morning fixing for people who should have known better.

The soft glow of the screen rested across a face that had learned how to balance composure with quiet fatigue. Her fingers hovered above the keyboard, not because she did not know what to say, but because she understood exactly what this invitation meant.

When she finally answered, the message arrived measured and dry in the way only Mary could make affection sound like discipline.

Mary: *Define quick, because your version of quick and mine have a history of disagreement.*

Marlie read it next, standing in her office with the city stretched wide behind her, contracts open across her desk, two emails flagged, a garment bag slung over the visitor chair, and life continuing in that relentless, forward-moving way that refused to pause just because something inside her still needed more time.

One hand rested against the edge of her desk while the other held the phone, her reflection faint in the window as she reread Marsha's message, then Mary's, then let the truth settle.

This would be the first time they sat in a public room and felt Mia's absence not as a hospital necessity, not as visiting policy, but as shape. A real, visible shape at the table.

She typed with a clarity that surprised even her.

Marlie: *Quick means we leave before it gets heavy.*

Marsha answered instantly, as if she had been waiting for someone else to name exactly what she had been refusing to soften.

Marsha: *Exactly.*

That one word carried everything else—the understanding, the urgency, the refusal to let sorrow turn into stagnation if they could help it.

Mary closed her laptop halfway, the decision settling into her body before she had fully analyzed it.

Mary: *I can do an hour.*

Marlie slid her phone into her tote, already reaching for her keys.

Marlie: *Send location.*

Across the state line, in a room that had begun to smell more like effort than fear, Mia's phone buzzed on the tray table beside her.

She had just finished a session she was still angry about, one shoulder sore from repetition, one thigh still trembling faintly from standing longer than she wanted to acknowledge.

The therapist had gone. The room had gone quiet. The black sneakers were off and placed neatly under the chair.

Her hand moved toward the phone with less hesitation than it would have a week ago, and she read the thread once, then again.

Her expression did not collapse.

It tightened.

Not because she felt forgotten.

Because she understood exactly what it meant.

And because understanding, lately, had become the one thing she could trust to arrive on time even when everything else did not.

She did not type.

Not yet.

She simply looked out the window for a second longer than necessary and let the moment pass through her without naming it too quickly.

The restaurant Marsha chose was understated in a way that felt deliberate, warm lighting casting soft shadows across polished wood, low music threading through conversations that stayed close to the table, the kind of place that didn't demand attention but rewarded presence.

Marlie arrived first, slipping into the booth with practiced ease, her bag settling beside her as her eyes instinctively scanned the table—and there it was, immediate and unavoidable.

Four women. Four seats. One empty space that did not need to be acknowledged to be felt. Her fingers brushed the edge of the table once, a fleeting contact, before she pulled them back into her lap and smoothed her sleeve as if adjusting fabric instead of emotion.

Mary entered next, her presence calm and grounded, her gaze finding Marlie at once. In that look was everything—recognition, understanding, restraint.

She did not take the seat across from her. Instead, she slid in beside her, shoulder to shoulder, closing the space without comment. The adjustment was small, almost invisible, but meaningful all the same, a silent agreement that some things did not need to be spoken to be honored properly.

Marsha arrived exactly as expected—energy slightly ahead of her body, presence filling the room before she fully reached the table, her bag dropping beside her as she slid into the booth and looked between them with sharp, assessing eyes.

"Alright," she said, already settling into the seat. *"Nobody better start acting like this is a memorial. I came here to eat and remind myself I'm still fine."*

There was no cruelty in it. No denial either. Just protection—the kind women build instinctively when they know a moment can turn if they let it.

Marlie looked at her, really looked, and something in her chest eased just enough for the corner of her mouth to lift.

Mary let out a breath she had not realized she had been holding. When the waitress approached with menus and efficient softness, they ordered quickly, decisively, anchoring themselves in something tangible before the weight of the moment had a chance to settle too deeply.

For a brief stretch of time, the table held that familiar rhythm—water poured, menus closed, napkins adjusted, Marsha complaining mildly about the size of the glasses, Mary already deciding the lighting was kind but not flattering enough for bad decisions.

Then the silence came. Not awkward. Not uncomfortable. Just aware. It settled between them with a presence that asked to be acknowledged.

Marsha did it first, because of course she did. She wrapped one hand around her glass and leaned back slightly, her eyes moving between them with that direct, unflinching honesty that had always defined her.

"Alright, I'm going to say it so we can move past it," she said, her voice steady but intentional. *"This feels strange."*

The word landed exactly where it needed to.

Mary nodded once, her fingertips touching the edge of her napkin.

"Yes."

Marlie's gaze dropped briefly to the table before lifting again, meeting theirs with quiet clarity.

"It does."

Marsha leaned forward slightly, her expression shifting, not losing its strength but gaining something steadier beneath it.

"But strange doesn't mean wrong."

That distinction mattered more than anything else she could have said.

Mary adjusted her posture, voice calm and measured.

"No. It means different."

Marlie held their gaze, her shoulders settling.

"And we're allowed different."

That was the moment it shifted—not dramatically, not suddenly, but enough to let something new take root.

The food arrived in soft curls of steam and familiar scent, grounding the space in something immediate, something present.

Marsha reached for her fork with decisive urgency, as if refusing to let the moment slip back into heaviness.

"Because if we don't eat," she said, already cutting into her meal, *"this turns into something dramatic, and I'm not in the mood for dramatic tonight."*

That line, delivered with just enough edge to keep it honest, broke something open.

Mary let out a soft laugh, gentle but real.

Marlie followed, quieter but genuine, and just like that, the first laugh came—not forced, not careful, but natural, rising up from somewhere that had not disappeared after all.

It did not erase anything.

But it did not hurt.

As the meal unfolded, conversation began moving the way it always had—slowly at first, then more easily, weaving through familiar territories that reminded them who they had always been together.

Work frustrations surfaced in controlled doses. Small victories were shared without embellishment. A client had finally paid. Mary's coworker had managed to use the word *synergy* three times in one meeting and still expected to be taken seriously.

Marsha had eaten lunch at 3:40 standing near a copy machine and considered that a human rights violation. The world, rude and ordinary as ever, had continued.

Then, inevitably, the conversation turned—not because anyone forced it, but because life had already begun presenting itself in that other way too.

Marsha set her fork down and leaned back with the look that signaled she was about to say something she had already decided needed to be addressed.

"So are we going to pretend like the world didn't start noticing us again," she began, her tone sharp but controlled, *"or are we going to talk about it like grown women?"*

Mary raised one brow, expression composed.

"When did we stop being grown?"

Marlie leaned back slightly, watching them both.

"No, let her clarify. I'm interested in the definition."

Marsha shook her head, but the smile at the edge of her mouth had returned.

"I mean the DMs, the looks, the invitations, the 'accidental' run-ins. All of it."

As she listed them, it became clear all over again—life had continued to present itself, even while they had been standing still in parking lots and therapy hallways and waiting rooms.

Mary adjusted her posture, folding her hands neatly in front of her. *"I've declined most of mine."*

Marsha blinked. *"Most?"*

Mary didn't flinch. *"I am selective, not unavailable."*

There it was. That quiet assertion of self that had never disappeared, merely recalibrated.

Marlie's lips curved slightly. *"That sounded practiced."*

Mary took a sip of water and paused before admitting it. *"It sounded better in my head."*

Marsha laughed then, full and unrestrained, her shoulders relaxing as tension gave way to something lighter, something closer to what they had always known together.

"I knew it. I knew you were not sitting at home knitting your way through life."

Mary gave her a look equal parts correction and amusement. *"I don't knit."*

Marlie tilted her head, voice quieter now, more direct. *"But you're not uninterested."*

Mary met her eyes and answered plainly.
"No."

That single word settled into the space with quiet force.

Because it wasn't only about men.

It was about life.

Continuing.

When they stepped back outside, the evening air met them with a softness that felt almost intentional, the city moving around them in its steady rhythm, headlights cutting through dusk, voices blending into the background of something larger than any one moment.

Marlie paused on the sidewalk, adjusting her bag as she took it in, the weight of the day shifting slightly in her chest, not gone, but balanced.

Mary stood beside her, quiet, present.

Marsha rolled her shoulders back and exhaled slowly. *"That was necessary."*

Her voice was grounded enough to make it clear she meant more than the meal.

Mary nodded. *"Yes. It was."*

Marlie looked between them, then reached for her phone. Her thumb hovered over the screen for only a second before she typed into the place that had held all of them through every version of this story.

Ebony M. Elite

Marlie: *We went out.*

No explanation.

No justification.

Just truth.

The typing bubble appeared almost immediately, paused, then started again. When the response came, it was simple.

Mia: *Good.*

One word. But it carried everything—acceptance, understanding, strength.

Marlie stared at it for a moment, something warm and complicated settling into her chest as she turned the phone slightly so Mary and Marsha could see.

Mary smiled softly. *"That's her."*

Marsha nodded once, expression steady. *"Yeah. It is."*

Marlie typed again, fingers moving with more certainty now.

Marlie: *We saved you a seat.*

This time the pause stretched longer. A streetlight above them flickered once before settling into steady gold. Then the reply came.

Mia: *I'll take it.*

Marlie locked her phone slowly and slid it back into her bag as she looked out at the city again, her breath easing in a way it had not in weeks.

Because for the first time since everything had shifted, joy had returned.

Not loudly.

Not fully.

But honestly.

And that was enough to begin again.

Chapter Thirty-Two: The Weight of Beautiful Things

The first time they went shopping without her, it did not feel like an outing. It felt like a decision none of them had formally agreed to make, yet all of them had arrived at anyway through the quiet arithmetic of grown women adjusting to life after impact.

The mall stood bright and polished beneath midday light, glass doors opening into a world that moved at its own pace, indifferent to the private negotiations happening inside each of them as they stepped forward together.

Their reflections caught briefly in the shine of the entrance—three women still beautifully composed, still carrying themselves with intention, still very much themselves—and then disappeared into the larger flow of bodies, color, perfume, music, commerce, and ordinary life insisting on itself.

Marlie slowed for half a second just beyond the threshold, her hand adjusting the strap of her bag while her eyes moved through the wide, gleaming space instinctively, not searching for anything she expected to find, but still registering what was not there.

Four had always been their number in places like this. Four opinions. Four energies. Four rhythms blending into one fluid motion that turned shopping into strategy and strategy into pleasure.

Now the absence sat beside them like a shadow that refused to be ignored and refused, just as stubbornly, to be honored with too much ceremony. It was there. It was real. It was not the whole day.

Mary noticed the pause without turning her head. Her awareness moved that way now—quiet, exact, more observant than ever—and instead of naming the shift, she simply stepped a little closer to Marlie's side, closing the space with intention rather than commentary. Marsha, already moving a half step ahead with her usual forward charge, glanced back just long enough to read the air between them and clapped her hands once—light, controlled, purposeful.

"Alright," she said, her voice carrying just enough edge to keep all of them from drifting too far inward. *"We are not coming in here to walk around like ghosts. If we're doing this, we're doing it properly."*

Marlie exhaled, the tension in her shoulders easing just enough for her posture to reset. She lifted her gaze fully, let the brightness of the place land without resistance, and answered in the same calm, grounded tone she used whenever a room needed to be told who it belonged to.

"We are doing it properly."

Mary adjusted her glasses and glanced once at the directory, practical even in emotion. *"Then we begin with intention,"* she said, already moving toward the first store without waiting for further discussion.

Marsha smirked and fell into step beside them. *"See, this is why I like shopping with y'all. Everybody thinks it's about clothes, but it's really about strategy."*

The first store greeted them with low music and carefully curated displays, mannequins posed in attitudes of effortless elegance, fabrics draped in ways that suggested ease even when the prices clearly said otherwise. It smelled faintly of cedar hangers, pressed cotton, expensive perfume, and the kind of lighting design meant to flatter indecision into a purchase.

Marlie's fingers brushed a silk sleeve as she passed, the texture grounding her immediately in something physical, something known. Her eyes moved through lines, cuts, hems, shoulder shapes, hidden structure, the subtle decisions that always spoke to her before color did.

And then it happened.

A dress.

Deep, structured, elegant in a way that called memory without asking permission.

Mia would have loved it.

The thought came whole and immediate, and it stopped Marlie mid-step, her hand still resting lightly against the fabric while the image formed without warning—Mia standing beside her, tilting her head, studying the line of the waist, criticizing the sleeve, praising the architecture, offering that precise, beautifully irritating critique that always landed somewhere between fashion and philosophy.

Marlie's fingers stilled. For one suspended second, the store, the music, the movement around them all seemed to recede, leaving only the dress and the woman who was not there to see it.

Mary saw it from across the rack. Her gaze sharpened slightly, followed the line of Marlie's attention, then settled on the shift in her face. She crossed the small distance between them without hurry and let her voice enter the moment softly enough not to bruise it.

"It's her style."

Not a question.

An acknowledgment.

Marlie nodded once, her fingers finally pulling back from the fabric.

"Yes."

Marsha approached from the other side, her eyes scanning the dress first, then Marlie's face, then Mary's, reading everything none of them had yet fully said. For a brief moment her expression softened, something deeper moving behind her usual sharpness. Then she reached for the dress and pulled it from the rack with deliberate ease.

"Then we buy it."

Marlie blinked, caught slightly off guard.

"For what?"

Marsha looked at her as if the question itself were unserious.

"For when she's ready to wear it."

Mary's lips pressed together, her gaze lowering briefly before lifting again with a steadier warmth.

"That is not unreasonable."

Marlie looked between them, the weight of the moment shifting into something else—not lighter exactly, but forward-moving, useful, less helpless. Then, slowly, she nodded.

"Alright."

And just like that, the absence did not disappear.

But it changed.

They moved through the mall with more ease after that, their rhythm returning in pieces that felt both familiar and new, laughter surfacing in moments that did not feel forced, conversation flowing in ways that reminded them of who they had always been to each other even before grief and hospitals and rehab schedules had taught them harder versions of loyalty.

Marsha held up a pair of shoes with exaggerated seriousness, turning them slightly beneath the light.

"These say I have my life together, but I'm still approachable."

Mary adjusted her glasses and studied them with genuine thought.

"They say you are willing to be seen but not easily understood."

Marlie tilted her head, gaze narrowing with professional suspicion.

"They also say you'll be uncomfortable in about forty-five minutes."

Marsha laughed, full and unrestrained, the sound echoing just enough to turn a few nearby heads.

"See? This is what I needed."

She set the shoes back down, and her shoulders relaxed in a way that had not happened all morning.

The laughter came easier after that. It built naturally, layering over the movement of the day as they stepped in and out of stores, hands brushing fabrics, eyes scanning displays, opinions offered without hesitation.

They talked about texture, shape, color, and practicality with the same seriousness they once reserved for men who introduced themselves too casually.

They rejected two handbags for being emotionally shallow.

They approved one blazer because it looked like it came with a retirement plan. Marsha found a pair of earrings she declared were *"for surviving nonsense beautifully."*

Mary found a scarf in muted champagne tones and ran it through her fingers as if deciding whether it belonged to her or to the version of her she would become next.

Marlie purchased nothing for herself in the first three stores and still somehow made the whole experience feel curated.

It wasn't the same.

But it was still them.

By the time they settled into the small café tucked between two boutiques, the late afternoon light had softened, spilling through the windows in warm gold bands that wrapped around the room and turned every table into a small stage for ordinary life.

They ordered without much discussion—drinks first, then something light to share, the kind of choices that came from familiarity rather than debate.

Marlie leaned back slightly in her chair, her phone resting loosely in her hand, the group chat still open from earlier. Her thumb hovered for a moment before she typed.

Ebony M. Elite

Marlie: *We're shopping.*

Mary watched her from across the table, gaze steady.

"You're telling her."

Marlie nodded once.

"Yes."

Marsha leaned forward slightly, elbows resting on the table, her expression more thoughtful now than performative.

"Good," she said quietly. *"Because she needs to see that we're still moving."*

The typing bubble appeared.

Paused.

Mia: *Send pictures.*

The reply came quicker this time, stronger, and the force of it moved through all three women with almost physical clarity.

Marlie's lips curved slightly as she lifted her phone, angling it just enough to capture the table, the shopping bags, the amber light filtering in around them.

She snapped one picture, then another—this time of the dress, carefully folded in its bag, the handle looped over the back of Marlie's chair like a promise.

She sent both.

The reply took longer.

When it came, it carried more than any of them had been ready for.

Mia: *That dress… is mine.*

Mary exhaled softly, a quiet smile forming.

Marsha nodded once, satisfied in a way that looked almost reverent.

Marlie typed back, her fingers steady.

Marlie: *We know.*

They sat with that for a minute, the food arriving and the glasses sweating on the table while none of them rushed to fill the space.

Outside the café, the mall kept moving. Teenagers drifted by in clusters. Couples passed with shopping bags and private irritations. A woman in a camel coat talked too loudly into her headset near the escalator. Somewhere, someone was buying perfume they did not need and calling it self-care. Life remained beautifully, offensively normal.

Marsha broke the silence first, but this time without forcing brightness.

"I'm glad we came."

Mary looked at her, then down at the bag holding the dress, then back up.

"So am I."

Marlie rested one hand lightly against the strap of her bag.

"Me too."

The words sounded simple.

They were not.

When they left the café, the evening had begun settling in fully, the mall lights shifting into their softer nighttime version, storefront glass glowing, music from somewhere upstairs drifting down with the smell of cinnamon, pretzels, and expensive skincare.

Marlie adjusted her bag again, the weight of the dress inside it noticeable now—not heavy, but present. A reminder of something they were carrying forward, not leaving behind.

Marsha rolled her shoulders once and looked around with that familiar, restless spark returning to her face.

"Alright. What's next? Because I'm not going home yet."

Mary checked her watch, then looked up.
"I have time for a movie."

Marlie considered it for only half a second before nodding.

"Then we go to a movie."

Marsha grinned immediately, already stepping ahead.

"See? This is what I'm talking about. We're outside again."

Marlie followed, Mary beside her, their steps aligning as they moved toward the next part of the day, the next piece of life that had been waiting for them to return. And somewhere between the lights, the motion, the shopping bags, the dress meant for later, and the small photograph now sitting in Mia's phone, the guilt softened.

Not gone.

But no longer leading.

And that, more than anything, meant they were beginning to find their way back.

Chapter Thirty-Three: Rooms That Opened When They Walked In

The movie theater was colder than it needed to be, the kind of air that wrapped around your arms the moment you stepped inside and reminded you that comfort was always negotiable in public spaces, and Marsha complained about it immediately—of course she did—her voice cutting through the low hum of pre-show chatter as she adjusted the sleeve of her jacket.

"Why do they keep it like this? Are we preserving ourselves for later?"

Mary gave her a look that suggested both agreement and restraint, her hands already moving to fold her scarf more tightly around her neck as her eyes scanned the seating with quiet precision.

Marlie paused at the entrance to the aisle, letting her eyes adjust to the dimness, the glow of the screen washing over rows of strangers who had come to sit in the dark and disappear into something that wasn't theirs.

For a brief moment, she allowed herself to feel it—the contrast, the choice, the quiet truth of being here without Mia beside them. It didn't tighten her chest the way it had days ago. It didn't stop her steps. It simply passed through, acknowledged, then set aside with care instead of resistance.

Mary leaned slightly forward, already deciding.

"Middle."

Her voice was low but certain as she stepped into the row, guiding them toward seats that offered balance—neither hidden nor exposed—and they followed without discussion, their movement still choreographed in that unspoken way that years of friendship had refined into instinct.

Marsha slid into her seat first, stretching her legs out briefly before pulling them back in, her eyes scanning the room in that habitual, observational way that always noticed more than it needed to.

She leaned just slightly toward Marlie, her voice dropping as if sharing something confidential.

"Okay... I see at least three situations in here that I would entertain under the right circumstances."

Marlie lowered herself into her seat beside her, shaking her head as the corner of her mouth lifted.

"You haven't even sat down properly."

Mary adjusted her bag beneath her seat, gaze still forward, but her voice carried that dry, effortless acknowledgment that made everything sound like a well-considered thesis.

"Observation does not require full physical commitment."

Marsha let out a quiet laugh and settled back, satisfied.

The lights dimmed further, the room folding inward as the screen brightened, and for a while, the world narrowed into story and sound. Their bodies relaxed into the shared stillness of watching something unfold that had nothing to do with them.

It wasn't escape—it was relief. A place where they didn't have to carry the weight of interpretation, where emotion could arrive without being managed, where silence didn't ask for explanation.

Halfway through the film, Marlie's phone buzzed softly in her lap, the vibration subtle but enough to pull her attention for a second. She glanced down, careful not to disrupt the moment, and saw it.

Ebony M. Elite

Mia: *What are we watching?*

Marlie's thumb hovered for just a breath before she typed, the soft glow of the screen lighting her fingertips.

Marlie: *Something dramatic that we are pretending not to judge.*

The response came quickly.

Mia: *I would be judging.*

Marlie's lips curved, her gaze lifting briefly toward the screen before returning to her phone.

Marlie: *We know.*

She slipped the phone back down, her attention returning fully to the film, but something inside her had shifted again—not heavier, not lighter, just… connected. The thread between them remained intact, stretched but unbroken, present even in the quiet spaces where words were minimal.

—

When the movie ended, the lights rose slowly, pulling everyone back into themselves. Conversations began in soft waves as people gathered their belongings, jackets sliding back onto shoulders, phones lighting up, reality returning in pieces.

Marsha stood first, stretching her arms slightly as her body recalibrated from stillness to movement.

"That was better than expected."

Mary rose beside her, smoothing her coat with that same composed efficiency.

"It held its structure."

Marlie stood last, slipping her phone back into her bag, her gaze moving between them with quiet satisfaction.

"And it didn't waste our time."

They moved with the crowd toward the exit, the flow of bodies carrying them forward until the glass doors opened and the evening air met them—cooler now, softer, layered with the hum of night settling in.

Something about it felt different.

Fuller.

Open.

Like the day had stretched just enough to make space for something they hadn't planned.

It happened without announcement.

Marsha slowed mid-step, her eyes locking onto something ahead, her posture shifting just slightly—the kind of shift that meant attention had been claimed without effort.

Marlie caught it immediately, her gaze following the direction without turning her head too quickly. Mary registered it without looking at all.

He approached with intention.

Not rushed.

Not hesitant.

Grounded.

His suit was tailored without being loud, clean lines, quiet confidence. His expression held itself without effort, and when he spoke, his voice carried the kind of ease that came from knowing how to enter a moment without disturbing it.

"Good evening."

His gaze settled first on Marlie, then acknowledged the others with respect.

"I hope I'm not interrupting, but I would regret not saying hello."

Marsha's eyebrow lifted, interest sharpening immediately.

Marlie held his gaze, her posture steady, her voice calm and unhurried.

"You've already interrupted."

There was no edge to it.

Just truth.

A hint of a smile touched his mouth—not offended, not thrown.

"Then I'll make it worth it."

Mary's gaze shifted slightly, assessing now, measuring tone, presence, intention. Marsha leaned just enough into the moment to feel it fully.

"That's a strong opening," she said quietly.

He inclined his head once.

"I believe in using time well."

Marlie felt it then—that subtle recognition of energy that didn't disrupt, didn't demand, but matched. That rare alignment that didn't need to announce itself to be understood.

Mary spoke next, her tone precise, direct without aggression.

"And what is it you think you're using this time for?"

He met her gaze evenly.

"Connection."

The word settled.

Unadorned.

Unrushed.

Marlie watched him for a moment longer, then asked the question that mattered.

"And what makes you think we're available for that?"

He didn't hesitate.

"I don't."

A pause.

"But I'm available to be introduced."

Marsha let out a soft, approving sound under her breath.

"I like him."

Mary's expression didn't shift dramatically, but something in her eyes softened just enough to signal openness.

Marlie exhaled slowly, something in her chest aligning—not excitement, not resistance, just awareness.

The world had not stopped.

It had simply waited.

She met his gaze fully.

"Then introduce yourself."

And he did.

—

Later, when they parted ways and the night settled into its quieter rhythm, the group chat came alive again—not urgent, not heavy, just present.

Ebony M. Elite 💬

Marsha: *So we're outside AND being approached properly. I need everybody to acknowledge growth.*

Mary: *We were approached with intention, which is a notable distinction.*

Marlie sat in the quiet of her car, the city lights moving past her window in soft streaks, her body finally registering the fullness of the day. Her phone buzzed again.

Mia.

Mia: *Tell me everything.*

Marlie smiled—slow, genuine, earned—and began typing.

Marlie: *We went to a movie. It was good. And then we were introduced to someone who understood how to speak.*

The typing bubble appeared.

Paused.

Mia: *Good.*

A second message followed, slower, more deliberate.

Mia: *I like this version of things.*

Marlie stared at the screen for a moment, something deep and quiet moving through her chest, then responded.

Marlie: *So do we.*

She locked her phone and leaned back, her gaze lifting to the city beyond the glass—the motion, the light, the constant unfolding of everything continuing whether you were ready or not.

Because now something else had returned.

Not just joy.

Possibility.

And it did not ask for permission.

It simply arrived… ready to see who would meet it where it stood.

Chapter Thirty-Four: The Invitations That Knew Their Names

The invitations did not arrive all at once.

They never did. They came the way opportunity tends to come when it has been watching first—measured, intentional, spaced just far enough apart to feel like coincidence until the pattern revealed itself.

A message here. An introduction there. A follow-up that did not feel forced. By the time the third one appeared, it was no longer something to question.

It was something to acknowledge.

Marlie noticed it first, not because she was searching for it, but because she had always been attuned to shifts in energy that did not announce themselves loudly.

She sat at her desk with her laptop open, emails resting in quiet expectation, her phone placed just within reach.

When the notification appeared, she did not reach for it immediately. She finished the sentence she was reading, closed the document with calm precision, and only then lifted the phone, her expression composed, her posture unchanged.

"We would be honored to have you attend..."

She read the message once, then again, her eyes scanning not just the words, but the intention beneath them, the tone between the lines. It was not casual. It was not random.

It was specific.

Curated.

She did not respond.

Not yet.

Instead, she placed the phone down and leaned back slightly, her gaze drifting toward the window where the city moved in quiet, constant rhythm.

There had been a time when invitations like this would have been filtered quickly—accepted or declined based on schedule, convenience, or curiosity.

Now, they required something else.

Alignment.

—

Mary's invitation came differently.

Printed.

Delivered.

Placed neatly into her hand by a colleague who understood the language of presentation, the envelope thick enough to suggest importance without needing to announce it.

Mary stood in her office doorway for a moment after receiving it, her fingers resting lightly against the seal, her expression unreadable in that way that meant she was processing more than she intended to reveal.

She did not open it immediately.

She carried it to her desk, set it down with care, and continued her work for another ten minutes, finishing what had already been started before allowing herself to engage with what had just arrived.

When she returned to it, her movements were deliberate. She broke the seal cleanly, removed the card, and read.

"An Evening of Influence…"

Her eyes moved slowly across the page, taking in not just the event, but the room it represented—the conversations, the hierarchy, the subtle expectations that would not be spoken aloud but would be present all the same.

She closed the card gently, her fingers resting against it for a moment longer than necessary as she exhaled.

This was not about attendance.

This was about positioning.

—

Marsha's came the way most things did in her world—unexpected, slightly disruptive, impossible to ignore.

Her phone buzzed while she was in the middle of explaining something to someone who had already asked too many unnecessary questions.

She glanced at the screen with irritation that shifted instantly into something else.

Curiosity.

"You were recommended..."

She blinked once, her posture straightening as she stepped away from the conversation she had already decided she was done with.

"Hold that thought," she said, already turning, her voice carrying the kind of finality that did not invite response.

She moved toward the window, attention fully captured now as she read the message again, her lips pressing together slightly as something settled into place.

Recommended.

Not found.

Not stumbled upon.

Seen.

Her reflection met her in the glass—steady, aware, fully present.

"Well," she murmured under her breath, *"alright then."*

—

The chat came alive later that evening, not with urgency, but with awareness.

Ebony M. Elite

Marsha: *So are we all going to pretend like we didn't just get invited into rooms we didn't ask to be in?*

Mary read it from her living room, her glasses resting beside her now, the invitation card placed neatly on the table in front of her. She considered her response before typing.

Mary: *We did not ask. We positioned.*

Marlie saw it next, seated at her kitchen counter, her phone resting against a glass of water she had forgotten to drink. Her gaze lingered on Mary's words before she added her own.

Marlie: *And we were seen.*

Marsha responded immediately.

Marsha: *Exactly. That's what I'm saying. This isn't random.*

There was a pause.

Mia: *Tell me everything.*

The message came stronger now, more immediate, her presence in the chat no longer tentative but engaged. Marlie smiled slightly, her fingers moving with ease.

Marlie: *Invitations. Intentional ones.*

Mary: *Curated environments. Specific audiences.*

Marsha added, unable to resist sharpening it.

Marsha: *People with sense and resources.*

The typing bubble appeared again.

Paused.

Then—

Mia: *Good.*

But it did not end there.

Another message followed, slower, more deliberate.

Mia: *You belong there.*

The words settled differently.

Not encouragement.

Recognition.

Marlie felt it first, something warm and grounding moving through her chest as she read it again, her gaze softening just slightly. Mary adjusted her posture, thoughtful. Marsha leaned back, her head tilting as she exhaled.

Because coming from Mia… It meant she still saw them clearly.

—

The next day, Mia stood between the parallel bars, the room carrying the same quiet intensity it always had, the kind that left no space for distraction. Her hands rested lightly against the metal, her focus sharp, her breath measured as she prepared for the movement she had already decided she would complete.

"Again," the therapist said gently.

Mia exhaled, her jaw tightening just slightly before she shifted her weight forward. Her foot moved with careful intention, her balance catching, adjusting, holding.

The step came.

Not perfect.

But hers.

She paused, her breath steadying, her eyes lifting—not to the wall, not to the room, but somewhere beyond it.

Something further.

"Good," the therapist said.

Mia did not respond immediately.

Instead, she released one hand from the bar, her fingers flexing as she tested the space, the independence, the possibility. The air felt different when she was not holding on.

Her mind moved then—not fully formed, not fully spoken, but present.

Beyond recovery.

Beyond this room.

Beyond this version of her life.

The thought did not complete itself.

But it stayed.

—

That evening, preparation unfolded in separate spaces with the same underlying intention.

Marlie stood before her mirror, adjusting the line of her dress, her fingers smoothing fabric that did not need correction. Her eyes studied not just the reflection, but the presence it carried. She was not dressing to impress.

She was dressing to arrive.

Mary selected her outfit with quiet precision, each piece chosen for message rather than effect, her posture already aligned with the room she would soon enter. There was no hesitation in her movements, no second-guessing. Just clarity.

Marsha moved differently—fluid, expressive, her energy bold but controlled, her reflection meeting her with a confidence that did not require validation. She did not try on multiple versions of herself.

She chose the one that was already ready.

And somewhere, in a room that looked very different but held its own weight…

Mia sat on the edge of her bed, her phone resting in her hand, her reflection staring back at her from across the room. Her hair had been done earlier, her nails clean, her clothes simple but intentional. For a moment, she allowed herself to imagine it.

Walking in.

Being seen.

Not as who she had been.

Not as who she was recovering from.

But as who she still was.

Her fingers tightened slightly around the phone before she opened the chat.

Ebony M. Elite

Mia: *What are we wearing?*

The responses came quickly.

Marsha: *Power.*

Mary: *Clarity.*

Marlie's lips curved as she typed.

Marlie: *Presence.*

Mia read the messages slowly, her gaze softening as something deep and quiet moved through her chest.

Mia: *Good.*

A pause.

Mia: *Take pictures.*

Marlie responded without hesitation.

Marlie: *Always.*

—

Later that night, as each of them stepped into their respective rooms, the shift was immediate. Not dramatic. Not overwhelming. But undeniable.

Conversations opened.

Eyes noticed.

Introductions carried weight.

They were no longer simply present.

They were received.

And back in her room, Mia sat with her phone in her hand as the first photo came through.

Marlie—standing in a room filled with quiet influence, her posture effortless, her presence undeniable.

Another.

Mary—composed, centered, exactly where she was meant to be.

Then Marsha.

Alive in the moment, her energy unmistakable, her smile carrying something that had not been dimmed.

Mia stared at the screen for a long moment, her chest tightening—not with sadness, but with something layered.

Pride.

Longing.

Recognition.

Her fingers hovered, then moved.

Mia: *That's exactly where you belong.*

She set the phone down slowly, her gaze lifting toward the window, the night stretching beyond it—full of motion, full of life, full of everything that continued whether you were ready or not.

And for the first time…

She did not just watch it.

She began to think about how she would re-enter it.

Chapter Thirty-Five: The Quiet That Started Asking Questions

The quiet did not arrive suddenly.

It had been building—layer by layer, day by day—settling itself into the spaces between conversations, stretching into pauses that once filled themselves effortlessly with laughter, quick replies, and commentary that moved faster than thought.

Now, those pauses lingered just long enough to be noticed.

Not by outsiders.

Not by anyone who wasn't paying attention.

But by the women who had learned how to read one another far beyond words.

Marlie felt it first in the way Mia responded—not absent, not withdrawn, but measured. Each reply carried weight now, as though it had been turned over, considered, tested before being released. It wasn't distance.

It was processing.

And Marlie understood that instinctively, long before she allowed herself to name it.

That afternoon, the rehabilitation center moved with its usual rhythm—structured, predictable, filled with the quiet sounds of effort layered over routine. Machines hummed softly.

Therapists spoke in calm, guiding tones.

Somewhere down the hall, laughter broke through—brief but intentional, the kind that came from someone refusing to let frustration define the moment.

Marlie signed in with the same composed ease she had developed over the weeks, her name written neatly, her visitor badge clipped into place before she moved down the hallway with quiet purpose. Her presence was no longer unfamiliar here. It was expected.

Recognized.

When she reached Mia's room, the door stood partially open, the light inside softer than usual, filtered through thin curtains that shifted gently with the movement of air. Mia sat near the window, her body angled toward the light, her hands resting in her lap, her gaze not fixed on anything in particular — but not unfocused either.

Thinking.

Marlie paused for just a moment before stepping in, not out of hesitation, but out of respect—for the moment, for the space, for whatever was unfolding inside Mia's mind.

"You look like you're having a conversation with yourself," Marlie said as she entered, her voice calm, her tone light enough to arrive without disruption.

Mia's head turned slowly, her eyes finding Marlie with a clarity that hadn't always been there in the earlier days.

"I am."

The words came carefully, but more fluidly than before. There was still effort—but less resistance.

Marlie closed the door gently behind her, setting her bag down with practiced familiarity before moving closer, her posture relaxed but attentive.

"And how is that going?" she asked, lowering herself into the chair beside her.

Mia exhaled slowly, her shoulders shifting slightly as she adjusted her position, her gaze drifting back toward the window for a moment before settling again.

"Productive."

The word was chosen deliberately.

Marlie studied her, her eyes narrowing just slightly—not in suspicion, but in recognition.

"That sounds like a serious conversation."

A faint curve touched Mia's lips.

"It is."

She paused, her fingers brushing lightly against each other as if grounding herself before continuing.

"I've been thinking about... after."

The word settled between them.

After.

Not recovery.

Not therapy.

After.

Marlie felt it immediately—that shift, that quiet but undeniable turn in direction—and she didn't rush to fill the space that followed. Instead, she leaned back slightly, allowing the moment to open on its own terms.

"After what?" she asked, her voice steady.

Mia lifted her gaze fully now, meeting hers with clarity that did not ask for permission.

"After this."

Her hand lifted slightly, gesturing—not just to the room, but to everything it represented.

The process.

The struggle.

The rebuilding.

Marlie nodded slowly, her breath even.

"That's a good conversation to have."

No dismissal.

No softening.

Just acknowledgment.

Mia held her gaze for a moment longer before looking down at her hands, her fingers tightening briefly before releasing again.

"I don't think I'm going back the same way."

The words came quieter now.

But no less certain.

Marlie felt something tighten in her chest—not fear, but recognition.

"You're not supposed to."

Mia's eyes lifted again, searching her face—not for reassurance, but for truth.

"No… I mean everything."

The room shifted.

Not physically.

But in weight.

Marlie leaned forward slightly, her elbows resting against her knees, her attention fully present now.

"Talk to me."

Mia inhaled slowly, her breath controlled, her thoughts aligning as she spoke.

"The house… the routine… the way everything was set up…"

She paused, her brow tightening slightly as she searched for the right word.

"…it all feels fixed."

Marlie didn't interrupt.

She didn't rush.

She simply held the space.

Mia continued, her voice gaining clarity as the thought formed fully.

"And I don't feel fixed anymore. I feel… different. Slower in some ways. Stronger in others. But not…"

She exhaled softly.

"…not that version of me."

Marlie nodded, slowly, letting the truth settle exactly where it belonged.

"That makes sense."

Mia looked at her, and something close to relief moved across her face—not because the answer solved anything, but because it didn't dismiss what she felt.

"I don't know what that means yet."

Her voice softened.

Marlie leaned back slightly, her posture easing.

"It means you're paying attention."

Mia let out a small breath, her shoulders lowering just enough to be seen, her gaze drifting back toward the window as the light shifted again—softer now, more evening than afternoon.

For a while, neither of them spoke.

The silence wasn't empty.

It was full.

—

Later that evening, the group chat moved the way it always had—but something beneath it had shifted, just slightly, just enough to be felt by those who knew how to listen.

Ebony M. Elite

Marsha: *I just got home and I need everybody to understand that people are outside behaving like they were raised without guidance.*

Mary read it from her couch, one leg crossed neatly over the other, her posture composed even in rest as her fingers moved across the screen.

Mary: *That is not new information.*

Marlie sat at her kitchen counter, her phone resting in her hand, Mia's words from earlier still moving quietly through her thoughts. She read the exchange, the corner of her mouth lifting slightly before she added—

Marlie: *What happened?*

Marsha responded immediately.

Marsha: *A man tried to explain my own schedule to me.*

Mary adjusted her glasses, even though she was already home.

Mary: *That is a bold strategy.*

Marlie shook her head, a quiet laugh slipping free before she typed—

Marlie: *And how did that go?*

Marsha didn't hesitate.

Marsha: *He is now aware that I do not accept external management.*

The humor landed.

Familiar.

Intact.

Then—

Mia.

The typing bubble appeared.

Paused.

Mia: *You've always been consistent.*

Marsha leaned back in her chair, her expression softening in a way she didn't always allow to show.

Marsha: *And you've always been observant.*

There was a pause.

Then Mia again.

Mia: *I've been thinking.*

The chat slowed.

Not dramatically.

But enough.

Marlie felt it immediately, her posture straightening slightly, her attention sharpening.

Mary's gaze shifted.

Marsha's fingers hovered.

Mia continued.

Mia: *About what comes next.*

The words settled into the space between them, heavier than the conversation before—but not unwelcome.

Marlie responded carefully.

Marlie: *We can talk about that.*

Mary followed.

Mary: *When you're ready.*

Marsha added, her tone steady, grounded.

Marsha: *We're not going anywhere.*

The typing bubble appeared again.

Paused.

Mia: *I know.*

Mia set her phone down slowly after that, her gaze lifting toward the ceiling, her body settling into the quiet of the room as her thoughts continued to move — deeper now, more intentional.

Because the conversation she had started earlier… wasn't finished.

And whatever came next — would not be small.

Chapter Thirty-Six: The Reveal They Felt Before It Spoke

The shift did not begin with the announcement.

It began with the way Mia had started looking past the room.

Not through it. Not beyond it in the vague, restless way people did when they wanted escape.

Past it with intention. As if the walls of the rehabilitation center had stopped being the shape of interruption and become, instead, a waiting room for a decision she had not yet set down in language.

By the time the week curved toward its end, that energy had settled into her so completely that even the women who loved her most could feel it moving beneath the surface of ordinary conversation.

> She still did therapy. Still corrected her scarf when it sat wrong. Still rolled her eyes at bad coffee and cruel fluorescent lighting and the audacity of people who used motivational voices before noon.

But something inside her had gone quieter in a way that did not feel like sadness.

It felt like choosing.

Marlie noticed it in the timing of Mia's silences.

Mary noticed it in the precision of her questions.

Marsha noticed it in the way Mia had stopped talking about *when I get back home* and started saying *later* instead, leaving the destination unnamed.

None of them forced the conversation. At this age, real women understood that some truths needed enough space to become undeniable before they could be spoken without distortion.

That evening, rain had not come, but the sky held that silver-blue softness that often made the world look paused even when it wasn't.

The rehabilitation center moved through its usual late-day routine—carts rolling, shoes squeaking, televisions murmuring too loudly in rooms where loneliness needed background noise, aides calling names in practiced tones.

Inside Mia's room, the light had turned warmer. Someone—probably Mary—had adjusted the curtains just enough to let the last of the day in without turning the room into glare.

The black sneakers sat beneath the chair. A cardigan Marlie had brought lay folded over the armrest.

Marsha's hand cream stood on the side table like part of the permanent décor now. Evidence of witness lived everywhere.

Tonight, all three of them had managed to overlap.

That almost never happened anymore.

Mary had come straight from work in a deep camel coat and soft scarf, her notebook tucked beneath one arm, the edges of fatigue visible only in the second blink she gave before sitting down.

Marsha arrived twenty minutes later with the kind of entrance that managed, somehow, to announce itself even when she was trying to be respectful of policy.

Her tote was overstuffed, her perfume slightly faded from the day, her lipstick refreshed in a parking-lot mirror with more confidence than precision.

Marlie came last, directly from a call she had taken in her car with one hand still on the steering wheel and the other answering questions from people who had no idea how different her calendar felt now from the outside.

When she stepped into the room, the air told her immediately that something had already arrived before she had.

Mia was not in bed.

She was seated near the window in the straight-backed chair she had claimed as her place whenever she wanted to feel more like herself and less like a patient under observation.

Her scarf was tied in a smooth, low wrap that framed her face cleanly. Her posture was upright, not from force, but from decision. The notebook on her lap was closed.

Her phone rested face down on the tray table. She looked less tired than she had the day before, but more resolved.

Marsha was in the middle of a story about someone at work who had the nerve to use the phrase *touching base* three times in one meeting and still expect respect.

Mary sat listening with that composed expression that meant she was only half listening because the other half of her mind was reading the room.

Mia smiled in the right places. Responded when needed. But the current beneath her remained unchanged.

Marlie set her bag down quietly.

"Did I miss anything important?"

Marsha looked up first.

"Only the death of professionalism and my patience. So, yes."

That earned the correct degree of amusement from the room.

Mary's mouth softened.

Marlie stepped closer, kissed Mia's forehead lightly, then moved to the chair nearest the bed and sat.

"How was therapy?"

Mia's eyes shifted to her with unusual steadiness.

"Useful."

Marsha turned her head at that. Mary did too.

Useful.

Not hard.

Not irritating.

Not *I survived it.*

Useful.

That alone was enough to make the room recalibrate.

Marlie leaned back slightly, one leg crossing over the other. *"That sounds suspiciously mature."*

A small smile touched Mia's mouth.

"I'm trying... something new."

The line landed lightly, but it did not dissolve the feeling underneath it. Even Marsha let the joke pass through without trying to build on it too quickly.

The women who knew Mia best had learned that humor sometimes arrived first because it made the truth easier to approach.

The aide knocked then—briefly, politely—just to remind them that overlapping visits were tolerated tonight only because the center was quieter than usual. Not too loud. Not too late. One of them would still have to leave first.

Marsha nodded like she was doing the building a favor by accepting civilization.

"We're behaving."

The aide, clearly unconvinced but too wise to argue, left.

Silence settled after that. Not awkward. Not empty. Simply ready.

Mia's fingers moved once against the closed notebook. Then stopped. Her gaze shifted from Marsha to Mary to Marlie, as if measuring not whether they could handle what was coming, but whether she was prepared to say it in a way that did not ask for rescue.

Mary saw it first.

Of course she did.

She lowered her notebook onto her lap and spoke gently, without pushing the moment too hard.

"You have something on your mind."

Mia looked at her.

Then nodded once.

Marsha straightened almost imperceptibly, all of her casual sprawl disappearing into alertness.

Marlie did not move, but the air around her sharpened.

Mia inhaled slowly. The room waited without rushing to make it easier.

"Yes."

The word came clearly.

That, too, mattered.

Marlie's voice entered the room like a hand laid flat against a table—steady, grounding.

"Then say it."

No pressure.

No performance.

Just permission.

Mia's eyes dropped briefly toward her own hands before lifting again. When she spoke, the words came more slowly than thought but with more force than any of them had expected.

"I don't think… I'm going back."

Silence followed.

Real silence.

Not confusion. Not interruption. Not the kind people fill out of panic because they cannot bear what stillness reveals.

This was the silence of impact. Of three women hearing a sentence that instantly meant more than it had said aloud.

Marsha was the first to breathe differently.

"Back where?" she asked, though all of them already knew.

Mia held her gaze.

"Home. The house. That whole… version."

Mary's fingers tightened once around the edge of her notebook. Marlie's face did not change, but something in her eyes deepened into full attention.

No one corrected her. No one softened the sentence into speculation.

Mia continued, because once truth had crossed the room, it wanted completion.

"My family and I... have been talking." She paused, not because she doubted the thought, but because her body still required patience from her. *"Really talking. Not just about rehab. About after."*

There it was again.

After.

Not theoretical now.

Not reflective.

Active.

Marlie leaned slightly forward, forearms resting on her knees.

"And?"

Mia looked toward the window for one second, as if drawing strength from distance, then brought her gaze back to them.

"We're selling the house."

The sentence landed harder than the first one had.

This time the silence cracked visibly.

Marsha blinked once. Then again, as if her eyes had become briefly unreliable. Mary's lips parted, then closed.

Marlie remained very still, but now the stillness had weight in it.

Mia's voice, when it came again, was quieter, but somehow even more final.

"We're moving to Georgia."

No one spoke.

Not immediately.

Because this was not one revelation. It was several. The house. The move. The family already inside the decision. The geography of separation changing from visits and scheduling to mileage. The future stepping into the room wearing a stranger's address.

Marsha sat back like the words had reached across the room and physically pressed against her chest.

"Georgia?"

Mia nodded.

Mary's voice came next, but lower than usual, her calm now threaded with something unmistakably emotional beneath it.

"How long have you known?"

Mia swallowed, her eyes dropping once before she answered.

"Not long. Fully? A few days. In pieces... longer."

That felt true. They could all hear it.

Marsha looked away first, toward the wall, the tray table, anywhere but directly at Mia while she tried to pull her own reaction into order.

"That's why you've been..." She stopped, then tried again. *"Quiet."*

Mia's expression softened with something close to apology, though she did not actually apologize. She had grown too honest for that.

"I needed to know... what I meant before I said it."

Mary lowered her eyes to her notebook but did not open it. *"Why Georgia?"* she asked, and the question was practical enough to give the room something to hold besides the ache itself.

Mia answered with more ease now that the truth had finally crossed the distance between them.

"My cousin is there. My daughter's been looking too. More help. More space. Different pace." She paused, then added, *"Less history in the walls."*

That one hurt the most.

Because they understood it immediately.

The house she was leaving was not just property. It held the architecture of her former life—the routines, the rooms, the assumptions, the version of herself who had lived there before the stroke, before the chat paused, before the world outside had started calling their names in ways that mattered. Selling it was not merely logistics.

It was a surrender.

A release.

A refusal to drag one version of life into another when the structure itself no longer fit.

Marlie sat with that for a moment, her gaze never leaving Mia's face.

"Do you want this?"

The question stripped everything else away. Not *Is it smart?* Not *Will it help?* Not *Are they convincing you?*

Do you want this?

Mia looked at her for a long time.

Then nodded.

"I think... I do."

Marsha let out a breath that sounded almost like anger because sadness often arrived to her that way first.

"I hate that I understand it."

Mia looked at her immediately. *"I know."*

Marsha laughed once, but there was nothing amused in it.

"Of course you do." She pressed her palms against her knees and leaned forward again, emotion finally showing through the edges of her control. *"I hate it, but I get it. I get the space. I get the support. I get the different pace. I even get the walls thing."* Her eyes filled, and she did not bother pretending otherwise. *"I just do not like seeing the map change."*

Mary closed her eyes once before opening them again, because she, too, had felt the map move beneath her.

"When?"

Mia's answer came quietly.

"After I'm discharged. Not immediately. But soon."

Soon.

That cruelly practical word.

Not tonight. Not next month exactly. Not a date they could hold and resent properly. Just the knowledge that this version of their proximity now had an ending on it.

Marlie rose then—not abruptly, not dramatically—and crossed the small distance to Mia's chair. She crouched slightly so that they were almost eye level.

"Thank you for telling us before it became logistics."

Mia's eyes filled faster now.

"You're my people."

The sentence came imperfectly. Beautifully. Entirely enough.

Marsha turned her face away for a second and wiped once at the corner of her eye with the heel of her hand like she was annoyed by moisture on principle.

Mary set the notebook aside completely and stood, moving closer, no longer interested in pretending this was a moment for composure alone.

The four of them stayed there in that quiet, altered room while the sun finished lowering outside the window.

No one rushed to transform the revelation into a plan.

No one said *we'll make it work* too quickly, though all of them would.

No one insulted the truth by trying to make it prettier than it was.

Eventually, Mary's voice returned first, careful and steady.

"Then we need to think about what this means."

It was not a rejection of feeling. It was how women like them loved—by beginning, even in heartbreak, to build structure around the thing that hurt.

Marsha nodded slowly, eyes still bright.

"And we are not doing this quietly."

Mia looked at her.

"What do you mean?"

Marsha sat up straighter, the old force returning not because the pain had gone, but because she had found something to do with it.

"I mean if you are leaving, we are not letting you slip out of here like a forwarded address and some tears. Absolutely not. We are giving this chapter the exit it deserves."

Mary's gaze sharpened through the emotion.

"A gathering."

Marlie stood again, looking from one face to the next as the first shape of what would come next began assembling itself between them.

"Not just a gathering."

Marsha caught it instantly.

"A proper one."

Mia stared at them, something between disbelief and love moving visibly across her face.

"You're already... planning?"

Marlie's mouth curved, but the expression was gentler than triumph.

"We are women. We process in layers."

That did it.

The first laugh came through tears.

Small. Broken at the edges. Real enough to count.

Even Mary let herself laugh, one hand briefly covering her mouth.

Marsha shook her head like she had expected nothing less from all of them.

Mia's shoulders loosened for the first time since the reveal began.

And in that moment, the room changed.

Not because the news hurt less.

Because the love rose fast enough to meet it.

By the time the aide knocked gently to remind them that overlapping visits had run long enough, the four women had not solved anything, but they had done something better. They had named the truth. They had survived the first hearing of it. They had let the map move without pretending it hadn't. And beneath the ache of what Georgia would mean, another current had begun to gather—not joy yet, not fully, but the first electric outline of an event.

An ending with style.

A goodbye with dignity.

Something worthy of the lives they had already lived and the ones they would have to keep carrying across state lines, chat threads, and time zones.

When Marlie finally stepped outside into the evening, her phone buzzed in her bag, some invitation or confirmation or man with good timing still trying to enter the larger movement of their lives. She did not look at it right away. Not because it no longer mattered.

Because now something else mattered more.

Inside that room, the future had spoken.

And all three women who loved Mia had heard it clearly enough to know one thing for certain.

Whatever came next would not leave quietly.

Chapter Thirty-Seven: The Night They Chose to Celebrate Anyway

The planning did not begin with excitement. It began with resistance—not spoken aloud, not argued over in long messages or dissected in careful conversations, but present in the way each of them approached the idea of gathering. Not as something they wanted at first, but as something they understood they needed.

Because the truth of Mia's decision had settled into them fully now, not as shock, not as something still unfolding, but as something real, something with shape, something that would soon become distance measured in miles instead of minutes. And none of them were willing to let that transition happen quietly.

Marlie was the one who named it.

Not dramatically.

Not emotionally.

Just clearly.

The message landed early in the morning, clean and direct, the way Marlie handled things when she had already made up her mind.

Ebony M. Elite

Marlie: *We are not letting you leave without a proper exit.*

There was no follow-up. No explanation. No elaboration on what *proper* meant, because it did not need definition.

Mary read it first, seated at her dining table with her laptop open and a list in front of her that had nothing to do with what she was about to respond to. Her eyes moved across the message once, then again, and when she typed back, it came with quiet alignment.

Mary: *Agreed.*

Marsha did not answer immediately, not because she disagreed, but because she felt it. She stood in her living room with her phone in her hand, reading the message with a stillness rare for her, her mind already moving ahead of the moment, already imagining what this would require—not just in planning, but in presence. When she finally responded, it came with the kind of energy that marked a shift.

Marsha: *Then we're doing it right.*

Mia read the exchange from her room, her phone resting lightly in her hand, her body still in that in-between space she had come to know too well—the space between recovery and readiness, between strength and uncertainty, between what had happened and what she was now choosing next. She did not answer right away. She simply stared at the screen a little longer than usual, her chest tightening as the meaning beneath their words settled into her.

Not goodbye.

Celebration.

When she finally typed, the sentence came slowly.

Mia: *You don't have to do that.*

The response came immediately.

Marlie: *We do.*

And that was the end of the discussion.

The venue revealed itself the way everything meaningful had begun revealing itself in their lives lately—not through searching, but through alignment.

A rooftop space in Newark, elevated just enough to separate itself from the noise below while still holding the city close, glass panels framing the skyline, soft lighting already woven into its structure as if waiting to be activated by the right people.

Mary handled the logistics with quiet precision, her movements efficient, her decisions measured, her understanding of space and tone guiding every choice. She didn't overdecorate. She didn't overcomplicate. She curated. Tables were placed with intention. Lighting was adjusted to enhance rather than overwhelm. The flow of the room invited movement without crowding it.

Marlie oversaw the aesthetic with the kind of eye that caught details before they fully formed. She adjusted the fall of linens, corrected the balance of the color palette, reconsidered the seating arrangement until conversation and ease could exist in the same breath.

Marsha handled the energy—music, timing, the pulse of the evening itself, the atmosphere that didn't just exist but moved.

During one of their planning calls, her voice came through the speaker low but absolute, cutting through indecision before it could root itself anywhere.

"We are not doing sad," Marsha said, the firmness in her tone leaving no room for negotiation. *"We can feel what we feel, but we are not making this heavy."*

Mary, still looking down at her notes, answered in the calm, grounded way she always did when refining chaos into shape.

"Balanced."

Marlie nodded once, eyes still on the layout in front of her.

"Intentional."

Mia listened from the other side of the call and said nothing, because something in her chest was already full.

The night arrived with a kind of quiet anticipation that did not need to announce itself loudly to be felt.

The air held that early evening softness that always made city light look more expensive than it was, the skyline stretching beneath the rooftop in lines of movement and glow while the sky shifted slowly from blue into something deeper, richer, more willing to hold emotion without exposing it.

Marlie arrived first.

Of course she did.

Her dress moved with her in a way that suggested both structure and ease, her posture aligned, her presence immediate the moment she stepped onto the rooftop. She paused just long enough to take it in—not critically, not analytically, but appreciatively. It was right.

Mary followed, her entrance calm and composed, her gaze moving across the space with quiet approval, each of her earlier choices now visible in the environment without needing acknowledgment. She stepped beside Marlie, her hands resting lightly at her sides, and after a long enough look to make the judgment matter, she said softly, *"This works."*

Marlie's eyes stayed on the room another second before she answered, *"Yes."*

Marsha arrived last, exactly as expected, but when she stepped onto the rooftop, she did not speak immediately. Her eyes moved slowly across the space, taking it all in, her usual commentary held back for one brief, unguarded moment as something deeper settled into her. Then she exhaled and shook her head once, a smile touching her mouth before the words came.

"Okay... this is right."

And just like that, they were ready.

Mia arrived with assistance.

But she did not enter like a patient.

She entered like herself.

The elevator doors opened slowly, and for one suspended second, the space stilled—not because anyone had planned it that way, but because presence had a way of commanding attention without ever needing to ask for it.

Mia stepped forward carefully, her movement deliberate but controlled, her posture upright, her expression composed, her outfit chosen with the same level of intention she had always carried into a room. She was not who she had been before.

But she was not less.

Marlie moved first, closing the distance between them with a steady grace, her eyes soft but clear as she took Mia in fully.

"You look exactly like you're supposed to."

Mia's lips curved slowly.

"I feel like it."

Mary approached next, her presence grounding, one hand resting briefly against Mia's arm in a gesture so simple it almost escaped notice.

"That is the point."

Marsha stood a step back at first, her eyes scanning Mia from head to toe, not critically but carefully, letting herself absorb what the moment deserved before she nodded once with visible approval.

"Yeah," she said, the tenderness beneath the line arriving without disguise. *"We did good."*

Mia laughed then.

Soft.

But real.

And with that, the night began.

It unfolded the way only certain nights do—without forcing, without pushing, just allowing itself to build naturally, moment by moment, conversation by conversation, laughter layering over music that moved through the space without dominating it. Glasses lifted. Voices blended.

The women moved between one another and the room with an ease that had returned not fully, but honestly. Men were present—not overwhelming, not intrusive, but aligned.

Introductions were made with intention. Conversations were held with respect. Attention was given without demand.

The same man from the theater approached again, his presence steady, his demeanor unchanged, his timing still excellent in that rare way that made it noticeable without making it irritating.

"You chose well," he said quietly as he reached Marlie, his eyes moving once across the room before settling back on her.

Marlie tilted her head just slightly, one brow lifting in calm acknowledgment.

"We always do."

Mary found herself in a conversation that matched her pace, her intelligence, her preference for substance over performance. The man speaking with her knew how to listen without using silence like bait, and that alone was enough to make him memorable.

Marsha laughed more freely than she had in weeks, her energy returning in waves that felt familiar without becoming reckless, her body language easing into the kind of brightness that only came when she was no longer carrying every emotional corner of the room by herself.

And Mia—

Mia moved through the night in her own way.

Not everywhere.

Not constantly.

But enough.

Sitting when she needed to. Standing when she could. Engaging when she chose. Watching when she wanted. Receiving the evening without trying to prove anything to it.

Present.

Fully.

At some point, Marsha lifted her glass, not loudly, but clearly enough to gather attention without demanding it.

"Alright," she said, her voice carrying just enough to pull the night in around her. *"Before we get too far into pretending we're not emotional beings, I need to say something."*

The space shifted.

Not heavy.

Focused.

Mary turned first. Marlie stilled. Mia watched.

Marsha looked at Mia before she looked at anyone else. Then she let her gaze move across the women who had become, by now, more than friends and more than history. Her words came without flourish.

"We didn't get here by accident."

She let that settle.

"And we are not standing here tonight because things were easy."

Mary's fingers tightened slightly around her glass. Marlie's posture remained steady, but something behind her eyes shifted. Mia's chest rose slowly.

Marsha kept going, her voice deepening not with drama, but with truth.

"We are here because we stayed. Through silence. Through fear. Through change. Through all the parts nobody posts and nobody claps for."

She raised her glass a little higher.

"And now we're celebrating the fact that we're still here... even if here is about to look different."

She looked directly at them and finished simply.

"To us."

Mary lifted hers first.

"To alignment."

Marlie followed, her glass catching the city lights.

"To evolution."

Mia raised hers last, her hand steady enough to count and then some.

"To staying connected."

The glasses touched.

Softly.

Intentionally.

And for a moment, the entire rooftop seemed to hold still around the sound.

Later, when the music lowered just enough to let the city lights speak louder than the speakers, the four of them found themselves drawn slightly away from the crowd—not by design, but by instinct.

They stood closer than before, the skyline stretching behind them, the noise of the gathering fading into a textured hush. No one spoke immediately. No one rushed to rescue the moment from what it held. They did not need to.

Mia looked at them.

Really looked at them.

Her gaze moved from Marsha to Mary to Marlie, her expression steady but full, her voice quieter when it came.

"I didn't expect this to be the hardest part."

Marlie's brow softened.

"What part?"

Mia exhaled slowly, the city wind catching just slightly at the edge of her scarf.

"Leaving you."

It landed.

Clean.

Honest.

Marsha looked away first, her jaw tightening before she let out a breath that wasn't quite steady. Mary shifted her weight, her composure holding but her eyes softening visibly.

Marlie did not move, her gaze locked on Mia, her presence steady enough to hold all of it.

"You are not leaving us," Marlie said, her voice low but certain. *"You're moving."*

Mia shook her head slightly, not disagreeing, but feeling the difference too sharply to pretend otherwise.

"It's not the same."

Mary stepped closer, her voice calm, grounded, but carrying something deeper beneath it.

"No. It's not."

Marsha finally looked back at her, the edge gone from her tone now, leaving only the truth.

"But it's still us."

Silence followed.

Not empty.

Not uncomfortable.

Full of everything they had been, everything they had built, everything they were trying not to lose.

Marlie reached out then, her hand finding Mia's, steady, intentional, grounding.

"We didn't build this on proximity," she said. *"We built this on presence."*

Mia's eyes closed briefly.

Because that—

That was true.

It did not solve the miles. It did not soften the coming distance into something easier than it would be. But it told the truth about the foundation beneath all of it. And at this stage of life, truth mattered more than comfort.

Marlie reached into her bag then and pulled it out—the clicker. Small. Black. Unassuming. Meaningful.

"Alright," she said, letting the softness of the moment shift just enough into motion. *"We are not leaving without this."*

Marsha let out a quiet laugh.

"Of course not."

Mary adjusted her posture. Mia smiled.

They positioned themselves together, the skyline stretched behind them, the city alive below them, their bodies aligned in a way that felt both familiar and new.

Marlie lifted the clicker—but this time, she did not press it right away. She looked at them first.

Really looked.

At who they had been.

At who they were now.

At who they were becoming.

Her voice, when it came, was barely louder than the wind.

"Ready?"

Marsha answered first, but all of them were in it.

"Always."

Marlie pressed the button.

Click.

The moment captured.

And for one suspended second, they did not move.

Because they knew.

They felt it.

This one mattered.

Mia's phone buzzed softly in her hand.

She looked down.

The image had already been posted into the place that had survived every version of this story with them.

Ebony M. Elite

No caption.

No filter.

Just them.

Then the messages began.

Marlie: *Same time. Different place.*

Marsha: *Don't start acting new because you moved.*

Mary: *We will coordinate.*

Mia stared at the screen, her vision softening just slightly as her thumb hovered before she typed.

Mia: *I'm not going anywhere that this can't reach.*

She hit send.

The notification glowed between them.

Alive.

Still theirs.

Still moving.

And this time, none of them needed to say anything out loud.

Because they all understood.

The chat had not paused.

It had expanded.

Epilogue: The Continuation

The quiet in Georgia did not feel empty. It felt intentional.

Morning arrived differently there—not rushed, not layered with the constant hum of traffic and movement, but stretched, softened, allowed to unfold at its own pace.

Light filtered through the windows in long, unbroken streams, settling across the floors, climbing the walls, resting gently against spaces that had not yet been fully lived in but were already becoming familiar.

The air carried a soft southern warmth, thick but gentle, wrapping around everything instead of rushing past it, the distant hum of cicadas weaving into the stillness like a quiet reminder that life here moved on its own terms.

Mia stood near the kitchen window, her hand wrapped around a warm mug, her body steady in a way that had taken time to return.

Outside, the trees moved slowly in the breeze, their rhythm unbothered, their presence grounding.

The house was quieter than the one she had left behind, but not in a way that made her feel alone—just recalibrated.

She shifted her weight slightly, testing the strength that had been rebuilding day by day, piece by piece, the kind of progress that didn't announce itself loudly but revealed itself in moments like this—standing longer, moving easier, breathing without thinking about it. Not who she had been, but no longer who she was at her weakest—something in between, something becoming.

Her phone buzzed softly against the counter.

Ebony M. Elite

Mia smiled before she even picked it up.

The rhythm of them had not disappeared.

It had expanded.

She tapped the screen.

"Good morning beautiful people. Who's up?" — Marsha

Mia exhaled a quiet laugh, her thumb already moving.

"Georgia is up."

The response came almost immediately.

"Of course you are. You always trying to be first in a different time zone." — Marsha

Mia shook her head slightly, the smile lingering as another message appeared.

"How are you feeling this morning?" — Mary

Direct. Steady. Always paying attention.

Mia leaned her hip lightly against the counter, considering the question, not rushing the answer.

"Stronger."

There was a pause in the chat—not empty, just felt.

Then—

"We like stronger." — Marlie

Mia's chest tightened slightly, not in pain, but in recognition, because that word had weight now.

—

By midday, the house no longer felt like a place she was settling into. It felt like a place she was shaping.

The living room held small traces of her already—blankets folded just the way she liked them, a book resting open on the table, sunlight marking the exact place she preferred to sit.

Boxes had been unpacked slowly, not rushed, not overwhelming, each item placed with intention instead of urgency.

Her family moved around her easily, not hovering the way they had in the beginning, not watching every step, but still present in ways that mattered—checking without crowding, supporting without suffocating.

The kind of care that had learned how to breathe.

Mia moved through the space carefully but confidently, her hand grazing the back of a chair, her steps measured but no longer hesitant. She paused near the mirror in the hallway, catching her reflection—not critically, not searching for what had been lost, but acknowledging what was there.

Still her.

Just… evolved.

Her phone buzzed again.

This time, a video call.

Marlie.

Mia answered, angling the phone slightly as Marlie's face appeared, composed as always, but softened by something unspoken.

"Let me see you," Marlie said, her tone calm but carrying a quiet demand.

Mia stepped back slightly, adjusting the frame. *"You see me."*

Marlie's eyes moved across the screen, taking her in fully, assessing without judgment.

"I do," she replied, her voice quieter now, *"and I like what I see."*

Mia smiled, shifting slightly as she leaned against the wall.

"I'm getting there."

Marlie shook her head once, gently.

"No... you're already there. You're just continuing."

Mia held her gaze for a moment longer, because that—felt true.

—

That evening, the air cooled just enough to invite her outside. The porch had become her place quickly, a space where she could sit without feeling confined, where the world stretched just far enough to remind her that life was still moving beyond her, but not without her.

She settled into the chair slowly, her body lowering with control, her breath steady as she leaned back, her gaze lifting toward the sky as it shifted into dusk.

Her phone rested in her lap.

Quiet.

For a moment.

Then—

Ebony M. Elite

A new message.

"So… we're not going to talk about this trip or…?" — Marsha

Mia blinked once, then again, because there it was—not hesitation, not fear—forward.

Mary followed quickly.

"We should begin planning early. Timing, accessibility, accommodations."

Mia could almost hear her voice—measured, structured, already building.

Then — Marlie.

"Location first."

Mia sat up slightly, her body responding before her mind fully caught up, her thumb hovering, then moving.

"Georgia is warm."

The response came immediately.

"Oh so now we coming to YOU?" — Marsha

Mia laughed, the sound fuller now, freer than it had been weeks ago.

"You said we're not stopping."

There was a pause.

Then—

"We're not." — Marlie

"We're definitely not." — Marsha

"We will coordinate." — Mary

Mia leaned back again, her gaze lifting toward the sky as the evening settled fully around her, and for the first time since she had left, it didn't feel like distance.

It felt like expansion.

—

Inside the house, her things continued to find their place. Outside, her life continued to take shape.

And somewhere between Newark and Georgia, between recovery and rediscovery, between what had been and what was becoming—the connection remained.

Not fragile.

Not forced.

Just… true.

Mia picked up her phone one more time, her fingers moving with quiet certainty.

"Next time... we dress up again."

The replies came instantly.

Marsha: *"Obviously."*

Mary: *"Coordinated."*

Marlie: *"Elevated."*

Mia smiled, her eyes softening as she looked out into the night that no longer felt unfamiliar.

Because this — This was not an ending.

It was not a pause.

It was not something left behind.

It was movement.

It was continuation.

It was a different version of the same bond that had carried them through everything they had already survived.

And as the group chat continued to glow softly in her hand—alive, active, unbroken—Mia exhaled, her body settling deeper into the moment, her spirit no longer catching up, but finally walking in step with where her life was taking her.

Forward.

Together.

Still.

The chat never paused.

It simply learned how to reach further.

Note to the Reader

Thank you for stepping into this space with me. *When the Chat Paused* is more than a story about four women — it is a reflection of what it means to grow, to reconnect, and to rediscover yourself in seasons of life that are often overlooked, but deeply transformative.

Marlie, Mia, Mary, and Marsha represent something real—friendship that evolves, conversations that carry weight, and the quiet understanding that life does not end at a certain age… it expands.

If you have ever found yourself in a moment where things felt different—slower, quieter, or uncertain—this story is for you. Not as a reminder of what was, but as an invitation to embrace what is becoming.

The chat may pause. Life may shift.

But connection—true connection—finds its way to continue.

Thank you for reading, for reflecting, and for allowing these women to share a piece of their journey with you.

To stay connected beyond the pages of this book, you can also find me across social media where I share story updates, conversations with readers, and glimpses into the growing world of the Platinum Chocolate Universe.

Simply search for ***"Platinum Chocolate Romance"*** *and you should be able to find me across:*

• *YouTube*	• *Facebook*
• *Instagram*	• *LinkedIn*

You can also visit my online home at: ***platinumchocolateromance.com***

Your support, your presence, and your belief in these stories mean more than you know.

Until we meet again on the next page... Keep dreaming. Keep loving. And keep reading.

With gratitude,

LongTemple

Continue the Journey in the Platinum Chocolate Universe

The **Platinum Chocolate Universe** is a growing collection of interconnected stories celebrating love, resilience, friendship, healing, and the beautifully layered lives of grown people finding their way through the world.

The Ebony M. Elite Series

Friendship. Romance. Sisterhood. And the unforgettable adventure of women rediscovering love later in life.

Start with:

• **Caramel and Steel**

• **Searching for Platinum Chocolate**

• **When the Chat Paused**

The Rhythm Series

A soulful romance shaped by music, faith, ambition, and the kind of love that grows stronger through time. Start with:

• **Rhythm & Design**

• **Rhythm's First Lady**

Then discover the emotional continuation:

• **When Love Learns to Heal**

Reflective Companion: When the Heart Learns to Heal

The Run Series

A powerful family saga exploring loyalty, survival, love, and the complicated bonds that shape a lifetime. Start with:

- **Flip & Run**
- **Just Run**
- **Run with Denim** (June 2026)

Stand-Alone Platinum Chocolate Romances

Stories of love, rediscovery, and the courage to begin again.

• **The Colors of Us**

• **A Heart's Anchor**

• **Cotton Sheets and Velvet Dream**

Stand-Alone Platinum Chocolate Psychological Sagas

Stories of Interior life, struggles, resilience and survival

- **Luxuries & Lies**

- **Between Grace & Fire**
- **Loved in Chaos**
- **What Survives the Pressure** LongTemple & Fielder Whitley
- **Kansas Spoke** (April 2026)
- **Built Not Chosen** (May 2026)

Coloring Companions - Black & White Line Art

- **Caramel & Steel**
- **Searching for Platinum Chocolate**
- **The Colors of Us**
- **A Heart's Anchor**
- **Cotton Sheets & Velvet Dreams**
- **Rhythm & Design**
- **Rhythm's First Lady**
- **Flip & Run**

Wherever you begin, the story continues.

www.ingramcontent.com/pod-product-compliance
Lightning Source LLC
LaVergne TN
LVHW020647110826
845149LV00012B/1941

* 9 7 8 1 9 7 2 2 1 7 2 3 8 *